Veronica Stallv ... ated
abroad, and no ... has
worked in the l... ury and more recently
in Lincoln College library. Her first crime novel,
*Deathspell*, was published to great critical acclaim
and became a local bestseller, as did her second
novel, *Death and the Oxford Box*. She is currently
working on her next book, which will be the third
novel to feature Kate Ivory. When she is not writing,
Veronica Stallwood enjoys going for long slow runs
in the country, talking and eating with friends, and
going to the opera.

Praise for Veronica Stallwood's previous novels:

'Some Rendell-like skewed psychology ... welcome,
individual qualities, chief of which is an evident gift
for characterization ... irresistibly readable'
William Weaver, *The Financial Times*

'Novelist Kate Ivory snoops with intelligence, wit
and some nice insights'
Marcel Berlins, *The Times*

'Not only plausible but, in my view, absolutely
compelling'
Gerald Kaufman, *The Scotsman*

# Oxford Exit

## Veronica Stallwood

**HEADLINE**

First published in 1994
by Macmillan London Limited

First published in paperback in 1994
by HEADLINE BOOK PUBLISHING

10 9 8 7 6 5 4

ISBN 0 7472 4808 7

Printed and bound in Great Britain by
Caledonian International Book Manufacturing Ltd, Glasgow

HEADLINE BOOK PUBLISHING
A division of Hodder Headline PLC
338 Euston Road
London NW1 3BH

For Cora Cécile Frances Stallwood
and in memory of
Frank Stallwood (1910–1978)

With thanks for their help and indispensable encouragement to Sandra Bailey, Deirdre Barber, Glenys Davies, Richard Gartner, Sally Gutowski-Smith, Robert McNeil, Annabel Stogdon and Maryanne Tubb

# i

## First Person Narrative

*Welcome to the creative writing course. During this term, we shall be covering the basic techniques of fiction writing and I shall be setting you an assignment to write each week which you may hand in for my comments, if you wish.*

*The first thing I want you all to do is to write from your own experience. However uneventful you feel your life has been, it contains elements that are unique to you, and it is these that I want you to capture on paper.*

But you wouldn't want to hear how I killed Jenna, would you, Mrs Dolby? Not yet, anyway. Descriptions of death should be kept for black and white photographs, not shown in colour, or given in detail as an exercise in a creative writing class. Death should happen off-stage, or as in this case, off the motorway, out of sight of the slip-road: on the Oxford Exit. But that's a joke I won't be sharing with you just yet.

She knew, she must have known, what was going to happen. First of all the red and white cones, the notices apologizing for the roadworks and promising to have them completed on a date already two weeks gone. She must have had some premonition, as I drew off the slip-road and took the track made for the contractors' vehicles. The light was going from the sky, and the earth gleamed a sullen yellow in the rain that poured out of the low clouds and bounced off the roof of the car. In that flat landscape the sky seemed immense, the rain unending. She tried to run when I told her to get out of the car, and for a moment I thought she might get away from me, but her smooth rubber soles were slipping on the wet surface; she stumbled, scrabbling at the earth, sobbing; and I soon had hold of her. Her hair was soaked, plastered to her fore-head in rats' tails, but it didn't matter, since it had never been pretty hair. I pulled up the hood of my shell-suit to protect myself from the rain. Did you know that a shell-suit sheds no fibres, and picks none up? I knew. No fibres on my clothes, no evidence inside my car (not that I was ever on anyone's suspect list, but it pays to be careful). I was wearing thin, matt-surfaced plastic gloves when I grasped her by her hair and pulled her head back.

*Be specific. Describe the place, the time. Tell me how it feels, how it smells.*

But I'm going to concentrate on describing the why and

the when; someone else may write the who and the how.

Afterwards, I looked down at her: little Jenna, really no more attractive in death than she was in life, but given importance by my act. I gave Jenna her fifteen minutes of fame, you could say.

I opened the boot of the car (I had lined it with black plastic sheeting before leaving home) and brought out a spade. The light had nearly gone now, and I was working by the dim reflection from the clouds, but the ground had been recently worked by the road builders, and it didn't take long to dig her grave. I placed her in, straightening her limbs, making sure that she looked decent, arranging her tidily in the embracing earth. Then I threw in her backpack and shovelled the earth over her.

I replaced the spade in the black plastic in the boot, added my muddy gloves, closed the boot and climbed into the driver's seat. I switched the headlights on for a moment to make sure that I had forgotten nothing. It was only a small mound – she was not a big girl – so similar to other mounds in the pitted and cratered landscape. But I could not leave her grave unadorned like that, after all. A cassette was still playing in the car; Mahler's Fifth Symphony, I remember. I went back to the boot and took out the flowers I had cut for her funeral wreath. I had meant to float them down the river in her memory, but instead I placed them on top of the mound, pushing the stalks into the soft earth, and watched as the rain soaked into the pink petals. She would have liked the music. Do you know the *Adagietto*? Visconti used it in *Death in Venice*. Yes, it is very pretty.

I'm sorry, I missed that. I must have been day-dreaming. What is it you're saying, Mrs Dolby?

*In this course we are going to be dealing with the writing of fiction. Many writers start by taking the material of their own lives and putting it in order and heightening the effect until it forms a shape that we call a story. Often the most rewarding period, because of the intensity of our feelings at that time, is our childhood. So, for your first exercise, I want you to take some strongly felt incident from your own childhood and write about it, in the first person, but as though it happened to someone else. The 'I' of the story is someone outside yourself. Try to be objective, but keep the underlying emotions of the original experience.*

I'll start with my first memory: a front-doorknob, hard, white, shining porcelain, like an over-boiled egg, and smelling of my mother's hands. In the background the radio is playing.

This is the first house I remember living in, and it is in St Antony's Road, Summertown, Oxford: a street of tall houses, built of greyish-yellow brick, with fanciful Gothic turrets and pointed windows, topped with grey slate roofs, their gardens stuffed with overgrown shrubs, their garages full of croquet sets and bicycles.

Our house has a pattern in the brickwork at first- and second-storey levels, like a few rows of red and yellow Fair Isle knitted into a plain grey pullover, and it has yellowing foliage and overgrown geraniums straining against the glass of a decaying conservatory which leans against our back wall.

In spring the street is bright with the pink flowers of plum and cherry; in autumn the pavement is thick with their soft brown leaves. Rain falls silently here, as though unwilling to disturb professors in their studies, teenagers working for Oxbridge entrance, and mothers listening to the radio as they mash the potatoes for dinner.

So God alone knows what Mum and I are doing here, occupying this house between the Woodstock and Banbury Roads, no resident man in evidence. Our front door is bright blue instead of ox-blood brown, and it crashes shut behind us with enough noise to set the dogs howling; our unlined curtains have a pattern of sunflowers as large as elephants' ears; our radio is the loudest in the neighbourhood.

This morning Mum is mooching round the kitchen, looking at yesterday's bills in their torn brown envelopes, grumbling at everything I do. Some mornings she floats in from her bedroom as though on to a West End stage, her pink dressing-gown floating behind her, satin mules clacking on the floorboards in time with the lilting music on the radio. She spreads her arms wide, so that a scent of jasmine and perspiration gusts over me, and she speaks in a funny deep voice, like someone on the television. When she is like this I know that whatever she is about to say is, if not exactly a lie, somehow less than the truth. This morning I'm watching Mum and pretending to eat my breakfast at the kitchen table when the telephone rings.

She comes to life like a marionette jerked upright by its strings. 'They want me after all,' she sings out, sailing into the hall to answer it. 'Everybody loves me,' she carols, lifting the receiver. 'Hallo. Yes?'

I know what's going to happen next, so I wrinkle my nose, open my mouth and drop my toast and Marmite on the floor. She is still talking in her low, murmuring voice, as I let out the first grizzle and push over my mug of warm milk with its topping of wrinkled skin. It forms three distinct pools on the table, in which spoons and knives, butter and cornflakes packets stand marooned like islands.

'I have to go out,' she says, when she puts the phone down. 'Not for long. I shan't be gone for long. Just a few minutes, really.' She doesn't look at me while she speaks. The music in the background growls with drums and brass.

I grizzle harder, and let out a really loud howl.

'Selfish little beast!' she shouts. 'You only think about yourself. What about me, then? I can't be expected to stay here all day on my own with you, can I?' She comes up close and stares into my face. 'Children are supposed to love their mothers,' she hisses at me. 'So why don't you show how much you love me by shutting your noise. I'm going out, do you hear? And if you're a very good boy, I'll be back before lunchtime.'

Then her glance falls away and takes in the toast and the spilled milk, and she hits me, fast, on my bare legs, twice, so that I gasp and choke, but quietly this time, while she hugs herself in her fluffy pink dressing-gown.

'It's not my fault,' she says. 'You shouldn't blame me.

And, anyway, I shan't be gone for long.' She goes into her bedroom and dresses, while I dabble my fingers in the milk and keep my lips pressed together. The shouts, the cries, the tears, must all stay locked up inside my head, for if I am not good enough, perhaps she will never return.

She is doing something to her hair when she comes back into the kitchen, pushing it up on top of her head, pulling at a curl that falls in front of her left ear. She has long hair, thick and waving, of a reddish-brown colour. She smiles at herself in the round black-framed mirror on the sideboard, purses her lips and paints on lipstick, then brushes something over the top that shines like a snail's slime. She pokes out a pointed red tongue and licks the lipstick from her top teeth.

'Beautiful you are, girl. Beautiful,' she says, in a silly voice, and wriggles her hips. She takes a tube from the drawer and squeezes out a long white worm of cream and then rubs it into her hands and wrists. The smell reaches me from across the room. 'Be good, now,' she says to me in her other voice, the one that sounds like eggshells cracking. 'You're a big boy now, so don't make a fuss.' She lifts me down from my chair and sets me on the Marmite-smeared rug. 'You can listen to your music while I'm out.' And she turns up the volume of the radio and twiddles with the dial until music hovers round the kitchen and mingles with the smell of coffee and burning toast. 'Third Programme: it must be educational,' she says. 'You just listen to that while I'm out: you might learn something.'

I follow her to the door, though she shushes me and

shoos me back like a bad-tempered goose. 'Pity I didn't have time to get you dressed,' she says, as she slips her pink toes into high-heeled white sandals by the front door. The door slams and I hear the rattle and slap of her feet down the brickwork path, the clang and snip of the latch on the gate, and then the diminishing click of her heels as she walks down the road and out of my morning.

The music shouts 'No!' on a rising fifth, then it bounds off over fields, through meadows starred with wild flowers, down to a tree-lined lake where a cuckoo calls from the edge of the woodland, while I stand here with my mouth full of doorknob: cold, hard, porcelain, like an oversized, over-boiled egg. If I hold on hard to the door knob, it might bring her back. The house is dark as evening with the curtains closed.

Three quick footsteps approaching the front door. Not Mum's. I step back. The hard sound of boot on stone, then the thrust of letters through the flap. Two brown envelopes fall to the carpet; a third, larger, is caught in the aperture. I reach up and pull the envelope through with my right hand while I keep the flap open with my left. It is a wide, deep letter-box, with a light spring. When I stand on my toes I can see through, a long, thin view of the outside world. The sun is shining and the view is brilliantly lit.

There are grey bricks, laid in a herringbone pattern to form the path from front door to gate. I can just see the gate, flanked by tall, papery scarlet flowers with the sun shining through them, standing open the way my mother left it.

A figure appears, and behind her on a well-stretched lead is a solid yellow-furred dog. They pause at the hyacinth blue gate and the dog piddles against the gatepost. The woman, in her old camel-hair coat, says, 'Come along, George!' in a bossy voice, and pulls at the lead. They move on, two well-brushed North Oxford residents, making plain their opinion of my mother and me.

Nearer to the house, on the right-hand side, huge white peonies droop over the path, casting their petals to the ground, like sliced-off ears. It must be summer outside in the garden as well as here inside the music. Slanting sun lights the leaves, illuminates the whole forest of jade-green stems with their scarlet flowers. To the right of the frame are the peonies. Even as I watch, one of them splinters in the breeze, spilling more tender white ears on to the front path.

Another woman appears on the left of the frame, younger this time, green-jacketed, followed by two children, bigger than me, but still too young for school. They stop and stare through the open gate, and I wonder whether they can see my returning stare through the open letter flap. Then their mother reappears right of frame, takes their stiffly resisting arms and hauls them away, right. I hear her disapproving, scolding voice diminishing into the distance.

Mum has been gone for a long time, it seems to me, as I stand here, trying to score the hard white surface of the doorknob with my teeth. I wander back to the sofa and put my head down on the cushion, dreaming of white peonies and dead babies until someone shakes me awake, her hands hard on my shoulders, her long loose hair brushing my face. There is a nasty smell all around me, and the sofa is warm and damp.

'Filthy child! Disgusting, filthy child,' she is shouting as she shakes me. 'What did you have to do that for? You only did it to spite me!' She lifts me under the armpits and sets me on my feet. 'You stink! You've made the house stink!' Her face wavers as though seen through the smoke of a bonfire. Then she picks me up again and carries me at arms' length, our faces level, and dumps me in the bath. Cold water is gushing out of the tap and over me and she is scrubbing at me with a flannel. I feel the places where her thumbs dig into my shoulders, the precise shape of them, small black petals, through the ache of the cold water. I am a strong child, and I want to kick and punch, but know better than to do it. Neither do I cry. I stand very still, keeping everything tied up inside me. I can feel it trembling, bunched up, trying to escape through my eyes and mouth, but I hold on tight and I wait for the storm to pass, when she will sit me on her knee and talk to me. The black petals of her thumbs are painted indelibly on my shoulders.

It was a good carpet, she told me. Does it still lie on the floor in some North Oxford house, faintly smelling of incontinence – a reminder of the babyhood from which we all came, a pointer to the senility towards which we inexorably travel?

Later, when I am clean and dressed, she sprawls on the sofa and pulls me on to her knee and talks to me, murmuring into the hair above my ear. 'There now, darling, you know Mummy loves you, don't you?' Her arms are strong and pull me against her so that I can smell her hair, her scented sweat and her peppermint breath.

'You won't be naughty again, will you? You won't ever cry again when Mummy has to go out. And then, I didn't really leave you alone, did I? You made that up in that imagination of yours. You'll stay quiet if they ask you about it, won't you? You'll never say a word, like a good little boy.' There is the slightest of threats in the way her hand is stroking my head and neck and I nod my agreement, to show her that I will never speak again if that is what she wants.

She has cut the dying peonies from the bush and they lie on the floor by the bin, speckled with brown, decomposing. I watch as a long, sinuous insect wriggles out of a flower head and disappears under the sink. I close my mouth to stop the words from escaping and she smiles her lovely smile at me. She has the curliest lips I have ever seen, even to this day, the upper lip with a heavily indented bow, then dipping, drooping over the lower before lifting in elfin points at the corners. Mobile, flexible lips. Who needs dimples when they have long, curling lips, painted a rosy pink?

'We understand each other, you and me, don't we, Viv? We have a marvellous time here together on our own.'

'Tell me the story of the princess with the hair,' I venture.

She laughs and picks a lock of her own hair between her fingers and brushes it down my cheeks and across my lips. 'Did she have longer, thicker hair than me, do you

11

think?' She runs fingers through it so that it cascades over her shoulders and the light from the window behind her turns it to fiery gold.

Is there anything I could have done to change what happened? Even looking at it now, so long afterwards, I can't see what I could have done. How do you walk into someone else's fantasy and tell them to return with you to reality? No, you're standing for ever out there in the rain, with your nose pressed to the lighted window, wondering how you can break your way into the bright bubble where the happy families live. Maybe one day the princess in the tower will let down her hair and let me climb up and in through her window and I can join her and the rest of her family by the fireside.

I sit and suck my thumb while her words caper around me and fill up the empty hole where my heart should have been. I know it is a good story by the tone of her voice. But I don't hear everything she says because I am waiting for the telephone to ring again.

Have I got the right effect there? Is it perhaps overwritten? Are there too many adjectives? But I have got the main themes in, I think, and some quite nice imagery. You'll have to wait to find out what their significance is (if any) and how they relate to future chapters. Just remember that this is a work of fiction, an exercise in imagination. Don't worry if you find some of it disturbing: it is the business of the writer to leave you moved and to question your assumptions and prejudices. If indeed this really is fiction . . . if there really is an author.

*This piece of work shows fluency and a gift for striking imagery.*

*You have dealt with the question of where very well, as I suggested you should in an opening page. The question of when is a little less well dealt with. Is this happening in the present day? In the fifties? In the thirties, even? I think we should get a more precise picture before the end of the first page, unless, of course, there is some reason, to do with the plot, that stops you from giving it away.*

*On a technical note, are you sure that you could sustain this use of the present tense? It is tricky to use for more than a page or two, and can be tiring – not to say tiresome – for the reader. I like the way that you see the story through the eyes of the child, though perhaps he is a little young to notice all that this little chap seems to take in! And the mother's motives do remain obscure. Shouldn't we get some hints about her and what she is doing? She seems a rather two-dimensional figure next to the child.*

*But don't let my criticism put you off. This is an ambitious piece, and a mature one, and I'm sure I'm going to enjoy reading more of your work during the coming term. E. J. Dolby.*

# Chapter One

The clear blue sky of early summer fills the upper half of the window, reminding her that on the outside there are trees in fresh green leaf, the scent of wallflowers, and a city harvesting its early crop of tourists. After enduring a cold, windy March that battered the daffodil buds into the mud, she would like to walk out into the warmth of the morning, but if she lets her gaze drop below the sky it falls on to a stretch of scrubby grass, dotted with the corpses of narcissi and, below that, the line of the window-sill and the pale grey expanse of a computer screen with a couple of lines of text reminding her to stick to essentials or she will have no money to pay the mortgage.

The room smells of the three mugs of coffee that she drank earlier, there are biscuit crumbs on a plate, and pervading it all, the bass line of some rock music from her neighbours' stereo.

Kate Ivory chewed on the end of her pencil and told herself to stop day-dreaming and get on with her work, but the only ideas coming to her involved murdering the neighbours. Perhaps she would give up for the rest of the morning and walk into Oxford and buy the new biography that she wanted to read. Reading other people's books was so very much easier than writing her own. She stretched and tipped her chair back. At this time of year she awoke from her winter lethargy and dreamed of gambolling in meadows starred with daisies in the company of an attractive man. She squashed the pleasing picture and let her chair right itself. Time to exit. *Exit, save, exit.* She pushed the power button off and the gentle whirring stopped so that she could hear the neighbours' music more clearly. A shouting voice had joined it. She wrote herself a note for her next session: 'Rewrite chapter 4, it fails to convince.' Then she tidied her desk, picked up the three empty coffee mugs and the plate, and thought how nice it was to be her own boss so that she could take a walk into Oxford any time she wanted to.

The phone rang.

'Kate? Andrew here.' Andrew Grove, old friend. 'Growing tired of your life of leisure yet?'

If prunes and custard could speak they would sound like Andrew Grove: sweet, glutinous and covered in a thick yellow sauce. His question, in any case, was unanswerable, since she didn't want to argue with him over whether a writer's life was one of leisure. Perhaps if she wrote something less popular than historical romances, Andrew would take her seriously. She screwed up the piece of paper on which she had doodled a large bunch of daisies and lobbed it into the wastepaper basket.

'Are you making me an offer, Andrew?'

'It's time you settled down and found yourself a proper job.'

'You sound like my mother. You'll be wanting me to get married and produce children next.'

'I wouldn't dream of intruding on your personal life, but as to work, there's a little something that's come up. It would suit you down to the ground.'

'I'm writing. I'm busy.' She hardly felt the twinge of guilt at the way she had been planning to waste her own time.

'I'll call in this evening,' said Andrew, ignoring her. 'Sevenish?'

'Six thirty,' said Kate.

'Very well. It won't take long.' And she was left with the buzz of the disconnected line in her ear. She just hoped that the person she was expecting for dinner at seven thirty would be late. He and Andrew disliked one another: they bristled at each other like terriers meeting in an open gateway.

She turned away from her computer screen and started making a list on a piece of scrap paper. Smoked salmon. Lemon. A small wholemeal loaf from the good baker in Summertown. Real butter, softened so that it would spread without reducing the bread to a heap of crumbs. She started doodling another bunch of daisies.

Andrew had brought his new girlfriend, Isabel, with him and they turned up five minutes early. They arrived just as Kate was about to change out of her *ad hoc* track-suit (the one with different shades of navy blue in its top and bottom) and wash the salad dressing from her eyebrows and hair. Isabel smelled deliciously of Diorissimo, Kate less deliciously of olive oil and crushed garlic.

Andrew was only slightly apologetic about Isabel's presence, but Kate could see that she and Isabel would never have much in common. For one thing the girl was so *young*. She had soft fair hair caught up in a waterspout above her left eye, huge blue eyes, pouting lips painted a shiny plum colour, was wearing a very short skirt and showing the sort of thin, straight legs that you usually only find on an eight-year-old. There was, however, little point in feeling jealous: since she didn't want Andrew for herself, she should feel glad that he had got himself a new girlfriend. *Girlfriend*. It was the only way to describe someone like Isabel.

'Whisky?' she asked them.

'Peppermint herb tea if you have it,' replied Andrew. 'So much more cleansing than whisky, don't you think?'

My God, the man was serious, so Kate went to dangle three tea-bags in three mugs, while Andrew and Isabel sat very close together on her pink sofa and Isabel showed off even more slim thigh and a pair of eight-hole DMs.

Andrew was looking sprightlier than the last time she had seen him. His ill-defined face had a slight glow, probably due to Isabel's presence. His red hair was fading and receding, but then this made his forehead seem higher and gave him a suitably academic air.

'Expecting someone for dinner?' Temporarily detached from Isabel, he had followed her into the kitchen and was leaning over her shoulder.

'Just a friend,' she said, as she poured boiling water into

the mugs and pointedly ignored the expensive bottle of claret breathing on the dresser, the fresh herbs she had been chopping on the table and the opulent smell coming from the oven.

'Smoked salmon,' murmured Andrew, opening the fridge and prodding with a plump finger. 'Yummy. You may find it hard to get rid of us if you tempt us like this, Kate. Or would it be that you're expecting that elusive Music don of yours?'

'He's not elusive, it's just that he's not very sociable at the end of a hard day's work, and he's apt to disappear again if he thinks I'm entertaining other friends.'

'In that case, I'm quite sure that Isabel and I should stay and help you show the uncivilized brute that he can't dictate to you like that. Does he like you to dress so informally, too?'

'I'm going to change into something sophisticated before he gets here.'

Andrew looked at his watch. 'When's he due? Seven thirty? You haven't got much time for a major transformation,' he said.

'Why don't you tell me why you're here, Andrew, instead of irritating me.'

'Do you remember when you worked for us at the Bodleian back in '88 and '89?'

'When I learned more about cataloguing a book than I ever wished to know?'

'I seem to remember that you were the star pupil in your cataloguing course.' He opened the oven door for an appreciative sniff. 'What's this, lamb?'

'From the Real Meat Company,' said Kate, without thinking. 'I go to that marvellous butcher in Cumnor.'

'It needs just a little more garlic, I think. Have you given it a sprinkle of virgin olive oil, a hint of brown sugar, a sprig of fresh rosemary?'

'Yes, and I've scrubbed some new potatoes.' The small kitchen was filled with Andrew's bulk and she felt hot and cornered. Would she have time for a quick shower before Liam arrived?

'But why the questions about cataloguing? Am I still expected to remember about name-title added entries? Uniform titles? How to deal with a work with more than three authors?'

'I knew you were a bright little thing, Kate.'

'Bright, yes. Little and thing, no. And take your nose out of that saucepan.'

'And such a good memory for rules.' He had picked up a fork and was prodding at the saucepan's contents. 'Are you sure there's enough for four, Kate? We don't want to be mean with our portions, do we?'

'There's plenty for two people, Andrew, for just two greedy people.'

'Just teasing, Kate. Just checking on what I'd given up when I introduced you to that long thin streak of Music don.'

'You don't seem to have taken to celibacy for very long yourself,' she said, thrusting a mug of peppermint tea into his hands and carrying the other two ahead of him into the sitting-room. 'And you'd better tell me why you were subjecting me to that cataloguing test.'

Andrew rearranged the cream crocheted tablecloth that was draped over a shabby Victorian chair.

'Haven't you had this re-covered yet, Kate? It would look quite pretty in blue, I think.'

'It will be pink velvet when I get round to it,' said Kate, placing an embroidered cushion squarely on the crochet cover and then sitting on it. 'Now speak, Andrew.'

'Computer Abuse Act 1990,' he said, settling back on to the sofa and placing his hand on Isabel's knee. 'Section 3, to be precise.'

'How can you abuse your computer?' asked Isabel, puzzled.

'It's about hacking, and viruses and things like that, Izzie darling,' said Andrew, fondly. 'There was no such crime before, you see, you had to rely on the Criminal Damage Act 1971, or accuse people of stealing electricity.'

'How could you find people in possession of stolen electricity?' asked Izzie.

'Maybe we should let Andrew explain what he's talking about and tell me how he thinks I can help him,' said Kate, glancing at the clock and wondering if she could shift them out of her sitting-room in under twenty minutes. Throttling Izzie would do it, but then Andrew might object.

'We believe that someone is hacking into the Libraries Computer System and altering records. You'd be ideal to look into it for us: you were there when the system was first set up, you remember how to catalogue – oh yes, you do, Kate – and then you're so good with computers.'

'Only at an elementary level.'

Andrew had got to his feet again and wandered over to her mantelpiece. He picked up a blue pottery hedgehog and blew the dust off it. 'I've seen you whizzing your little cursor up and down your screen, calling up your database, switching chapters of your book around your word-processor. I even caught you talking about sixteen-bit and thirty-two-bit external transfer the other day.' He put the hedgehog back on the mantelpiece in its correct place.

'Oh, shut up, Andrew.' But with only fifteen minutes to go, she couldn't afford to argue. She rubbed at the oil spots on her track-suit top.

'We have so much to offer you in return, Kate.' This time he had picked up a small enamel egg and was polishing it between finger and thumb. 'Salary (modest, but regular), holiday pay, sick pay, coffee and tea breaks. What more do you want?' Again he replaced the ornament in its rightful place and his fingers hovered between an Art Deco scent bottle and a glass paperweight.

'You're sure we're just talking about computer criminals here?' demanded Kate. 'Polite men, totally lacking in aggressive instincts? Men – or women – who wouldn't know their way into a deserted house, and wouldn't want to attack me and drown me in two feet of water?'

'Pussy cats,' said Andrew. 'Gentle people who are kind to their mothers and take in stray puppies. Their only fault is to be a little too brainy and to accept the challenge of outwitting the system. Satisfied, Kate?'

'I'd like to know who I'd be working for, but I haven't got time just at the moment to go into all that,' said Kate, leading him back to the sofa.

'But you'll do it?' He sat down and put his hand back on Isabel's knee.

'All right, Andrew. Yes. OK. I'll think about it. I'll consider it. I'll come and talk to you about it.' Now *go*.

'I knew you'd see sense. I'll come and see you tomorrow at half-past eleven and we'll work out the details.' He glanced at his watch. 'Time to go, Izzie darling. We've got just four and a half minutes to get to the restaurant.'

Izzie whispered confidentially to Kate, as she was leaving: 'You've got to do something to yourself before your man gets here, even if you only change into a jacket and skirt.' Kate thought about the long black jacket and colourful skirt that were waiting for her upstairs. 'Have you got one of those thick silk scarves from Liberty's? No? If you had something in deep gold – you know, a Van Thingy sort of colour – it would be a knockout with your colouring.'

'Thanks for the advice, Isabel,' said Kate, fixing a smile to her lips. 'And what is your interest in this library business?' She only meant to change the subject, but Isabel replied:

'Oh, Jenna and I were friends . . .' For a moment her face lost its childlike clarity, and a new, serious Isabel stood there.

'Three and a half minutes, Izzie darling,' said Andrew, and took her firmly by the arm. Isabel smiled at Kate and picked up her handbag.

'But I need to visit the bathroom,' she said. 'And Kate will show me where it is.'

At the top of the stairs, and out of sight of Andrew, Izzie

pulled Kate into the bathroom and whispered rapidly:

'Andrew doesn't want me to talk about it, but she was a friend of mine and I think she was killed because of what she knew. When she got back from California she hinted that something was going on, but she didn't tell me what it was.'

'Hurry up, Izzie!' shouted Andrew from downstairs. 'Kate wants to get showered and changed, you know.'

'Who was she? What was she doing?' Kate asked.

'I'll have to go,' whispered Izzie, and flushed the lavatory. 'But please try and find out what really happened to her.'

They went back downstairs and Kate watched Andrew hand Isabel into his car and help her with the seat belt. He waved at Kate, then smiled like a middle-aged cherub.

Hmm, she thought. You planned that little scene quite carefully, didn't you, Andrew? Including the interruptions by Isabel. And you're trying to hide something from me. Well, I'm tired of your manipulations, and if I decide to take this job of yours on, it's because it's in my interest and because I want to do so.

Then she raced upstairs and tore her clothes off, throwing them into the linen basket to keep the room looking tidy, showered and washed her hair rapidly. She dressed and looked in the mirror. Was she getting a bit staid? She put on a fresh layer of scarlet lipstick and a gaudier pair of earrings, and pushed her hands through her damp hair so that it stood on end in what she hoped was a youthful way.

\* \* \*

Liam was ten minutes late. They talked too much, as usual, and it didn't seem to lead anywhere useful. Maybe she should try wearing a stretchy skirt the size of a wide belt, purple lipstick and Doc Martens instead of the tasteful silk top and Liberty skirt she had put on for Liam. Or perhaps no one should try to dress like Isabel once they had hit thirty without stopping.

The meal was very good, but it was interrupted by a telephone call. Why hadn't she remembered to put her machine on?

'Kate? It's Emma Dolby. Look, I was wondering whether you'd like to take over my creative-writing class for the rest of the year. I'm—'

'No thanks, Emma. I couldn't face a roomful of little old ladies all wanting to write rhyming couplets about sparrows in the snow.'

'It's not like that. It's—'

'I've got to go now, Emma. I'm in the middle of dishing up the main course. Speak to you again soon. Bye.'

Liam left soon after midnight.

'How do I get to know you, Kate?' he asked suddenly, holding her by the shoulders and looking down at her. 'It's impossible to get behind the writer to the woman. I know you no better now than when we first met.'

But what else was there to know? Work took up most of her life, but writing was something you did, rather than talked about. Getting closer to Liam was impossible, too: her alarm clock was set for ten to five, so that she could get a substantial amount of work done before the neighbours started thundering up and down their stairs, and after that she went out for a run, before showering and changing, eating a substantial breakfast and facing the rest of the day. Liam, on the other hand, often didn't finish his work until late at night. If he was producing an opera or attending a concert, he ate late, wolfing down whatever happened to be available at that time of night, which meant Indian or some sort of junk food. And his idea of an early morning was to be out of bed at five to eight rather than five past. Kate liked to eat early in the evening, and it had to be something healthy, with a salad, and a glass of mineral water, or an occasional glass of wine. By ten thirty in the evening she was very bad company. And if anyone wanted to know what took up so much of her life and her concentration, they would have to read her books. What she was was there on the page.

She started clearing up, and as she gathered together the mugs that Isabel and Andrew had used, the plates and glasses from dinner, she started to feel better. She wiped her hands and went to change the CD on the player. She had had enough of Mahler for one evening, and the machine squeaked, whispered and then filled the sitting-room and kitchen with the nicotine-dark voice of Bruce Springsteen. The place was beginning to belong to her again. It was too small to share. It even smelled of other people at the moment as though the air in the rooms retained their exhaled breath.

What did she want from a man, anyway? Someone who was there when she wanted company or comfort, and who disappeared without a murmur when she wanted to get on with her work? Someone who got up early and didn't want to stay up late? Someone who was domesticated to just the same degree as she was, and who would take over and cook her a meal when she didn't feel like making one for herself? Impossible to find such a paragon. But she wasn't a complete hermit, she reassured herself. She went running – mostly on her own these days – to keep fit, and she had a well-ordered social life. She had thought that Liam fitted in there to fill up her emotional needs, but perhaps she was wrong. And wasn't he just as wrapped up in his own work? They said that creative people had to be selfish to survive, and maybe they were right. But that was a wide bed in her bedroom upstairs, and sometimes she wished that there was someone to share it more frequently than Liam did. She would never admit the word *lonely* into her vocabulary. If she was on her own, it was because she enjoyed solitude, not because she lacked a choice. And if just occasionally she wished there was someone there at the end of the day to lie under the duvet and share her satisfaction with her work, or her despair when it went wrong, to give her a cosy, warm feeling of belonging, then she reminded herself just how little creative work was produced by the domesticated woman, and she forced herself to welcome the cool, metallic feeling of independence.

She spent a restless night dreaming of a glowing green cursor jumping all over her screen while a masked man stole all the best chapters from her new book.

Next morning she was still wrestling with conflicting decisions about catching hackers, or just finishing her novel. She tried to get some work done on the next chapter, but the neighbours had put something loud on their stereo, so that the repetitive thumping bass came through the communal wall and filled her head with its mind-numbing noise. She countered with Bruce Springsteen and turned up the bass. It blotted out the noise from next door, but she still couldn't think against it. Time to go out, she thought, and went upstairs to put her running shoes on.

' 'Ere!' It was the eldest and most streetwise Toadface child, waiting for her at the gate. 'You going to be an investigator, then?'

'What makes you think that?'

'With that voice of yours, everyone knows,' he said. 'But you got a lot to learn: you're going to need lessons.'

'In what?'

'Well, for a start, there's your driving.' They both looked at Kate's car, parked at an angle to the kerb and a couple of feet away from it. 'Can't be an investigator if you drive like a girl. I'll organize something. See ya.' And he disappeared back inside the house.

She ran through a light drizzle down the tow-path towards the centre of town. What was the point of sitting at home on her tiny income, trying to get on with her book all day, when the only hours she could count on for uninterrupted work were the same as those she was restricted to when she was off at a full-time job? She might as well be paid for doing something else during the day, since she couldn't concentrate on her creative work. And then again, although she liked to think of herself as a completely dedicated creative artist, interested only in her writing, she had to admit that she was more than a little intrigued by the thought of outwitting a hacker, or whatever the computer criminal was. Her feet slapped on the greasy path and the tower of Magdalen College loomed at her through the haze, when a cyclist, instead of going straight past, slowed down and rode alongside her.

'Hallo there,' he said.

'Paul? Paul Taylor?'

'You're speaking to me, then? I thought maybe after our last meeting you wouldn't want to.'

'Oh, I'll forgive you, eventually,' she said, trying to forget how she had been so very much in the wrong on their previous meetings. 'What are you doing these days?'

'Just checking that you're following a completely law-abiding path and keeping out of trouble.'

'I'm writing one of my popular books,' she said. 'And I have a job offer that I have just this moment decided to accept.'

'Lion tamer? Private detective? What would suit your personality and qualifications?'

'I am going to be working for a while at one of the most boring and law-abiding jobs going. Not a hope of any excitement whatsoever.'

He raised an eyebrow. 'Undertaker's assistant?'

'Close. I'm going to be a librarian.'

'You'll never manage it! You'll be sacked for unladylike behaviour on duty.' Detective Sergeant Paul Taylor laughed and started to cycle away from her.

On an impulse, Kate called: 'Do you know anything about a girl called Jenna?'

He paused for a moment, then said something over his shoulder that sounded like *Dead Girl with Peony*.

She must have misheard, and she called out her question again, but this time there was no reply and Paul Taylor's black Lycra cycling shorts moved swiftly ahead of her and disappeared round the next corner. *Dead Girl with Peony*? It sounded like the title of a painting – something Pre-Raphaelite. Or then again, perhaps it meant just that: Jenna was dead, whoever she was. It would probably be months before she saw Paul Taylor again.

Maybe that was what suited her best: a man who appeared from nowhere, exchanged three or four lines of dialogue, intrigued her and then disappeared.

## ii

### The Unreliable Narrator

*This week, I want you to move one stage further back, and show your story through the eyes of a narrator whose view of the events described is not necessarily accurate. Don't worry if you don't give in your work when it is done. Not everyone likes their early efforts to be read by an outsider. But do try to complete the assignments that I set you each week.*

I haven't been back to Oxford for oh, I don't know, it must be twenty-five years, and I thought I had forgotten the Aunts. But when there is a death, you have to go; it is expected. You have to say your farewells and hope that the dead body will then rest quietly in its coffin and not come shuffling out at night to haunt your dreams, the way the living do.

Twenty-five years? Maybe it's been a whole century, maybe not that long, for if I lean my head back against the seat of the train, close my eyes and touch the smooth petals of the flowers, the Aunts loom over me, brightly coloured and smelling of violet cachous, from a different world from the one I inhabit now.

They smiled at me with purple lips.

'Your mummy has had to go away for a while,' said the first.

'Of course, she didn't want to leave you,' said the second, 'she'll be back as soon as she can.' A round face, puckered like a pink balloon on the morning after a party, bent down towards me, exhaling a vapour of Devon violets.

'You can call me Aunt Dilly,' it said, or so memory tells me.

The second woman was taller, gruffer, darker-eyed, with a soft grey moustache and false teeth that glinted pale green against the tanned leather of her face.

'Aunt Nonie,' she said. (And again, this is what memory dredges up from the silt that time has deposited. Her letter yesterday was signed only with the initial A.)

'We love you, Viv,' Nonie would say. 'Of course we love you.'

'You are our own little Vivvy,' said Dilly. 'Our own little love.'

Why did they have to keep saying this? Is love brought into being by saying the word out loud? It was not something that I could ever say, myself. I don't know why. I can't think why.

Behind them, in the dimly lit kitchen, the radio poured out music rich with trumpets and drums, the dark *oompah* of a tuba and the jangle of tambourines. Aunts? No, I recognized them for what they really were: Ugly Sisters, Witches. I was trapped in their enchanted house.

'I've cut the crusts off your sandwiches,' said Dilly.

'Bloater paste,' said Nonie. 'And sliced tomato. Special treats.'

'With Heinz salad cream. It's Liberty Hall here, Viv. You'll soon get used to us,' said Dilly. Daylight streamed through the coloured glass panels of the front door and lay in jewel-coloured pools on the threadbare carpet and spangled the hair and faces of the two women.

'It's not her fault; you mustn't blame her,' they both said. 'We're sure she's done her best.' Their faces bobbed and danced in front of me as their eyes tried to make contact with mine. 'But now you're going to be our very own little boy.'

The music rose to a crescendo and I thought that at any moment a trapeze would come swinging across the room above my head, or a girl in fishnet tights would balance her way along the washing line strung from one side of the kitchen to the other.

'We've always wanted a little boy,' said Dilly.

'And now here you are,' said Nonie. And we sat down to fish-paste sandwiches and shared a sliced tomato, sprinkled with salt and dipped in salad cream, before it was time for me to clean my teeth, pass a damp flannel over my face and go to my early bed.

'We've got you your own room. Nonie painted it blue, specially for you.' Hyacinth blue, like the door of our house in North Oxford.

Dilly read me a story before I went to sleep, from the old book of Grimms' fairy tales. I liked the sinister black and white pictures. I dreamed all night of a tower and a princess but when I climbed the Fair Isle pattern of its smooth brickwork, trying to reach the lighted window at the top, I kept slipping back into the tangled briars at its base.

'Can I go home now?' I asked the empty room next morning. I had been kidnapped by the Aunts. My mother didn't know where I was, but one day she would come back and rescue me.

I went downstairs to an unfamiliar smell, something sweet and heavy. My nose must have twitched, for Dilly said: 'We're boiling up the cat's meat.'

'Horse,' said Nonie. 'We get it every Wednesday from a man in the market.'

What did they do with the hoofs and the ears?

And then I saw the cats. Striped and spotted like their big brothers at the zoo, they stretched and groomed themselves and came purring and twining their elastic bodies around my grey school socks. Brass band music still rolled out of the wireless, and Aunt Nonie's grey hair stood up stiffly from her head, like a peaked cap.

'Will my mother come for me today?' I asked.

'Perhaps,' said Nonie.

'If she gets back from her journey in time,' said Dilly.

'What journey?' I asked.

But Nonie was stirring her witch's brew, lifting long strings of meat up to the light on a wooden spoon, and Dilly was standing on a kitchen stool, bringing down the washing from the line. Perhaps now the girl in tights and spangles would balance her way across it.

And all this even before Nell turned up.

The smell of cooking horse followed me to school every day: just one more thing to keep me apart from the other children – not that I wanted anything to do with them, anyway. I marched to the *oompah* beat of that brass band, while they tripped along to some gentler measure.

I sat in class dreaming of my mother's face. She held me by the shoulders so that I felt the black petals in the soft skin above my armpits, and the sweep of her long hair against my face.

'I will return,' she said, in the voice of a tearful cello. 'You will not weep for me Viv, but you will remember me every single day.' And she shook me slightly, so that the petals fluttered against my skin, her hair shimmered, and I looked into the green pools of her eyes and drowned. Then she walked away and left me. I watched her go. She started to hurry, turned towards me, and a smile touched her lips, curling them up at the corners.

The Aunts were not keen on washing. Hot water was rationed in that house, coaxed in a thin, spiteful stream from the corroded copper spout of the vicious geyser. It had it in for me, that geyser. It was only waiting until I should be on my own in the bathroom and then the water would dry up entirely and the whole machine would heave and roar and blow up in an expectoration of pipes and gas and blue flames. No, the safest thing, for the Aunts as well as for me, was a quick rub over with a damp, smelly flannel. The whole house was soaked in a fusty, ancient smell. Each room had its own, but hanging over it all was this odour of the three of us, our individual body smells, never completely eliminated by the bowls of tepid water and reconstituted tablets of soap that we used on Saturday evenings in front of the coal fire in the sitting-room. They never opened the windows.

They took me to the local school. Aunt Nonie, buttoned up tight in grey tweed, let me scamper through the gates on my own, while she disappeared in a cloud of blue smoke from a Balkan Sobranie. But in the afternoon, Aunt Dilly turned up early and waited for me, standing apart from the circle of duffle-coated mothers. She wore a brown overcoat and a cowpat of a beret pulled down over her forehead and skewered into place with a wicked hatpin. Her feet overflowed from ladylike pointed shoes and she walked with them placed constantly at ten-to-two. The horse-meat smell clung to both of us.

'Let them talk about us,' said Dilly, stoutly. 'See if we care!' And she marched me off down the road, while the tower of St Barnabas' church raised its admonishing finger at us, demanding in vain that we conform to the standards of life in Jericho.

I lived in the silence of my own company; I invented stories and companions. I juggled with the music and the words that swirled around the house, as though they were brightly coloured balls.

Then at school I found that it was not only a mother that I was lacking.

'Have I got a dad? Where is he?' I asked the Aunts.

'He's much too busy to come visiting here,' said Aunt Nonie.

'I have got one, then?'

'Everyone's got a dad,' said Aunt Nonie.

'He had to go abroad,' said Aunt Dilly. 'To India or China or one of those places.'

'Like Mum.'

She gave me a funny look. 'Yes, you could say that.'

'Will she come back today?' I still asked the question from time to time.

'There'll be a letter for you soon, I'm sure,' said Dilly. 'And maybe one from your dad, too.'

'I expect she's in Australia by now,' said Nonie. 'And that's a hard place to get away from.'

I imagined a country where the earth was glue beneath her feet. I tried hard to get them to send me back to her, but they just changed my sheets every morning and ignored the awful stench that hung about my room.

'Is she coming today?' I asked, like an incantation.

'I expect she'll be here to see you next week,' one of them would answer.

'Or the week after,' the other would add. The same story was repeated, as though it had been written down and imprisoned in cardboard covers like the other bedtime stories they read me.

'Tell me the story about the princess with the hair,' I said then, and I closed my eyes and grasped the glossy red-brown tresses and started to climb. The hair filled my nose and mouth and I thought that it might strangle me, but if I kept climbing I would at last reach the top and scramble into the golden firelight of the room where I would find her at last.

We went away to the seaside. The days slid into one single day, with a pewter-grey sea, pearl-grey skies and an ashy-grey beach with a narrow frill of white foam.

I wanted to sit there in the dunes, with the singing grass around me and watch everything. But they kept talking to me. All the time. 'Look over there, Viv,' they said. 'That's a wading bird.' Or, 'Look at the seagulls up above us. They're searching for their breakfasts.' And they would laugh and keep walking, their knobbled feet escaping through the open spaces of their unfamiliar sandals and desecrating the innocent surface of that grey strand. I wanted to listen to the gulls: I knew that if I could only hear them undisturbed, we would understand each other, the birds and I, and I would learn the truth at last.

I watched the waves rolling in, and lapping at the shore with their woven strands of seaweed, thick reddish-brown like the hair of my princess. I imagined it, lit by the candle in the room behind her head, as though she was surrounded by a bright halo.

Then Aunt Nell came to stay.

I was lying in the bath, trying to forget that the geyser might explode at any moment, turning the misty patterns of cracks on the ceiling into pictures of dragons and witches and monsters, when I heard the front door knocker sound, and the gales of unusual sounds, that clarified into a loud guffaw and a heavy tread up the stairs. The bathroom door was flung open and she stood there, wreathed in clouds and curls of steam, like the villain at the pantomime.

She was huge, a giant scarlet satin balloon topped by a hat that sprouted feathers.

'I,' she announced, 'am your Aunt Nell,' and she paused, as though for applause and the throwing of bouquets.

'No, you're not,' I answered, hiding as best I could behind my small face flannel, cross at this invasion of my privacy.

'Oh, yes, I am,' she repeated.

They moved me out of my own bed into a narrow, folding one, and Aunt Nell and I shared my bedroom for the next week. The strangeness of her presence kept me awake at first. Nell herself fell asleep immediately she lay down. I knew she slept, for in the dim night light I could see the flesh of her face melting away from her bones like heated wax. Then air escaped from her various orifices with a *whooeff* sound. I had never been present at anyone's death, but with just such gentle expulsions of gases do I imagine the soul to leave the body.

Our room subtly changed its customary smell to encompass her strong peppermints and the big blue bottle of Evening in Paris that she uncapped each morning and dabbed all over her skin before hoisting herself back into her pink corsets and grey lisle stockings, snapping on the suspenders with their round rubber buttons.

At meal times Nell asked: 'Is there onion in this stew, Dilly dear?'

'How else do you make a stew?' barked Dilly.

Nell ostentatiously removed grey slivers from her portion and draped them over the side of her soup plate. 'Onions disagree so, don't you find?' she said.

Many things disagreed with Aunt Nell, whose whalelike bulk contained a refined and dainty constitution, it seemed. The disagreements expressed themselves in gentle burpings that she caught delicately in the recesses of her scented handkerchief.

She unlocked the piano for me. It lived in the front room and although I had seen its upright form, topped by a lace-edged linen runner, and had even pulled the brass candle-holders in and out a few times, I had never been allowed to touch its keys, yellow as a smoker's teeth.

Aunt Nell's bottom filled the seat of the piano stool and overflowed the edge like a Yorkshire pudding, then she sat me on her feather-bed lap and her huge arms came round me. I had to lean against her corseted chest so that she could reach the keys. My arms were pinned to my sides by hers so that I couldn't cover my ears, and I breathed the smell of her Evening in Paris and strong peppermints.

Aunt Nell thumped her way loudly through some late-Victorian ballads before she stopped with a spasm of throat-clearing and coughing.

'Can we listen to Mahler now?' I asked, when she came to a halt. But I don't think she understood.

She met me from school, with her red velvet hat flaming on her hennaed curls and a small rusty fox crouched round her shoulders.

'And who do that snot-nosed lot think they are?' she said, in her carrying voice, as we collected another disapproving dozen of Looks. She grasped me by my unwilling hand and set off with me down the road.

She started to sing. It was probably something like 'Pack up your troubles', or 'It's a long way to Tipperary'. I kept my mouth firmly shut. How could she sing in the street like this? We don't do that sort of thing in Oxford; not even in Jericho.

'Breathe from the diaphragm,' she commanded me, when she had got to the end of a verse. 'Head up, shoulders relaxed, arms loosely at your sides.' The habit of obedience was still with me then, and I did what she said. By the time we reached the terraced house, we were both bellowing out 'Roll out the barrel', *fortissimo*, loud enough to rattle the windows in their frames all down the street.

'That's better,' she said as she unlocked the front door and followed me in. 'I don't like to see a child so quiet and cowed. Just remember the diaphragm, Viv, and they'll hear you at the back of the gallery.'

On the next Saturday I found out what the gallery was. The seats we sat in at the theatre were covered with dusty red plush, worn into bare patches by decades of suburban bottoms. The curtains, too, were red, decorated with gold braid, green in places, rubbed and hanging in thin gold strands in others. There lingered over it all a faint aroma of long-extinguished cigars.

And then people came on to the stage and talked to us. We sat near enough to see the white paint on their faces, the black rings around their eyes, the false lashes, the dots of red in the corners of their eyes. There was a princess, dressed in white; at least, that is the way I remember it. She sang and she danced, her little blue satin shoes moving around on the wooden boards of the stage, and it must have been dusty, for the soles of the shoes were dark with dirt.

'Is it real?' I asked in the interval.

'Real? What do you mean, dear?' asked Aunt Nell.

'I don't know,' I said. 'It doesn't matter.'

Aunt Nell took my hand and led me to join the queue for ice creams. By the time I had licked my way through a strawberry and vanilla cone, the teasing questions faded into insignificance and we went and found our seats for the second act.

The princess came back on stage, wearing pink satin shoes this time, and a fresh layer of pale powder on her hot face. She sang a new song. The audience clapped and cheered. That's what I want to do, I thought. Stand up in front of people and pretend to be something different. Speak things that are made up as I go along. That must be the best thing in the world: to invent stories and make people believe that they are really happening.

The princess had dressed up as a boy, wearing beige tights on her thin legs, and hiding her hair under a cap. She didn't fool me, though. But at last she revealed herself to the prince, doffing her suede cap with a flourish, so that her long hair cascaded over her shoulders, down her back to the hem of her doublet. It rippled in the scarlet spotlight and glimmered with a thousand tiny flames. No wonder the prince fell in love with her.

When it came to an end, the actors lined up and the

lights shone down on them, and the audience applauded until I thought they would never stop, and the palms of my hands were stinging with the pain of it.

'Bravo!' shouted Aunt Nell, at my side. And from a box to one side of the stage, someone threw down flowers. They lay there on the boards, ten fat pink peonies, until the leading actress, she whose curly scarlet lips had smiled at me, picked them up and bowed and kissed her fingers to the young man who had thrown them down to her. She held up the bouquet and bowed and smiled again. One of the blooms, exhausted by the hot, bright lights, burst and scattered its petals on to the stage. They lay there, little hands lopped from dead babies.

Even when the curtain had come down for the last time, and I stood there until I was quite sure that none of them would come out for another bow, Aunt Nell couldn't persuade me to leave. One of them might yet come dancing through the curtains and out along the aisle. The magic might begin all over again.

'Come along, duckie,' said Nell. 'Since you're so star-struck, we'll wait at the stage door so that you can see them come out there. I can see it's the only thing that will satisfy you.'

It was raining, I think, though I didn't care. There was a very small crowd, only four or five of us, waiting at the stage door, amid the dustbins and the cats with the long, swaying tails and the raucous voices.

The actors came out at last: they seemed small and ordinary, wearing beige raincoats, putting up umbrellas, lighting cigarettes, making off towards the bus stop.

'There she is,' said Nell, pointing. 'There's your princess.'

I didn't want to believe her. The woman, for she was no girl this one, was wearing a fawn raincoat and short brown rubber boots. Her head was bare and she must have forgotten her umbrella for her hair was wet and straggled round her face in forlorn rats' tails. It was short hair, of some nondescript dark brownish colour, and she was smoking a cigarette, the white tube stuck to her lower lip as she spoke to her companions.

'Where's her hair?' I must have spoken aloud.

'On her head, love,' said Nell. 'The other was just a wig. Didn't you know?'

I turned and watched as she walked off down the alleyway. From her right hand drooped a bunch of peonies, bluish-grey in the light from the street lamp on the corner. One of them was still shedding petals and they floated on the surface of an oily puddle, stirring gently and moving in idle circles as we set off down the alley for our own bus back to Oxford and Jericho.

I breathed from the diaphragm, but however hard I tried, I couldn't sing.

Aunt Nonie wrote to let me know when Nell died. The letter followed me from my previous digs and arrived this morning. I read it with the sleep still in my eyes and my hair uncombed. Nonie would have taken a damp flannel to my face, but after I had worked out train times and made myself a strong cup of coffee, I stood under the shower and scrubbed myself with a plump new tablet of scented soap. Then I dressed myself in my best suit, which was dark enough for a funeral, a dove-grey shirt and a black tie with a discreet silver spot. My hair was still damp and combed straight back when I looked at myself in the mirror. Aunt Nell would have approved.

I was leaving for the station in plenty of time for the next London train when I remembered that I should take some flowers. Nell had loved flowers and it wouldn't do to forget them. I had the ground-floor flat in the house where I was living, and use of the garden – a flat expanse of grass with a laburnum tree planted in a round hole in its dead centre. Nothing there for a funeral wreath. Next door lived a large and noisy family, and I had managed to get myself on terms of enmity with them. At this time in the morning they were all out: the children at school, the parents at work. Their garden, like mine, was mostly grass, worn into bare patches by the games of football played on it. But they did have a few shrubs and bushes around the perimeter: cotoneaster, forsythia, something anonymous with dark, sharp needles and, on the far side, a big bushy peony.

Here in late May the peonies were in full bloom, like exotic cabbages.

I didn't think about it: I vaulted the fence, damaging only slightly the forsythia, and ran across the grass. My penknife was out in a flash and I had cut them: one, two, three, a dozen fat pink blooms – and I was back over the fence, leaving a mute, broken-backed cotoneaster behind me.

I don't think Nell would enjoy this service. The singers

are flat, the organ wheezes and the vicar is having problems with his sinuses. But I stand beside Nonie and Dilly, though Nonie glares at my undisciplined bunch of flowers. At last it is over and I kiss their powder-scented cheeks and squeeze their gloved hands and murmur the words they expect from me.

'We had some good times together, didn't we, Viv?' Dilly says. 'In the old days, I mean.'

I remember the hard rasp of her flannel on my face, the hot shame I felt when I saw her waiting for me outside the school. 'Yes,' I say. 'Of course we did.'

'Remember the sing-songs round the piano? And the time we all went to the seaside?' says Nonie.

Painful notes from the upright piano and their voices, talking, talking at me when all I wanted was silence and the freedom to think my own thoughts. 'Great times, Aunt Dilly,' I say. 'I'll never forget them. Really.'

And now I am standing by the graveside, and the words are all spoken, the handful of dust is thrown. I lay my bunch of flowers on the ground beside the grave. Whatever rests inside that coffin, I have no sense of Nell's presence. She is gone, for ever, and with her the restraining hand that she has placed on my imagination. I breathe from the diaphragm and the words come sailing into my head, bringing the bright pictures of a new world with them. At last I am free to fly like the seagulls on that grey beach, and look for living food in the darker grey of the waves.

My neighbour has done me proud: the peonies have a colour so amazing that it can only have one of those vivid names like heliotrope or indigo, magenta, lavender or cardinal. Plain pink, the colour of blancmange and of old ladies' knickers, just won't do to describe it. I choose a single bloom to throw down on to the domed lid of the coffin. The flowerhead bursts as it strikes polished mahogany and petals drift across the shining surface and lie there, like little pleading hands.

*I'm glad you've changed to the past tense for this week's assignment: it's much easier to sustain, don't you think, and the shift to the present tense, when it comes, is most effective. Again, I find your writing as fluent and lively as ever, but I find myself longing, just sometimes, for a nice, ordinary, normal character to set against your grotesques. It reads as though you were brought up on Angela Carter as a child instead of Enid Blyton. Perhaps you could make next week's offering just a little shorter? Much as I enjoy reading your work, it can take me rather a long time to give it my properly considered opinion. Remember, if you can work to standard, to time and to length, your work will be professional and saleable. E. J. Dolby.*

# Chapter Two

Andrew turned up alone next morning, sliding his red Sierra expertly into the only parking space, pulling a face at the window of number 12 as he pushed open the gate of number 10.

'I've just seen a child with a face like a toad, poor little bugger,' he said, entering Kate's house. 'It put out a huge tongue, flattened it against the window and then licked its way up the pane like some primitive pink mollusc.'

'How gross. Did you pull faces at it?'

'I'm afraid I did.'

'Good. Please repeat the process on your way out. Would you like a drink?'

'Yes, please, a whisky would be fine, especially if it's that fifteen-year-old single malt from Oddbins that you've been hiding in the third cupboard from the left in the kitchen.'

'You're very cheerful, Andrew,' she said, pouring out mean portions of liquid gold and adding a splash of bottled spring water.

'I've misdirected my first two tourists of the season, and

that always puts me in a good mood. They asked the way to the University, so I pointed in the direction of Woodstock and told them to keep walking.'

They sat on the pink sofa and sipped their whisky. 'So tell me more about this job you want me to do for you. And tell me which "you" we're talking about.'

'The Libraries' Board Computer Security Team,' said Andrew. 'I've been co-opted on to it, and when this little problem came up, I thought of you.'

'Start at the beginning, Andrew.'

'Five years ago the University decided to catalogue the books in its libraries on to one great database so that students in colleges, academics in their offices and readers in the Bodleian could all consult this one huge list and see where to find the books they wanted. It wasn't just the Bodleian that would be involved; eventually all the colleges, the faculties and departments would send staff to be trained, and would add their own acquisitions and holdings into this Union catalogue. Not only could you sit at a public terminal anywhere in the University and see what books were available, but you could also see what was on order, what was out on loan and when it was due back. You could reserve a book and check what books you had already borrowed. And unlike the old card indexes, which showed only authors and titles, you could search the database by subject, or by an odd word in the title to find what you wanted. And through academic computer networks, you can look at university library catalogues not only in this country, but all over the world.'

'How many records have you got on the Oxford database now?' Someone next door had started to practise the saxophone and Kate hoped that the explanation wouldn't need much concentration.

'A million or two, perhaps. And we know that details of one book have gone missing.'

'If only one has gone missing, I don't see what you're worried about.'

'What if someone did it on purpose? And suppose this is just the tip of a very nasty iceberg.' The saxophonist repeated the same phrase for the eighth time; he still had it wrong.

'I see that if someone is buggering up your records you could find a large bill on your hands.'

Andrew sighed. 'Not just that. Think of the loss of goodwill. A lot of the money we've spent has been given by benefactors, and your modern benefactor likes to know that his money isn't being wasted, or walking off in the pocket of some con artist. If there's a hint of scandal, they'll give their money to the Welsh National Opera instead of to us. Opera's very big at present.'

'Ah. So that's why you want a quiet, undercover job done. Something that will stifle your hacker and never be reported.' The saxophonist was attempting to play 'Like a Virgin'.

'You always were a bright girl, Kate.'

'And a salary like mine could be written off as petty cash, I suppose?' Through the wall came a vocal accompaniment to the saxophone.

'As long you don't take too long over the job. We might have problems if you stayed longer than a month or so.

By the way, can we go next door and express our displeasure at the noise level?'

'Only if you want your features realigned. I imagine you think it's an inside job. But it's going to take me time to find my way around and meet all the likely suspects.'

'Now there we can help you narrow it down a bit. Once you've formally agreed to work for us, I'll give you a list of possibles.'

'But why is your hacker doing it? Just for kicks? That's usually the motive for someone young, not a senior library staff member.' The young female Toadface had found her drum kit. She was marginally more talented than the saxophone player. And louder.

'I'm afraid it's more sinister than that.' Andrew had raised his voice. 'It first came to our notice when someone rang up and grumbled about a missing record. He had found a book on the library system computer and then when he came to check it again a few weeks later, it had gone – the record, I mean. Are the neighbours always this noisy?'

'The children are on holiday from school, so this is the worst it gets. What about the book itself, are there any clues there?'

'It was an obscure work by an obscure writer: *Dead – and Alive!* by Eliza Baughn, published in London by Edmund Doyle in 1863.'

'Would anyone want to steal it? Is it valuable? Hasn't it just gone missing, the way a few hundred other books do from libraries every week?'

'The worrying thing is that it is not just the book that

has gone – as you say, that is too common an occurrence to attract such notice – but in this case, someone has deleted the computer record as well.'

'So maybe the book is still there, and someone just pressed the delete key by mistake. Happens to me all the time. Nothing to get worried about.' The noise next door halted abruptly. There was a thundering of feet on uncarpeted stairs and the front door slammed. Twice.

'It isn't that simple.' Andrew found that he had to lower his voice suddenly and considerably. 'You can't delete a record from a huge database like ours, where more than a couple of hundred people can use the staff side of the catalogue, without a very high authority level. And only thirteen people have that authority.'

'And they wouldn't be simple little clerical staff, I suppose, so you can't call them up to your office and grill them. But I still think you may be making a big fuss about a book that may well not have gone missing at all.'

'When you have a few million books in your bookstack you can't find them without a shelf-mark. And you can't find the shelf-mark if someone's deleted the record.'

'What about the old shelf lists? Can't you check them?'

'They're not being kept up by hand any more: the staff are fewer than they used to be and there are cut-backs all round. It seemed to be duplicating work that could be done better on a database, you see. And when old stock is put on to the computer, the card catalogues are usually destroyed: it's too confusing to have a multiplicity of catalogues lying around the place, and few libraries have the space. And why are you sitting on the edge of your seat looking so tense?'

'I'm waiting for Mrs Toadface to realize that her house is now unnaturally quiet and start to play her Tammy Wynette records.' There was another slam of number 12's front door and Mrs Toadface, head bent and a look of malevolence on her face, moved down the road pushing little Toadface in its buggy. Kate relaxed her shoulders and leant back in the sofa. 'So the book concerned might, or might not, be missing. Is there any way of finding out what other records might have been erased? Could we see some sort of pattern?'

'It would be a major task: there are so many new records being added every day. And obviously there are errors made, genuine ones. The only way would be to compare a previous back-up tape with the current one. Back-ups are made every night after the system closes down, and these tapes are archived and stored. The Automation Team are already at full stretch, keeping the system going, working on improvements to it, and answering users' queries. I don't know that we could ask them to take this on as well, not without giving them some extra staff. And the Libraries' Board wouldn't wear that in the present financial climate.'

'But I'm still not clear what I could do. And don't forget that I've got a book to write, as well.'

'You've done all the research and note-taking, haven't you? You've just got a bit of wording-in to do, as I understand it. No problem for you, Kate. Get up an hour earlier and you'll get a couple of thousand words a day written, no problem. That's eighty-five thousand words in six weeks, not counting what you've done already. Problem solved.'

'Thanks, Andrew, but I'm not sure I want to get up any earlier.'

'There's something else bothering you, isn't there? I know you've managed a full-time job as well as your writing before this, so I don't believe that that's it.'

'I haven't forgotten what happened last time I tried some sleuthing.'

'But you enjoyed it, you know you did. You enjoyed going round asking all those rude questions of complete strangers.'

'Yes. But I wasn't so keen on the ending. I'll never forget how it felt to be dragged across the floor: helpless, out of control and then the sudden release and fall. I thought for a moment that I would be pulled over the edge of that staircase and end up dead. I haven't been able to look down from any height at all since it happened: I even get dizzy on the stepladder. And when I realized that someone was drowning and that there was nothing I could do about it, how do you think I felt? I'll never quite forgive myself for that death.'

'Yes, very nasty. But it's all over now.'

'I still get nightmares.'

'Keep running: doesn't that give you invigorating, healthful sleep?'

'Has anyone ever told you that you're cold, callous and calculating?'

'Yes, they have. But now I've got Isabel who thinks I'm

a sweet and wonderful man who still cares too much for his old friend Kate, which is why I'm working hard at changing myself.'

'Isabel is an idiot.'

'Yes, but very pretty, don't you think?'

'I'm asking you to assure me that there is no physical danger involved in this job. No one is to get murdered, or even injured. Is that understood?'

'Of course. Would I let you get hurt?'

'Possibly. But who was Jenna?'

Andrew's eyes shifted sideways for a moment. 'I've never heard of her. It's an unusual name and I'm sure I'd remember it. No, Kate, we want you because there's a brainy job to do: a chase, a puzzle. Outwitting people. Solving the clues, drawing conclusions, reaching the final solution before anyone else does. You'll travel round to different libraries, listen to what goes on underneath the surface, discuss what is happening that the casual observer would miss. Hidden agenda, Kate, subtext. A job only you can do.'

'Interesting work *and* you'll pay me to do it, you say?'

'And it will fit in nicely with that strong moral sense that you like to pretend you haven't got. You'll be working for the good guys, I assure you, and ending a nasty and dishonest practice.' Andrew stood up. 'I think I'd better move my car before the young musicians return with their friends and practise disabling a car alarm and breaking into a Ford Sierra.'

'Probably a wise move.' Kate followed him out into the

street, narrowly missing being mown down by a skate-boarding Harley Toadface.

'I'll give you a couple of hours to think about it. Ring me at the Bodleian,' said Andrew.

'If I say yes, what happens next?'

'We go along tomorrow morning and meet a very interesting man.'

Andrew and Kate were walking through the centre of Oxford. On the corner of the Broad and St Giles' a busker was playing the flute. Kate dropped a twenty-pence piece into the open music case.

Andrew stopped in front of a door with a card pinned to it with the notice 'OULBCST: Visitors Must Ring and Wait'. He rang. They waited. The door was black and needed a new coat of paint. Kate tried muttering 'Owlbec-est' to herself, but Andrew said tersely, 'Just call them the Team; people who matter will know whom you mean.'

The building was grey, its façade eroded, and it looked as though pieces might drop off on their heads at any moment. Kate stepped back a pace, while at the same time a tinny voice snapped, 'Who is it?' through a grille on the right of the door.

'Grove,' replied Andrew. 'And Ivory. We are expected.'

'Don't you have to give the password?' hissed Kate, and giggled.

'Not yet,' said Andrew repressively.

The door buzzed at them, Andrew pushed it open, and they went in.

The hallway smelled of mildew and decay, of floorboards and joists rotting away with damp. As they walked through the building, Kate saw green and cream gloss paint bubbling and peeling from antique walls, while open doors gave glimpses of cupboards and even whole rooms full of mouldering, outdated, unwanted, forgotten files and furniture. She followed Andrew up the stairs and into a large room dominated by a grey marble fireplace and lined with bookshelves behind green-painted grilles. The smell of fungus followed them in as Andrew closed the door.

'This is Kate Ivory, the woman I told you about,' said Andrew. 'Kate, this is Charles.'

Didn't he have a surname? Apparently not for her. She walked forward and held out a hand. It was shaken by a few insubstantial fingertips in return as though he was unwilling to respond to such direct human contact.

He was in his early forties, and was thin, with receding mouse-coloured hair and the soft, papery skin of the sexually inactive.

'You can sit down, Kate,' said Andrew. His look told her that she could stop staring at Charles. He probably knew that she was taking mental notes and would insert the unfortunate Charles, gender changed perhaps, into her next novel.

Charles was frowning at her. He had surprisingly dark brown eyes, and the skin around them was yellowed and puffy. 'Are you sure that Kate understands the discretion she will need to do this job?' he asked Andrew, as though she wasn't there.

'I think you'll find her reliable enough.'

'I know how to keep my mouth shut,' said Kate. 'And I don't usually walk around with a magnifying glass asking intrusive questions, if that's what you mean by discretion.'

Charles sighed. As he walked back to his own chair, Kate saw that he was so thin that his beige corduroy trousers bagged around his legs and ended up above the ankles so that too much dark grey woollen sock filled the gap between turn-up and shoe. 'You'll need more subtlety than that if you're going to work for us,' he said in his wispy voice, as he seated himself behind his desk.

'I thought it was my way of finding out the truth that you were counting on, actually,' said Kate, ignoring Andrew's scowl.

'You'll have to tell people that you're a novelist and always looking for material for your books, of course, if they get suspicious. We don't want them to know that you're working for us,' said Charles.

'I'm not sure I want to work on those terms,' said Kate.

'Really? How much of your advance have you got left?' said Andrew.

'Stop trying to manipulate me, Andrew,' Kate snapped. 'I've made my own decision to do this job, because it interests me and because I think I'd be good at it, but I'm not going to be walked over by you and your friend. If I don't like the conditions, I shan't take the job.'

'You'll go home to the saxophone player and the budding Ringo Starr, will you?'

'Who? Oh, I forget how *old* you are sometimes, Andrew.'

'Let's get on with it, shall we?' said Charles, glancing

at his watch as though he had already spent too much time on such a junior member of his staff. He sat down behind the large, untidy desk. 'We haven't a lot of choice and I suppose Miss Ivory will have to do for our purposes. At least she knows how to catalogue a book.'

It had been too long since Kate had worked for anyone other than herself and she was resenting the dismissive way this Charles character was talking. She didn't like his humourless mouth and his clean, neat look of a nineteen-fifties schoolboy.

'One more question,' she said. 'Why all the secrecy? Why not just call in the police?' Andrew and Charles both grunted 'Huh!' simultaneously. 'Or send in one of your own people openly? Why the cloak, even if I'm not being issued with the departmental dagger?'

'Economic facts,' said Andrew.

'Money,' said Charles. 'As ever. Explain it to the lady, Andrew.'

'We're expected to raise money ourselves these days, rather than have it arrive as if by magic in our bank account,' said Andrew. 'And that means that we have to keep squeaky clean. If potential benefactors think that their donations – and we're talking millions here, Kate—'

'Do you think you could fill Kate in on the rest of the background in your own time?' interrupted Charles. 'She will have to be properly briefed, of course, while giving her only the information that you think is strictly necessary to complete her task. She doesn't need to know too much political background, don't you think?'

'I'll tell her what she needs to know,' said Andrew diplomatically.

'Make sure she meets Graham Kieler sometime. He's the Team officer who goes round libraries trying to impress them with the need to keep some kind of security: usually it's at the level of removing Post-it notes with the operator's password from computer screens, but he might have seen or heard something useful.' And Charles was standing up, assuming that they would do the same, while he fiddled with his brown tweed tie.

'And you're sure this is a simple investigation into the possibility that someone has tampered with computer records?' insisted Kate.

'Of course. What else were you expecting?'

'What on earth is the woman talking about, Andrew?'

'The unfortunate story of the trainee last year, Charles.'

'That had absolutely nothing to do with us, as I remember.' His mouth shut into a straight line. 'Now, to get back to relevant matters. We can appoint you to a Grade Three Clerical post,' he said, as though the matter were settled.

'Grade Five,' said Kate. And at the look of distaste on Charles's face, she added: 'Top of the scale.'

'First incremental point,' said Charles, 'since really you will have no supervisory duties to justify a Scale Five post,' and Kate had to concede him the victory since she didn't know what sums they were talking about, anyway.

They made their way back through the mould-scented air to the front door. On the ground floor she had a glimpse through an open door of a large room full of desks and computers, with a couple of operators tapping aggressively at keyboards, and a third pouring boiling water from an electric kettle into a stained mug.

'Do they live here? They look as though they sleep at their computers, too,' said Kate.

'They probably do. Shall I see if Graham is in?' asked Andrew. 'I could introduce you to the rest of the Team, too, while we're here.'

'Just get me out of this place before I start growing green mould all over!'

'That's what you call an interesting man, is it?' asked Kate as they walked back down St Giles'.

'You seemed to have an unfortunate effect on him. Did you have to be so aggressive?'

'Aggressive? I hadn't even started. I have no intention of ever being put in my place by boring little men like that.'

'Well, you'll have to tone down your style if you're going to be working in the University libraries. Many people work in libraries because they think they can hide there from the nastier aspects of life – like *people* – and spend their lives dealing only with books. They're wrong, of course. Libraries are about spreading information and interacting with people, but they don't think that when they go into the profession. You'll have to treat your colleagues as shy, wild animals. And if any of them make friendly overtures, take them up on it. It's by wandering into as many offices and listening to as much gossip as possible that you're likely to pick up what you need to know.'

They were crunching their way across the gravel in front of the Sheldonian Theatre.

'You did say that you could start work tomorrow, didn't you, Kate dear?' Andrew's voice sounded hollow and unusually solemn as it echoed in the stone archway leading into the Schools Quadrangle of the Bodleian Library. Ahead of them sunlight shone on golden Cotswold stone enclosing hundreds of scholars poring over their books.

'Mausoleum,' muttered Kate. 'Monument to dead authors and dead books.'

'Rubbish,' said Andrew briskly, as they strode across the flagstones and out into Radcliffe Square. 'There sit the coming generation,' he said, gesturing towards the Radcliffe Camera. 'Young, keen, idealistic undergraduates. Some of them are women even, Kate.'

They walked into the Lower Camera and as she looked around her at the rows of hard-working students, her heart softened. It was the business of librarians to make sure that the books these young people wanted were on the shelves when they were needed: it directly affected their exam results. At least for the moment she was a librarian – or, more accurately, a library assistant – and so she was part of that process. Apart from anything else, book-theft disturbed her sense of neatness, of achieving a job well done.

Andrew's office was through an inconspicuous door in the Lower Camera and she could hardly see him behind the piles of books and letters when he had seated himself at his desk.

'We've decided that the easiest way of getting you in

where we want you is to offer you as a Retrospective Conversion Cataloguer around the University system.'

'Is that as dull as it sounds?'

'Probably more so. There are around forty libraries on the computerized system at the moment, ranging from the Bodleian itself and its Dependent Libraries, through college libraries, down to small specialist outfits with a couple of shelves of books. They can keep up with the stock coming in week by week – and that's a couple of thousand items in the case of the Bodleian – but if they want to keep track electronically of who they've lent their books to, they have to put the mass of their collections on the system.'

'What's the advantage of that?' asked Kate, as it seemed to be her turn to say something.

'Before the computerized system some poor library assistant had to work her way through boxes of loan cards to keep check on who had what, and send out reminders when books were overdue. Dull, time-consuming work: just the sort of thing that computers were designed to do. The problem is finding the time to re-catalogue thirty or forty thousand books while getting on with their normal work. And that is where you will come in.'

'Will they be able to afford me? I can't see a small library willingly doubling its staff just to please you, Andrew.'

'You'll be cheap, Kate. Very cheap, since we'll be paying your salary and they will be asked to contribute only a nominal sum.'

'You'll tell them about my coffee breaks and the chocolate biscuits I like to eat with my tea, will you?'

'I'll make sure you get some training in the job you'll be doing. You won't be very popular if you can't do it without asking for help every five minutes. I'll assume that you can remember the basics of cataloguing, but I'll take you through a quick refresher course tomorrow morning. And in the afternoon I'll take you over to the Bodleian Cataloguing department for a crash course in the retrospective work.'

'You said something about a list of thirteen people who had the authority to delete records. Have you got it here?'

Andrew sorted through a few of the piles of papers and files on his desk while Kate studied the dull books in his bookcase. *How to Motivate the Under-Achieving Employee* was a title that caught her eye. She hoped that Andrew wasn't going to practise on her. At that moment he opened a drawer and pulled out a sheet of paper.

'You can't take it out of this room, so look at it and memorize the names.'

She took the typed sheet and looked down the list. The first three names would be easy enough to remember, anyway: Charles Trim (yes, his name would be Trim), Andrew Grove, Graham Kieler. Then there were the librarians of a couple of colleges, the head of the Kennedy Centre for North American Studies, and some other names that Kate didn't recognize.

'Those three work at the Bodleian,' said Andrew, pointing them out, 'and then there are a couple of faculty library heads and the last two are from Bodleian dependent libraries.'

He let her study the list in silence for a few moments while she committed the names to memory.

'But unless this investigation is going to take ten years, how do I catalogue thirty thousand books in each of four or five libraries, as well as questioning all the relevant people?'

'I've thought of that. What you will be doing is spending just a short time in each place, estimating how many books they have to catalogue, how easy the cataloguing is likely to be, and what they are going to need in terms of hardware and workspace. You'll spend a few days, catalogue a hundred or so typical books, and put in a short report so that they can cost the job, estimate how long it will take, and have some facts and figures to present to their governing bodies.'

'And then? We conquer the world?'

'Not until next Monday morning, when I deliver you to your first library.'

Next morning she was back in Andrew's office.

'Do I get to swear an oath about kindling fire in the Bodleian Library again?'

'No,' said Andrew. 'Once is quite enough for that. But you do have to get yourself a staff identity card. I'll take you up to the studio.'

'Studio' sounded arty and professional, but the photograph on Kate's new identity card made her look like a criminal with her white face, round staring black eyes and pale hair standing straight up from her forehead as though she had just been given a severe electric shock. RETRO-

CON said the card, ominously and incomprehensibly, as though she was some convict wearing a nineteen-sixties broad-arrowed suit. However, when she waved the card at blue-jacketed porters, they smiled and allowed her through into the illustrious depths of the Bodleian Library.

The thing that struck her first was the difference between the Bodleian's public and private faces. Its Schools Quadrangle drew crowds of tourists throughout the year, guides gave more or less accurate accounts of its history, and Kate herself had gasped at the splendours of the fifteenth-century Divinity School and sniffed at the beeswax-polish smell of Duke Humfrey's Library where books still stood on their original shelves and library assistants climbed up into galleries to find books for their readers.

But once she was through the Staff Only door, all glamour disappeared and she was in dark corridors, walking up gloomy staircases and sitting in a common-room that smelled like a very old ashtray, drinking nasty coffee from a machine.

Then she was back in Andrew's office, sitting at a terminal and going through a rapid refresher course in cataloguing.

At lunch time she went for a walk, setting off down St Giles', under the plane trees, past the secretive blank faces of Balliol and St John's. And behind them was the small medieval college of Leicester where Liam was working. No, not working at this moment, but sitting with the other senior members of his college, eating a lunch served by a

65

white-jacketed butler. Who else was there, and what were
they talking about?

She had arrived at Little Clarendon Street and
wandered down its length, staring in the windows. Then
she saw it. A deep gold linen jacket, fitted into the waist,
with a wide collar and deep revers. A Van Gogh of a
colour, as Isabel nearly put it. She went into the shop.
Yes, it was a size ten. Yes, Izzie was right, it looked quite
stunning against her hair. It cost so much money that she
lost her head and bought a cunning little blue skirt to go
with it. After all, she had pretty good knees, so she might
as well flaunt them.

# iii

## *The Use of Dialogue*

*This week I want you to write a scene involving dialogue. Try and bring out the personalities of your characters in what they say and how they say it. This isn't easy when you first start, but keep practising and you'll soon get the hang of it. Remember that the best dialogue has a subtext, or hidden agenda: something that the reader and one or more of the characters know, but the other character does not. This creates what we call dramatic irony and makes the dialogue much more interesting than the means for a simple exchange of information.*

Eventually I wanted to return to Oxford, the real Oxford of colleges and learning and academic excellence. I wanted to wipe out the picture I had of the two of us living in that house in North Oxford with the hyacinth door and the sunflower curtains, as well as of the peculiar household in Jericho. This time I would belong; I would be an insider.

I would have the quiet voice, the old car, the upright bicycle and the position of respect in a college that I had always coveted. I knew that it was what I should have, what I should be. It was only by some vagary of an unkind Fate that I had gone to a red-brick university and been awarded an indifferent degree.

Most of all, I wanted to belong in these libraries, to have the right to study their leather-bound books, to sit under their painted ceilings and breathe in the dust of several centuries. I had wandered in the Schools Quadrangle of the Bodleian Library with the crowds of summer tourists, and gaped up at the ceiling of the Divinity School. It wasn't enough. I wanted to own it, to devour it, to make it a part of myself. I knew that one day I would, but just for the moment I could do no more than buy a couple of souvenir postcards and go on with my Dream.

Which comes first, do you think, the Dream or the Action? I know that when I dream something like that, so that it passes in technicolour before the screen of my closed eyelids, that it *will* happen. Maybe not today. Give it time.

I have never liked the name my mother gave me: Vivian. It has a sexual ambiguity about it that can be quite embarrassing at times. So when I had the chance to change it and to improve my whole life at the same time, I took it. Isn't that a fantasy we all have? Haven't *you*, Mrs Dolby, wondered what it would be like to step out of the person that you have been for the past thirty years and step into a new one, as though you were discarding a worn-out cardigan and donning a smart new jacket? A new name, a new career. Leave behind the reputation you have built up and pick up someone else's. I would have the same face to look at in the mirror in the morning, but a different name, a whole new personality.

I suppose that anyone who has ever tried their hand at acting on the stage knows what I'm talking about. But the character in the play is given to you, together with the words that you must deliver, and this is why you often feel stiff and awkward inside his skin. But what I am talking about is a transformation. A metamorphosis. Caterpillar into butterfly. Or vice versa if you prefer it. Instant gratification. Well, that is what it was like for me.

I bumped into John in St Giles'. We both paused on the pavement, waiting for a couple of cyclists to pass so that we could cross Pusey Street, I to walk up to Little Clarendon Street where I was going to get my hair cut, he to carry on up the Woodstock Road towards the head-quarters of the international charity organization for whom he was about to start work. It is one of the felicities of Oxford that it is such a small town – if you don't count the tourists – that you will always bump into someone you know in any hundred yards of its central streets.

The day was hot and we stepped into the 'Bird and Baby' pub. (He, more formally, called it the Eagle and Child and remarked, as everyone always remarks, that this was the pub where Tolkien and the Inklings used to meet.) We walked through to the garden at the back, and ordered iced lagers.

'So,' I said, and I called him, naturally, by his name – the name that now belongs to me. You shall know him as

John, in the same way that you have learned to call me Vivian. 'John,' I said. 'What have you been doing with yourself since college?' John had got himself a very good degree – considerably better than the one that they awarded me.

'I went on to library school,' he said, mentioning a large and prestigious establishment.

I raised an eyebrow. John had surely been destined for a more exciting life.

'I am interested in the collecting, organizing and dissemination of information,' he said – rather smugly, I thought. 'Or at least I was, until it occurred to me that I had been privileged all my life and was now proposing to pass on this privilege to others of my own type and class. There must be more to life than this, don't you think?'

'Of course.' But no, I hadn't thought beyond the acquisition of a reasonable standard of life for myself, but then, I hadn't had John's upbringing. And for a moment I thought that John was going to say something truly embarrassing, such as, 'Have you found Jesus in your life?' But he merely composed his face, as if for silent prayer, and said, 'I was lucky enough to read the right books and meet the right people so that I understood where my lifepath should lead, at least for the next couple of years.'

Yes, it is comparatively easy to give up the good things of life when you have enjoyed them effortlessly for the past twenty-three years. It comes harder to those of us who are still striving to attain them, don't you think?

Even this early in our conversation the idea was coming to me.

I had often thought of becoming a librarian. The problem was that my degree was just not good enough. Good enough to get me into a library school, perhaps, but not good enough to get me the sum it cost to pay the fees and keep myself for a year or more. And, of course, not good enough to get me into a good library without the extra qualification. But here was a way to get round these difficulties. I might not have been born anywhere within licking distance of a silver spoon, but I could see an opportunity when one presented itself, and I could take it, especially if it had the buzz of added danger.

The sad thing about really good people – and at least for this time in his life I do believe that that was what John was – is the way they take you at their own valuation. If you smile, and sound concerned and caring, they believe that that is what you are. They do not suspect you of an ulterior motive – not beyond the wish to feel good about yourself. I sat, looking concerned, sounding caring, asking large numbers of impertinent questions. I learned a lot about John, from the name of his head of department at library school to the address of his widowed mother. I learned that he had given up on the pleasures of cigarettes, strong drink and the company of women. In fact, John had cut himself off from most of his former friends, since he no longer enjoyed the same things that they did. His new companions were serious and idealistic, and would seem to have nothing in common with the noisy, profane crowd of his student days.

I forget now the precise part of the developing world that John was travelling to to purge his over-privileged soul. I remember that it was obscure, and that I had to search for a long time on the map before I found it. And perhaps I would never have used all the information I gathered that day were it not for the coincidence, a few weeks later, of two pieces of news in the same issue of the newspaper. On one page there was an advertisement for a junior Assistant Librarian's position at the Bodleian Library, and on another there was a small item of news, not more than a column inch, I suppose, on the killing of an aid worker in . . . well, I still forget the name of the place. But I remember his name all right: John Exton. I looked at the job advertisement again. I hadn't a hope of getting it. John Exton would stand a very good chance, of course, but he was dead. It seemed such a waste of that golden academic career. Did I tell you that I hate waste? I'm like that character in *Cranford* who could never see a piece of butter left on her plate without using it up. And so the idea, which had started out as a tiny seed in the Eagle and Child, germinated and sent out an exploratory rootlet and two green leaves. I sat down and wrote two letters: one to the Assistant Secretary of the Bodleian Library, requesting further details of the post advertised in that day's quality newspapers, the other to the widowed mother of John Exton, expressing my extreme sorrow on the death of my dear and close friend. My approach to her was straightforward and manly.

Both my correspondents replied promptly, and only three days later I had details of the job at the Bodleian, together with an application form, and an invitation to visit John Exton's mother and attend his funeral (this had to await the shipment of his body from the developing country, I understood). The coincidence seemed too appropriate to ignore. I took a couple of photocopies of the application form and tried filling one of them in, in pencil, in the character of John Exton. They asked for references, and this worried me for a little, until I remembered that John had told me how large and impersonal both the educational institutions he had attended (with such glowing results) had been. If I wrote to the heads of department in each instance, they would probably consult some file and then send out a standard letter of reference. Another couple of hundred faces had passed before them since John's, after all, and you could not expect these people to recognize an individual student. I consulted the Reference section of the Central Library to discover the names and titles of these gentlemen.

Then I set off for the dull town in Hertfordshire where John's mother lived. This could have been trickier, but I remembered that John had cut himself off from his former friends, and that I was probably the only one to have contacted Mrs Exton when the news of his death was reported. I was perhaps foolhardy to make the visit, but I was not yet committed to anything, and it had occurred to me that I needed to know details like his exact date of birth, and also his National Insurance number.

Really, it was a doddle.

'It must be painful for you to sort through his things,' I said. 'Would you like me to help you?'

Of course I didn't touch any of the personal stuff: the old teddy bear, the childhood books and toys, his swimming certificates and school prizes. But I did remove all the dreary bits of paper that his mother no longer needed, and that would furnish me with his identity. And then I helped her to bag up his clothes and books and drove them all down to the nearest charity shop. Afterwards I made a pot of tea for us both and passed across the packet of tissues. In reality I could hardly suppress my excitement. I was embarked on a journey, and a change in the direction of my life, no less drastic than those which John himself had undertaken three months before.

I'm sure you realize by now that his name was not really John Exton. When it comes to the fictionalizing of real events, you can't even be sure that I have left the genders of the characters the same, can you? I learned early not to trust what people said, and if you are only just beginning to do so as a result of my writing, then you should thank me for a valuable lesson in life.

*You certainly have an unusual way of looking at things, Viv. This piece is presented with your usual flair and fluency, but perhaps is just a little too smooth and slick. I find it difficult to know what these characters of yours are really thinking. They present plausible faces to the world, but I am never sure what is going on behind the masks.*

*On a practical level, I would like to read a page or two that made do without adjectives and adverbs. Think more about producing lively verbs: remember that the over-use of the adjective is the mark of the amateur writer. E. J. Dolby.*

# Chapter Three

Kate had forgotten how much there was to learn before you could catalogue competently on the on-line system. In the long cataloguing room at the Bodleian, with its powerful up-lighters and rows of terminals and micro-computers, she was handed over to a tall young man with dark hair and tinted spectacles.

'Marc,' he introduced himself. 'Make yourself comfortable.' And he gave her a chair next to his, in front of the dark grey screen. 'I'd better run through the basics of the On-Line Public Access Catalogue – or OPAC for short – before we start cataloguing,' he said.

He tapped at the keyboard until a menu appeared in green on the screen in front of them. 'If a reader comes into any of our libraries and asks for a book, he will be directed to one of these machines and told to find its shelf-mark. He can then fill in a request slip and an assistant in the bookstack will locate the book he wants and bring it up to a reading room. So, from this first menu, let's tell the machine that we want to search for a book.' He typed a digit and pressed the return key. The message on the screen now asked whether the user wanted to search by the author's name, by the title of the book, or by subject.

'Well,' said Marc. 'There's really only one choice, isn't there? And he typed *1* to choose the first option, pressed the return key, and then typed in *Ivory, K*.

Fourteen lines of authors' names unfolded down the screen, with Kate's own appearing at line two. When he typed *2* and return, the screen displayed a list of all her book titles.

'How about calling up *Storm Across the Water*?' she said.

And there on the screen appeared the catalogue record for her book, showing all the details: its title, her name, the date it was published and by whom, how many pages it contained and how tall it was. Marc pointed to a set of initials and a date at the end of the record.

'There, you can see from the initials that I catalogued it myself, last November. Now we can look to see which libraries hold copies,' and he typed in another character so that the words *Copies held in Bodleian Library* appeared.

And there was the location of her book, BOD, and its shelf-mark, indicating the precise place in the bowels of the Bodleian bookstack where her book would be found on a shelf. It was the best moment of her day.

'But now we have to turn to cataloguing,' said Marc. 'And the first thing to remember is that we don't duplicate other cataloguers' work. We search other databases to make sure that no one else in a British university library, or the Library of Congress, has catalogued the book already. If they have, we transfer the record from their database to ours, and simply add the details of location and shelf-mark that refer to our copy.' And he was off, with an unending stream of instructions on record-matching, downloading, editing in Sidekick, retrieving from the Bibliographic Pool, record-keeping, card-pulling, CURL and OCLC.

By the end of the afternoon, Kate felt proud of herself and her abilities, especially when she discovered that she had talked Charles into paying her at a couple of grades higher than the other clerical staff around her.

At four o'clock she went down to the canteen with Marc for a restorative cup of tea. A few minutes later they were joined by another young man, who pulled up a chair close to Kate's. He had a pale, slightly spotty complexion, dark hair slicked back from his forehead, and was trying hard to be pleasant. He was tall, slim and broad-shouldered, and nearly good-looking, but there was something too self-satisfied in his expression, and his denim jeans were a size too small.

'Ian Maltby,' he said. 'I work up in the Conservation Department.' He smiled at Kate, showing gappy teeth. 'Why don't you come up and visit us?' he said, 'I'd be pleased to show you round.'

'Ian specializes in getting to know young female staff,' said Marc, cattily. 'There isn't a trainee in the place who's safe from him.'

'Nonsense,' said Ian, maintaining eye contact with Kate. 'I just like to make people feel at home, make sure they're finding their way round in a new environment.' And Kate realized that this was part of a Bodleian courting ritual.

She was about to refuse, when she remembered that she was supposed to be gaining as much information – or what one might unkindly call gossip – as possible, and any opportunity was to be welcomed. And it wasn't as though she would be working at the Bodleian any longer than necessary, so she wouldn't be landed with an unwelcome admirer.

'It will have to be a brief visit,' she said. 'I've got a lot more to learn about cataloguing this afternoon.'

His room was at the top of the building, through a corridor smelling of chemicals, and looked like a small laboratory, with benches and microscopes and strong lights. Above their heads were wooden racks like the clothes airers found in old kitchens, with large pads of cream-coloured felt sitting on them.

'Drying pads,' said Ian, seeing where she was looking. 'I've had to paste a sheet into this book, and I use the felt pad to press it while it's drying, so that there are no wrinkles when it's finished.'

Other work in the room seemed to involve water and balls of grubby cotton wool, and the whole set-up was so lacking in glamour and interest that Kate knew that she would never be able to use it in a story. But she continued her tour of the room, and listened to his account of his work and at the end she thanked Ian Maltby for his time. He flashed his gappy teeth at her as he urged her to return at any time, while behind him on the pinboard incongruously brilliant postcards sported silver beaches and cobalt seas to remind her that there was another world beckoning outside the library. On one card, scarlet and purple bougainvillaea rioted over a whitewashed wall, catching her eye. *Santa Luisa, California*, she read, before her attention returned to Ian Maltby and she refused an invitation to go to the cinema with him, said her goodbyes and left the room.

California, she thought. Young female members of staff. Had Jenna ever worked at the Bodleian? Since there wasn't a moment's respite from cataloguing for the rest of the afternoon, she was unable to ask.

'Brain-dead,' she said to Andrew, when they were sitting in the Crypt for a relaxing end-of-day drink. 'That's how I'm feeling. I'd forgotten the effect that hours of cataloguing have on you. My eyes are focused at a point eighteen inches away and I cannot uncross them. My fingers are stiff from hitting the same small selection of keys. My mind is numb from concentrating on those flickering green words and puzzling over trivial problems such as whether the main entry is or is not in the body. And the woman at the desk next to mine is a fresh air fiend and flings all the windows wide open, whether it is raining or not, while the man opposite her hates sitting in a draught and rushes up to close them all again as soon as she leaves the room. Then she returns and they bicker. I could happily drown them both.' She paused for breath.

'A bottle of the house claret, Patricia, and two glasses,' said Andrew into the brief silence, as they settled themselves in their usual corner. 'And if you could turn up the volume of the music just a smidgen, other people wouldn't be able to listen to what my friend was saying.'

'No one else is interested in your beastly computer, Andrew,' Kate said crossly. 'I shall talk as loudly as I want.'

'You'll be naming names as well as shrieking insults in a moment.' Andrew sighed. 'Bring her a chicken and bacon sandwich, Patricia, to raise her blood sugar level and keep her quiet.' The waitress disappeared towards the kitchen as though there was nothing at all unusual in Andrew's order. 'You're hell when your blood sugar drops,' he said to Kate as they waited.

'My metabolism has nothing to do with it: I'm making a perfectly reasonable series of comments on the cataloguing process.' She drank some of her wine and went on more calmly: 'I wanted to ask what I was looking for, especially. What books are likely to go missing, Andrew? Does someone intend to swipe the complete run of Mills & Boons from L Floor at the Bodleian, or are we looking for something a little more refined, do you think? Until I took to cataloguing, I never realized how many hundreds of obscure books were published every single week in this country. Where do I start to look?'

'In the college libraries, you'll find you are dealing mostly with undergraduate texts, and while of course text-books – law and medicine particularly – are expensive, I can't see anyone putting their career and liberty on the line for books that must be worth twenty or thirty quid at the most on the second-hand market. So, what you are looking for are the collections housed in some separate section or room. Some of these will go back over five hundred years and be worth large sums of money.'

'And you think they're going to confide in a simple cataloguer about them?'

'Here, eat some of your sandwich. You're turning up the volume again.'

She started to reply, but filled her mouth with food instead.

'I think there's going to be great opposition from some colleges to the publicizing of the whereabouts of their valuable books, and I don't think perhaps we're talking about very old, very valuable, books or manuscripts,' continued Andrew, ignoring the comment.

'Well? What?'

'I'm not sure. As you know, my own interests lie in the field of theology—'

'No, Andrew, I didn't know that, and it sheds an entirely new light on your character. Theology? Are you quite sure?'

'Finish your sandwich, have another glass of wine and try to talk sense.'

'But I've never even known you go to church. How can you be interested in theology, let alone be an expert on it?'

'That has nothing whatever to do with it.' He swallowed half a glass of wine and blinked at her through thick lenses.

'Does Isabel know about it? Should a theologian be going out with young, flighty girls like that?'

'Shut up about it, Kate. Am I quizzing you about that expensive-looking carrier bag that you have tucked between your feet? A bag which is acquiring a thick layer of sawdust that you are going to have great trouble removing from your new garment, whatever it might be.' Kate quickly picked up the bag and shook it. 'Let's get back to our subject, shall we? I think that what you have to look out for is a collection of books that isn't included in the undergraduate section, and yet is not so rare and valuable that copies have been hidden from outsiders on the system.'

'You didn't tell me about that possibility,' said Kate, giving up for the moment the opportunity to tease Andrew any further.

'Only four libraries have taken it so far: it goes against the spirit of a Union catalogue. It means that you can only see where a copy is kept if you are logged in from the actual college concerned. So I think you can disregard those holdings. Stick with records that can be read by anyone, anywhere.'

'I'm not sure how useful this briefing has been after all, Andrew. I don't believe you know any more about it than I do. Less, probably, since my crash course in cataloguing this afternoon.'

'Very probably. But I think that it would be a good idea in future for you to type me out notes on your daily activities, details of the people you've met, of anything that you've learnt that may be relevant to our investigation.'

'I'm not sure I fancy doing that after a day's work.'

'But think how useful it will be for you to sort out your ideas on paper – or screen, I suppose, in your case – every day, and what an invaluable reminder it will be if you want to look up some chance encounter in the future.'

'That makes sense, I suppose. All right, Andrew. But I

think I need a portion of chocolate fudge cake in compensation.'

'How gross.' But he caught the attention of a passing waitress and gave the order.

When she got home, the sun had only just set and Toad-face was out on the pavement, playing in a toy car. The noise level as its feet stamped up and down the road and incoherent shouts came from its toady little mouth was quite horrific.

She relieved her feelings by kicking the front tyre of her expensive cream car.

When she went inside, the phone was ringing: it was Emma again. Kate pulled the cord to its furthest extent and sat down in a chair. She had better make up for the other evening's terse conversation by giving Emma her full attention.

'Emma, how lovely to hear from you. So sorry I had to break off the other evening.'

'I guessed you had that man of yours there. Andrew, is it?'

'It was Liam, actually.'

'Well, anyway, I wanted to ask you about taking over my creative-writing class.'

Kate managed not to repeat her insult about the sparrow poetry. 'Well . . .' she said, which gave Emma the opportunity to break in again.

'It isn't at all what you're imagining. They're a varied crowd, about sixteen of them, different ages, men and women both. And we're doing a properly structured course. You could take it straight over: I've got my notes for all the rest of the sessions. It's only once a week.'

'Sorry, Emma, but I've just taken on a library job for a few weeks. I've got to get the first draft of my new book finished in the next six weeks, and I don't think I can take on any more work just at the moment.'

'Couldn't you think about it a bit more, Kate?'

Emma could not keep the note of pleading out of her voice, and Kate felt rotten at turning her down again. 'Oh, that's someone at the front door,' she fibbed. 'I have to go now.' And she put down the phone with another disloyal feeling of relief at her escape.

'Do you understand about relationships?' asked Kate. Though why she was asking her friend Camilla, who had only once (and that disastrously) been involved with a man, she didn't understand. Maybe it was because it was that expansive time after she had eaten and before she did her final hour's work of the day, and because Camilla was her oldest friend, that she had poured herself a small drink and dialled her number.

'I don't think I wish to answer that question,' said Camilla. 'And I assume that it is rhetorical and that you want to talk to me about Liam. Or Andrew. Or both. Or perhaps someone new.'

'Liam and I don't seem to have time to develop what could be described as a relationship. The times when we are both available are so few that we only get as far as covering what we've been doing in the days or weeks since we last met. We don't progress to anything more personal.'

'Had you thought of living together?'

'No.' Impossible to think of living with *anyone*. She hurried on. 'And it was Andrew I wanted to talk about. He's found himself a new girlfriend.'

'And you're jealous?'

'Certainly not!'

'So?'

'I like seeing him, but before he leaves, I wish he would go. If you see what I mean.'

'Barely. You're supposed to be the articulate one, but you've only scored three out of ten so far this evening.'

'I don't want Andrew around all the time, or even a lot of it, and it seems quite reasonable that he should find himself another woman, but why does it have to be someone so young and so stupid?'

'Did you ever meet Andrew's ex-wife?'

'He's never even mentioned her.'

'She was a year or two older than him and bossy. Rather like his mother, I imagine. Since he escaped from her, he's been running away from intelligent, managing women. What's this new girl's name?'

'Isabel. Izzie.'

'Well, with this Isabel it sounds as though he's succeeded. I should concentrate on your work and on getting to know Liam if I were you. What are the two of you running away from?'

'Nothing. And how are you and Carey getting on?' Carey was Camilla's disastrous man.

'I intend to carry on experimenting and travelling. Who knows what may be around the next corner?'

When Kate hung up, she still felt dissatisfied, as though life was moving on and leaving her behind before she could grasp what it was about.

Later when she had completed a thousand words of her novel on her word processor, she opened a new sub-directory, *Security*, and a new file which she headed *Notes* and dated with that day's date. Then she typed:

1. Two days ago: visit from Andrew Grove, of the Bodleian Library and the Security Team, together with his girlfriend, Isabel Ryan.
2. A book, with its corresponding catalogue entry, has gone missing from one of the college libraries, and the Security Team think that it may be an indication of widespread thieving.
   *Are they making a big fuss over nothing?*
3. Isabel mentioned someone called Jenna, who is dead. Paul Taylor also knows her name, though no one seems keen to give me any details.
4. Yesterday: meeting at the OULBCST office. Present: Andrew Grove, Charles Trim, self. I am to act as a retrospective cataloguer, looking at libraries and calculating how much work there will be to bring all their collections on to the computerized catalogue. There are millions of people, all over the world, who have access to the catalogue through their computer networks, but only thirteen, all senior and apparently respectable, who have the authority level

necessary to doctor the catalogue after stealing a
book, and the list is headed by Charles Trim and
Andrew Grove, and includes another member of
the Security Team, Graham Kieler (whom I
have not yet met). I did not like Charles Trim:
I thought him a self-important and pompous
man, with all the humanity and outgoingness of
a mechanical digger.
5. In fact, I did not take to the Security Team, in
their mouldering building, one little bit, and I
would love to find that the thief is one of them.

Kate·read through the last couple of points on her
screen and sighed. She couldn't print out this sort of
subjective stuff for Andrew. She should delete such
emotional responses to people from her notes. On the
other hand, she could just lift the acceptable paragraphs
and copy them into a second document, which she could
label *Report*, and give to Andrew. After all, she might
find that her initial reactions to people and situations
would come in useful later in the investigation. She
returned to her notes.

6. Spent the morning at the Bodleian, being
photographed and remembering how to
catalogue.
7. Afternoon spent at the Bodleian, in their
Cataloguing Department. The place was full of
people who were interested only in computers,
and who knew about nothing except modern

books, as far as I could tell. Met an anonymously pleasant young man called Marc.

8. Ian Maltby: a slimeball who intruded at tea time and insisted on showing me his office. I would love to think that he, too, is involved in crime. Works in a small lab, specializing in papers and inks. Nothing suspicious except his obnoxious character.

It only took a moment to block and copy the paragraphs, edit them for Andrew's eyes and she was finished. *Exit?* queried her computer.

*Yes*, she typed.

# iv

## An Exercise in Plot Development

*Plot is the one thing that all writers find difficult. But if you think hard about your initial idea, you will see how it can be widened and developed until it is big enough to fill up a whole book. Remember that all the best plots develop out of character. So this week I want you to take the piece you wrote last time and see if you can develop it further. Use your imagination and explore all possibilities.*

I doubt whether I can convey to you my feelings as I prepared to catch the bus into Oxford for my first morning at the Bodleian. Mixed with the triumph that was bubbling inside my head, was the fear that I would be exposed for what I really was: I expected that everyone, from the bus driver who took my fare to the porter who showed me the way to the Secretariat, would challenge me as to my true identity. I felt it was written in plain letters across my forehead: *This man is a fraud.* My palms were damp, my armpits gushing sweat and a small tic had developed beside my left eye. No one noticed. It was, in any case, considered normal behaviour to feel nervous on one's first day in what was Europe's leading research library.

I had thought carefully before accepting the position they offered me. You have probably been wondering how I would bluff my way through the professional minefields that lay in my path. But I knew quite well that the Bodleian, as England's oldest library, was proud of doing things in its own way. It catalogued and classified according to its own rules and was not interested in what was taught in library schools. Bodley was Best seemed to be their motto. Even the everyday words that other librarians used were different here: we didn't shelve books, we replaced them, shelf lists were called hand lists, and so on. There is only one Librarian, and the heads of administrative sections are called Keepers. The people who stamp and fetch and carry are library assistants. It was taken for granted that I wouldn't know what to do in my first few weeks, so I just kept my mouth shut, my eyes open and put my mind to learning fast.

The first thing that happened after someone had made me swear the Bodleian Oath, was that I went to have a photograph taken for my staff identity card.

You don't know what the Bodleian Oath is? You are imagining some round and blasphemous phrase to shout when a rare book goes missing. No, it runs as follows:

*'I hereby undertake not to remove from the Library, or to mark, deface, or injure in any way, any volume,*

*document, or other object belonging to it or in its custody, not to bring into the Library or kindle therein any fire or flame, and not to smoke in the Library, and I promise to obey all the rules of the Library.'*

You may think this has an old-fashioned ring to it, but at least we declaimed it in English rather than in Latin. And I am not entirely forsworn: I promise you that I have never kindled any fire, or indeed flame, in this library or any other. This oath is printed on the reverse of my staff identity card, which bears on the other side the photograph that was taken that first morning: white face, startled eyes, well-combed hair and something of terror in the tension of the lips.

Next, I was taken on a whirlwind tour of the Library by the Assistant Secretary, and historical facts and figures flew around my head as we raced through subterranean passages, high-ceilinged reading rooms, and huge, dim caves filled with shelves of books and the hum of distant machinery.

At last I was dropped off in the Cataloguing Department, the largest department in the whole place, and given a seat at a desk next to my mentor, an elderly gentleman whose duty it would be to initiate me into the ways of cataloguing a book according to Bodleian Rules. I sat and worked under his guidance like a medieval apprentice with his master. I enjoyed learning those cataloguing rules: they seemed designed to hide books so that no one, outside a small circle of initiates, would ever be able to find them again.

Since the main qualifications needed in this department were neat handwriting (there were no typewriters) and an unwillingness to take responsibility for one's own mistakes, I fitted in beautifully, and over the years I have prospered and moved up and across until I now hold my current position. As in every other situation where I have found myself, I notice that the ability to tell a fluent lie is a great aid to acceptance and advancement.

And that is the way it might have continued, if some forward-looking librarian hadn't decided to drag the Bodleian, with its dependent libraries, and even all the other libraries in the University, into the last quarter of the twentieth century. People started talking about computers, and systems, and databases and networks. People who had resisted the typewriter were forced to consider the keyboard and the visual display unit. New staff appeared to supervise and direct, people with a language of computerspeak and management jargon that were light-years away from our dark little caves.

Our library acquired a new manager, a large man whose hands could dominate a keyboard and whose Essex whine could be heard echoing round our bookstack, threatening that he would 'get rid of all this paper and ink. Drag the place into the twentieth century.'

'Does he mean the books, as well?' asked Betsy. 'And what about our manuscripts?'

He preached the gospel of 'information transferral' rather than reading and writing, and all the old guard scuttled away to their corners and wrote to the Pensions

Manager to find out what their chances of taking early retirement were.

There was consternation among some of my colleagues, there were resignations and early retirements, and those of us who took to the new technology found ourselves in positions higher up the scale than we might have expected. I saw that it might offer all sorts of opportunities and I learnt as much about it as I could. That is one advantage of working for an educational institution: they do lay on an awful lot of training courses for their staff.

And my own attitude? Well, it's a funny thing about computers, but as soon as I saw one, I wanted to give it a try: like a kid with a new toy. And when my fingers found those keys, I knew I could do it. It must be like giving a musical child a piano: I felt so at home, so comfortable. I was fast, oh, so much faster than they expected from me. Some of them never took to it. Betsy, for instance, stood staring at hers when they put it on her desk, as though it were something unspeakable that the cat had brought in and left, bleeding and pulsating, on her desk. Even after she got the Chaplain to come in from Leicester College and bless it for her – drive out the devils, dedicate its silicon soul to the Lord's own work – it was never quite godly in her view. She had to leave in the end. She's working over at Blenheim Palace now, taking parties of visitors round those profligate, dead rooms. Her feet are always killing her, but she likes the ambience, she says, and you meet a very nice class of person there.

\* \* \*

How many people sit down and decide to be rich? How many even know what they would do if they had a lot of money? But I did. Yes, I might answer, to both questions.

I suppose that a seminar on 'The Future of Automation in the Small Academic Library' is an unlikely place to start such an enterprise, but it was over sweet white wine and dry library conversation that I got to know – well, let me just call them Tom and Harry, since they would not wish to be identified any more closely in this manuscript.

We said nothing important to each other as we chewed on small biscuits spread with packet cheese and topped with half a teaspoonful of Branston pickle, but it was as though some secret signal had passed between us, and we agreed to meet again later, after the final sessions of the day. Perhaps there was nothing supernatural about it: perhaps we just recognized the economies that had gone into choosing our respective jackets and ties, the way our shoes were polished but worn down around the heels, the way we swallowed that unpleasant German wine, knowing that we could ill afford to buy anything better, and yet knowing, too, that if we could have afforded to, we would all have appreciated it.

Tom at least had a bottle of whisky and we met in his room, taking our tooth mugs with us.

'The problem with crime, as with other more conventional activities, is knowing where to sell your product,' said Harry, as Tom splashed whisky into our glasses.

'But the wonderful thing about this new technology that our masters are urging us to install and conquer is that it delivers just that: the entry to vast databases. The computer need not be, after all, our master, but our friend and colleague,' I said.

Harry has spent so long working behind the Reference desk of his library that he has forgotten that he has legs. The top half of him is smooth and well groomed, with a brushed and pressed jacket, a clean shirt and a respectable tie. But his trousers are creased, baggy and ill fitting, his shoes down at heel, as though they belonged to a different person.

We all drained our glasses and wordlessly passed them to Tom for a refill. The word 'crime' had sent a delicious *frisson* down my spine, and I was sure that it had done the same to Tom.

'You are right. And what is contained in these data-bases?' continued Harry, rhetorically. 'Why, all the information that we need to place our product precisely in its market niche.'

'Niche? Product?' asked Tom. 'What product?'

But we knew. Really, we knew.

Last month the seminar, with the same grey suits and pasty faces, had been on the subject of library security. What the three of us dealt in was books – all of them expensive, some of them valuable. But as Harry had said, once you had stolen your book, what did you do with it? How did you turn it into cash? And most important of all: how did you remain uncaught?

'Bookplates,' said Tom. 'Rubber stamps. Shelf lists. All are designed to halt the illicit removal of books.' (No mention of *theft*, you notice.)

Harry dealt with each problem in turn.

'What we have here in this room,' he said, pouring out a third, reckless, mug of whisky each, 'is a concentration of the expertise that we need. Tom here is in Conservation, an expert on papers and inks. I'm sure he knows how to remove something that we would rather not have present and replace it with something nearer our heart's desire. John we rely on to get the best out of computers and communicate via those clever little networks with possible markets across the world. For myself, I think I know a little about the sort of books that people would pay a lot of money for.'

'We could have our own bookplate and rubber stamp,' said Tom. 'Something solid and venerable-looking. We might even find ourselves in the reference books if we got it right.'

'Don't get too fanciful,' I said, for I knew the value of getting the lies just right. 'And we'll keep the computer part of the crime as simple as possible. Complicated computer crime is detectable because so few people are capable of committing it: only the professionals, the computer freaks. We must keep it to a level that is possible to any competent operator.' I thought of someone in my department – let's call her Josie since the rest of us are appearing pseudonymously in these pages – who irritated me daily with her chatter and her interruptions. She didn't get on with her own work and she prevented me from getting on with mine. 'And I could borrow someone else's password and make sure that it is used at a time when she could have been using the system but was off having her tea or chatting to someone.'

'How do you go about stealing a password?' asked Tom.

'Borrow, not steal. You choose someone stupid, careless and unimaginative,' I answered, with the image of Josie firmly in front of me. 'And there's a simple technique for blotting out records, so that no trace remains. Even someone junior could do it, if they knew how. I think of it as the Oxford Exit.' They both looked at me, but I was keeping my idea to myself for the time being until I had a chance to try it out a few more times.

'And our next priority,' went on Harry, 'would be to recruit any other experts that we needed.'

'Isn't that risky?' asked Tom.

'What do librarians, and more particularly library assistants, have in common?' replied Harry, and continued by answering his own question. 'I'll tell you: it's disaffection and resentment at the way they are treated. You'll hear them grumbling from Cornwall to Edinburgh about how no one recognizes their professional status or pays them enough money to enable them to live decently, or listens to what they have to say. No, put two librarians together and they'll find something to grumble about, from cataloguing rules to lack of shelf space. What we have to do is harness all that resentment.'

Tom agreed. 'And look at the colleges that have underpaid their librarians for years. They end up with a succession of unqualified people who have no understanding of systems. Have you seen the library at . . . (*and he mentioned a well-known Oxford college.*) Indexes not kept up to date, boxes spilled and the cards not replaced properly. They don't even do an annual shelf check. How could anyone possibly know exactly what they should or should not have on their shelves?'

'This is all going to be rich ground for us,' Harry said.

I had been thinking while the others were talking. 'You're right about these networks and databases,' I said. 'I can sit at my desk and look at the holdings of libraries all over the world. I can see what they have got – and what they are missing. We could do worldwide deals, couldn't we?'

'Are you sure that there are enough dishonest people to make the thing profitable and workable?' asked Harry.

'If we put it to them in the right way. If we show them that only really intelligent people – people like themselves – could get away with it, if we make it worth enough money and certain that no one would get caught,' said Tom.

We were all pitching in with ideas at this moment, and the room was full of the energy that comes from planning something exciting.

'All libraries have had to economize at various times in their histories,' I said. 'And what happens? For a year, or ten or even twenty, they have to cut back by whatever percentage the management decrees. They stop buying books and journals in whatever field seems least important. And somehow it is these very areas that now have come to prominence. And we all know how short a time most books remain in print. If the library doesn't buy when the book or journal is published, in most cases the chance to acquire that work is lost for ever. Unless we offer to replace it for them – at a price.'

'We present it to people as an exercise in marketing techniques,' said Harry. 'We would be providing a service to librarians worldwide. And I think that if we got ourselves established with what I believe is called a "front", no one need face the nasty fact that what we are doing is, in the strictest sense, illegal.'

'You're right,' I said. 'After we have established ourselves, we will acquire a certain validity of our own,' I said. 'I have an idea that I'll talk over with Tom. I think that eventually people will be coming to us, the way they go to specialist book searchers, to find the works they need to complete their collections. We'll be providing a much-needed service to libraries.'

'And they won't find us out?' asked Harry.

'No one can guarantee that,' I said.

They were right though. No one did catch on to what we were doing for a very long time. Perhaps we got over-confident. Perhaps we widened our group too far, though I believe that we were always selective in choosing new members – the Company, as we called ourselves, remembering perhaps spy novels that we had read, or is it the Mafia? Whatever the connotations, we liked the title. And we prospered, until Jenna turned up. Little Jenna with the bad complexion, the stringy hair and the fatal curiosity that led her to ask all the wrong questions.

# Chapter Four

'Can you tell me the way to the library, please?'

'Are you one of ours?' asked the thin white-haired porter behind the glass window at St Luke's College. 'I can't let you into the library unless you're one of ours.' His voice quivered and his pale blue eyes blinked rapidly as he looked at Kate's brilliant gold linen jacket.

'Not exactly. But I am expected,' answered Kate, rifling through her bulging handbag and finding the identity card with the criminal's photograph on it. 'Retrospective cataloguing,' she said triumphantly, holding it up for his inspection.

'I don't know about that,' he said doubtfully. 'I'll ring the library,' and he dialled a number. 'I have a Miss Amory here for you,' he said into the mouthpiece.

'Ivory!' shouted Kate.

'Virony. Says she's expected, but she doesn't look like one of ours. She is? You're sure? All right then, I'll show her through.'

He came out of his cubicle and stood beside Kate. 'I hope you're not going to need a special pigeonhole,' he said, as his blink rate hit a new record. 'Pigeonholes are very tricky, you see. We have quite a waiting list.'

'No. No pigeonhole,' said Kate quickly. 'Just some instructions on how to find the library.'

'You go through this archway here, round the quad to the opposite corner, then turn left and follow the wall round until you get to a small gateway, go through it and cross the next quadrangle, take the second archway on the left, go up the stairs in front of you and make for the small building on your right. You can't miss it.'

'Thanks,' said Kate, trying to remember what he had said.

'And if you want a hot lunch, you'd better sign the list in the buttery. You'll be eating with the undergraduates,' he said in a reproving voice. 'Library staff don't have much to do with Senior Members of College, you'll find.'

Kate stuffed her identity card back inside her handbag and crossed the first quadrangle. Ahead of her a low grey-stone medieval building blazed with green and gold creeper under a tender blue sky, and a magnolia tree with flowers the size of dinner plates guarded a small archway. She walked through the archway and back another few hundred years in time.

The library here was old and full of dust. Kate ignored the cold air and removed her jacket and hung it up on the bentwood coat-stand just inside the entrance before the dust could get at its golden splendour.

'Francis Tabbot?' she asked, as a grey-haired, grey-faced man approached. Grey woollen pullover, matching trousers, lopsided brown plastic spectacle frames, mended on one side with pink sticking plaster. 'I'm Kate Ivory,' she said, and tried a friendly smile.

'Are you going to be here for long?' he asked. The eyes behind the lenses were brown and unfriendly. 'I know it's a vital job you're doing for us, but . . .'

But you're a quill pen and homemade ink man, and you hate people who love computers, thought Kate.

'I'd better show you round,' he said, as though the faster he got her started the sooner she would be finished and out of his sight. Whatever her report said, she could see that it would be doctored to appear unfavourable for his governing body. He wouldn't welcome a stranger into his library to drag it into the current century. Even the card catalogue was in ancient wooden cabinets with brass fittings and Indian ink calligraphy on the indicator cards.

'We won't go into my office,' he said.

Through the glass door behind him, Kate glimpsed a jungle of green stems and leaves, tumbling down bookcases, curling around the filing cabinet, as though Tabbot channelled all his living into raising and caring for plants.

'It disturbs the humidity and temperature when we open the door.'

They moved through the reading room. Notices around the library, also hand-written, told the undergraduates that they were not to smoke, eat, drink, talk, run, put their feet on the desks, deface the books, meet their friends, take out more than six books or attempt to enter the building before 9 a.m. on weekdays or at all on Sundays. No wonder they all looked so cowed and miserable. On the other hand, the whole place was so old and venerable that it was unlikely that anyone had ever stooped to anything as vulgar as theft. A little long-term loan of a book, perhaps, but surely that was all.

'We use a modified Dewey Decimal classification,' said Tabbot, racing her around the tall dark bookshelves, past the tables full of the quiet undergraduates, and, 'Take your sports bag off the floor,' he said to a student without drawing breath. 'English Literature, History, Economics,' he said to Kate, who was nearly running to keep up with him. 'I'm sure you'll soon find your way around.'

'Can you tell me how long you've been using the Libraries' computer?' panted Kate behind him.

'Over a year, now. And a year too long, in my opinion.' His disapproval came back to her in his stiff-legged stride. 'Why do they want to make our library catalogues available to all and sundry? You'll be getting all sorts of riffraff asking to see your books if you go on like that. People from Ireland and Scotland, and even from abroad.'

'Is that a problem?' asked Kate. 'Do you lose more books if outsiders are using them?'

'I don't know about that. I'd have to look at my records. And how do you define a missing book, anyway?' On that unanswerable note, they rounded another corner and came face to face with a young, nervous-looking man.

'Michael Ennis,' said Tabbot. 'The Library Assistant.'

Ennis was under thirty, fair-haired, and wearing a V-necked Fair Isle pullover.

'Mick,' said the young man, and held out a hand to Kate.

'Yes, well, if you insist on the diminutive,' said Tabbot. 'And now that we've found you, I can hand Miss Ivory over to you for the rest of the tour of the library.'

'Kate,' said Kate, not wishing to be called Miss Ivory for the rest of her stay at St Luke's.

Tabbot disappeared and Ennis took her downstairs to a lighter, more modern room.

'This is the Science and Maths section,' he said. 'And our computer terminal for the use of the readers. Tabbot doesn't want to know it exists. All this year's library acquisitions are on the computer, and a few of our Special Collections, but the bulk of our holdings are still on the five-by-three card catalogue.'

'Aren't you worried that your terminal is rather out of the way?' she asked. 'Couldn't someone log into the database and start messing around with it?'

'It's a dedicated terminal,' said Mick. 'You can read what's already there, but you can't interact with it, or add or subtract any information. You'll be using a different machine for your cataloguing, of course.' And he led the way down a couple more steps and along a short corridor to what must have been a cupboard in the recent past.

'Well, yes, you can see what Tabbot thinks of modern technology,' he said, apologetically. 'It does comply with University standards of ventilation and lighting, though, even if it is so small, and that is a properly adjustable chair, so you shouldn't get backache or anything from a few days' work here. And that's not a bad PC: I've had it to myself up till now, of course. I'm sorry it's so crowded: Tabbot's taken over my half of the office upstairs for his plants, so I've had to move all my stuff in here. I can't think why they're bringing in an outsider like you to do this job. I warn you, it's making us all feel as though we're being spied on. You're reporting back to the Libraries Board, are you?'

'Really,' said Kate, as soothingly as she knew how, 'there's no need to feel nervous about me. My report goes to Mr Tabbot when I've written it. And it won't extend to more than a sheet of A4 at the longest.'

'They say you're a writer. I expect you'll be looking for material for your next book, too. We'll all have to watch what we say, or we'll find ourselves on your pages.'

'What as?' Kate said. 'I write historical novels and I don't think the pair of you would fit into my current book.' Or any other, she thought, unless I need a scene between a pair of immensely dull librarians. 'I'll be bringing in my own statutory large green plant,' she said firmly, to change the subject. 'It can stand on top of that photocopier over there.'

'Whose statute would that be? There are quite enough green plants in this library already. We don't want the copier damaged.'

'As advised by NASA,' she said, 'when working with VDUs. One plant per screen is the recommended rate. And it won't hurt your precious machine, don't worry.'

It would be the one living touch in the horrid little box, she thought, and Tabbot and Ennis would have to learn to like it. She sat on the chair and swung her feet around until she found the footrest. Yes, she supposed it would do. Mick was wandering round, chewing his thumbnail and frowning.

'What exactly is it you're going to do?' he asked. 'I

imagine it's just the undergraduate books you're interested in.'

'Not necessarily,' said Kate. 'What else have you got?'

'You'll have to speak to Tabbot about them,' said Ennis, huffily. 'I'm sure he won't be keen on having an outsider get their hands on anything valuable and put it in a catalogue that anyone can look at. I mean, people might start ringing up and writing in and asking to look at things.' His thumbnail had found its way back into his mouth and he was gnawing it. He was through skin and working on real meat. Kate looked away.

'And you wouldn't like any extra readers?' she said.

'Ask Tabbot about it,' repeated Mick. 'And anyway, you'd have to be issued with the Senior Key, and I'm sure he wouldn't agree to that.' He had removed his thumbnail from his mouth and hidden both his hands behind his back, as though stopping them from doing further damage.

'What about the Special Collections that are already on the computer?'

'Tabbot insisted on having the copies hidden, so unless you are looking at the catalogue from this terminal, you won't see them. Other University users can see that someone in the University system has got the books, but they can't tell who.'

'Is that popular with the rest of the system users?'

'No, but Tabbot insisted. It's short-sighted, too. Anyone who looks in the catalogue for a book and finds that the copies are hidden knows that library is likely to have lousy security. There are only four libraries on the whole system that hide their copies, so it really isn't difficult to find which one holds the book you want. And the chances are that if you want to nick it, it won't be that difficult. The library in question won't have security doors or full-time staff, probably.'

'You're assuming that the world is full of dishonest people.'

'The most unlikely people are dishonest when it comes to books.'

'Do we get a coffee break?' asked Kate. Maybe she could get more from the two of them over a cup of coffee if she offered to share her chocolate Hob Nobs with them.

Coffee, she was glad to see, emerged from an efficient electric machine and was made from something expensive from the shop in the Covered Market. The Hobs Nobs got a wintry smile from Tabbot's thin mauve lips, and he found china plates for them to eat from. Ennis took two, she noticed: obviously he needed to make up all that nervous energy he had spent on chewing at his thumbnails.

'Well,' she said, with a warm and cheerful smile at their doubting faces, 'I've had a look around, and taken a few sample books from the various sections. It all looks very straightforward, though the Modern Languages and Classics may be slower than average to catalogue.' Have I lulled them into boredom and acceptance of me? 'The only outstanding question hangs over your Special Collection.' The one behind the locked door.

'No need to include that in your calculations,' said Tabbot, while Ennis gave her a 'told you so' look over the remains of his second Hob Nob. 'There are no books there that need concern either the undergraduates or members of other institutions and colleges.'

Pompous sod, thought Kate. 'Shouldn't I look them over, though?' is what she said. 'Just so that I can make a complete report.'

'Nothing to do with you,' said Tabbot, through lips that were going such a peculiar shade of lavender that Kate was quite worried.

'Perhaps we should allow her a little peep,' said Ennis, skittishly. 'Just so that she doesn't think we're hiding anything . . . distasteful.'

'Finish your coffee,' said Tabbot, and gathered up the china plates, carefully scraping the crumbs into the waste-paper basket and piling the crockery up on a tray.

'Shall I wash up?' asked Kate, hoping to ingratiate herself with him.

'If you do, you will deeply offend our scout,' said Tabbot. 'And by God's Own, to coin a phrase, we have the most efficient scout that the college has ever employed. We do not offend him.'

And just as Kate thought she had completely blown it, he reached into the second drawer of his desk, pulled out a long steel key and said, 'If you insist on seeing our Special Collection, you had better come with me. You can look after the issue desk, Ennis, while we are gone.'

He led the way to the back of the library and up a small stone spiral staircase.

'We keep our archive up here,' he said, indicating a padlocked door on his left. 'And we keep our Special Collection in here,' and he unlocked first a padlock, then a thick dark wooden door on his right.

'Where does the collection come from?' she asked, as they walked into a small air-conditioned room and he switched on the strip lights over the shelves.

'The testamentary gift of an Old Member during the nineteen-sixties,' said Tabbot. He handed down a volume from a top shelf for Kate to look at.

Nothing old about that member, thought Kate, as she looked at the illustrations.

'The volume I have given you to look at is representative of the whole, but less indecent than some,' said Tabbot in his precise voice.

'Quite,' said Kate, closing the book and letting her gaze slide along the shelves to make sure that Tabbot wasn't trying to put her off the scent by showing her the one pornographic work in the whole collection. *The Pop-Up Kama Sutra* looked promising, but the others didn't attract her at all. As a general term, 'indecent' seemed to cover them.

'We follow Bodleian practice in giving such materials a shelfmark commencing with the Greek letter Phi,' said Tabbot in his prim voice, his eyes focused on the middle of Kate's chest. 'Then when someone requests such a work, we know exactly what it is a question of.'

'And you sit them at an isolated desk with the word "Unclean" on a banner above their heads, do you?'

Tabbot managed to frown, purse his lips, shake his head and keep his eyes on Kate's chest, simultaneously. It was a signal to leave the upper room and return to the main reading room of the library.

When she was free of Tabbot and Ennis she rang Liam on the internal phone.

'Sorry,' he said. 'I'm afraid I've got a rehearsal to take this evening. Tomorrow night I have to look over the costume designs, and Wednesday—'

'Sod Wednesday,' said Kate. 'It was this evening I needed a little sympathy and loving care.'

'I was going to say that on Wednesday I have to travel up to London to record an item for *Kaleidoscope* on the radio, but I'll give you a ring when I get back and we can fix something for later in the week.'

'Don't bother. I'll be in touch with your secretary about a future appointment,' she said, and put the phone down. It rang again, immediately.

'Kate? Andrew here.'

She felt quite pleased to hear from him. 'The Crypt at five forty-five?' she asked. 'I'll give you my report then.'

'Glad to hear you're taking your work seriously,' he said, and rang off.

She went back into the Science and Maths section to fill her trolley with some boringly representative books.

'Zilch,' said Kate, and helped herself to a glass of red wine.

'Is that it?' asked Andrew. 'The complete report?'

'Yes. But I've written it up and printed you out a couple of pages, so you can study them at your leisure. Why on earth did you choose the Rioja?'

'You'll get a decent claret when you have some proper news for me.'

'Wouldn't improper news count?' and she filled him in on her day's work.

'I'll ask around to see whether there's a market for the stuff you saw, but the book that went missing didn't fit into that category. It looks as though St Luke's is clean so far, in a manner of speaking.'

'They seemed too unimaginative and stuffy to be criminals. Though Mick Ennis looks as though he creeps up the stone staircase and spends his tea breaks in solitary conversation with the Special Collection. I'd really like to think that they are involved in something shameful and illegal, but I haven't come across anything yet. Do I have to stay much longer and catalogue their boring books?'

'Catalogue a hundred books, write them a report on a sheet of A4, and I should think you'd done enough. You can move on to the next place in a couple of days' time.'

'Gee, thanks, Andy.'

'Don't call me Andy if you want a second glass of wine.'

'I was tempted by the sight of your youthful and dashing tie.'

'You like it? It was a present from Isabel.'

'Oh.'

Toadface was hanging upside-down from the top of the climbing frame. Perhaps this position was not altogether voluntary – and indeed its face was going a nasty, purplish colour – for its sister – Shayla, wasn't it? – was sitting on the top with her strong fingers curled round its ankles like forceps. They were both being unusually silent. Kate had always hoped that one of them would bounce right off this dangerous-looking trampoline, which must be at least six feet off the ground, and disappear for ever over the fences and back gardens of Fridesley, like the recipients of some cruel medieval torture. She looked out her yellow foam earplugs and went downstairs to write a thousand words of her novel. When she had finished, she switched to her new sub-directory and entered her *Notes* file, heading the new screen with the day's date.

1. St Luke's College Library. An unfriendly place, with a collection of high-class pornographic books.
2. Librarian is Francis Tabbot. A man it is easy to dislike, especially since he appears to be carrying on a war against his readers. A quill pen man, not a computer enthusiast. But probably knows about books and what they are worth.
3. Mick Ennis, library assistant. I didn't take to him much, either. He had something to hide, and I have the impression it is something tacky. I would be surprised if he had the intelligence or initiative to take on anything at all ambitious. But I would like to think that these two are criminals.

She edited the notes so that they were suitable for Andrew's critical eyes, and saved both versions. Then she went to bed with a copy of Mary Shelley's *Frankenstein*.

The next morning, when she got to the library at St Luke's, she found that the Bursar wanted to see her, so she crossed the quadrangle and went into the college office.

'He's on the phone at the moment,' said the girl behind the computer screen. 'Take a seat.'

Kate wandered round the small room, staring out of the window at the green velvet lawn and the sundial on the wall opposite. In front of her on the window-sill was a mug with the initial 'J' painted on the side, full of cream and yellow freesias.

'How pretty,' she said, to pass the time. 'And don't they smell lovely.'

'They were her favourites, so I always keep some there in her mug, to remind me of her.'

Kate looked again at the girl at the desk. She was in her twenties, with a pale, shiny face, and small nose, full lips and badly cut mousey hair. She was wearing a nondescript dress with a grey hand-knitted cardigan over it. Oh dear.

' "J"?' asked Kate. 'What does it stand for?'

'J for Jenna,' said the young woman. 'She died nearly a year ago, but I like to think she's still remembered. It's bad enough dying when you're so young, but if no one still thinks about you, it all seems so pointless, doesn't it?'

'Did she work here?' asked Kate.

'She spent a few weeks in the library. She was a trainee, you see, and spent a month or two in a number of different libraries, to give her a grounding in the various skills for the job. I don't think they learned a lot, those trainees, but it gave them some practical experience before they went off to library school and buried their heads in textbooks again.'

'Where else did she go?' asked Kate.

The young woman was just about to answer when the door opened behind her and a man appeared and said, 'Sorry to keep you waiting, Miss Ivory. If you'd like to come in now . . .' And Kate had to answer questions about National Insurance and pension funds that she wasn't at all interested in. Maybe Jenna had nothing to do with the disappearing records, but everyone was so evasive about her that Kate just wanted to know more. When she came into the outer office again, it was to find that she was no longer there, and only the initial J on the mug and the smell of freesias were left in the room to remind her of Jenna.

Kate couldn't talk to Andrew on the telephone without the risk of being overheard by Tabbot or Ennis, so she made a nondescript call, fixing a date at the Crypt for after work. The word might get round that she and Andrew were an item, but she thought they could both live with that. If Liam heard about them on the grapevine and cared about it, it might ginger him up a bit, anyway. The thought that he might hear and not care at all was more depressing.

She set to work on the trolley she had filled that morning from the undergraduate section of the library and was half-way through her afternoon when Mick Ennis came down to tell her it was teatime.

'I'll just finish cataloguing this book. I've found a British Library record in the Pool database and I'm just going to transfer it to our system.'

The details of the book appeared on her screen and when she typed in 'yes' to affirm that the details were correct, another screen asked her if she wished to replace an existing item by this one. She was about to type in 'no', when Mick said:

'Aren't you ever tempted to type in "yes" and knock out someone's carefully made record of another book?'

She looked at him, startled.

'Don't worry, I'm only joking,' he said. 'Librarians can hardly tear up a catalogue card, let alone delete a computer record.'

Kate typed 'no', thoughtfully, put in the details of the accession number and shelf-mark of the book she was cataloguing and went upstairs to tea with Francis Tabbot.

She was running a risk of becoming seriously addicted to a half-bottle of wine after work, but Andrew ordered single glasses.

'I'm meeting Isabel later, and I'd better save myself for her,' he said, as he handed her a glass. 'What have you got for me?'

'A couple of things that may mean nothing.'

'But tell me about them anyway.'

'First of all, Mick Ennis showed me a method of zapping a record that could be used by any cataloguer – they wouldn't need the high level of authority that you thought they would, and it means that the list of thirteen suspects that you gave me is useless.'

'You'd better tell me how it's done.'

'It would be much easier to demonstrate than to explain.'

'I'll fix a meeting with Graham from the Security Team and see what he thinks about it. Anything else I should know about?'

'What can you tell me about these library trainees that go swanning around the colleges?'

'The University takes on about eight of them every year: young people who are taking a year between university and library school to get some practical experience. They get sent to various departments – they learn to catalogue, they do a week or two in the bookstack, they work in Accessions and in reading rooms and then they do a session in a college library or a department. It depends who is willing to take them on, since it's quite time-consuming to give them the training to make them useful during their stay with us.'

'And how would I find out where one particular trainee had been during her time here?'

'Who are you talking about?'

'Her name was Jenna, and it's a name that has come up a couple of times. And if she was moving around the system, then she might well have picked up on the scam we're investigating.'

'Where on earth do you find such awful words?'

'Stick to the question, Andrew.'

'I'm having a mineral water, would you like something else to drink?'

'Mineral water for me too, please. Fizzy, ice and lemon. Then tell me about Jenna.'

Andrew put the two glasses down on the table. 'I believe you asked me once before about her. After that occasion, I went back to Charles and checked. Jenna was a trainee, yes, in last year's intake. She had spent about eight months here – some of it in the Bodleian, some of it in other libraries – when she died.'

'How?'

'It's rather sordid and I really don't think it had anything to do with this problem of ours. She went off for the weekend with a group she belonged to, called Young Christians for Folk Song, or some such. They went off to do whatever they do on these occasions – pray and sing, I imagine, and eat healthy food and enter upon chaste and wholesome relationships.'

'Your prejudices are showing, Andrew.'

'What prejudices? Anyway, Jenna missed the train back to Oxford that the others took, and wasn't seen alive again. Her body was found on some ground where they were building a new slip-road on to the motorway.'

'Body? What had happened to her?'

'She had been strangled. It was assumed that since she had missed the train to Oxford she had accepted a lift from a stranger, and that he sexually attacked her and then killed her when she struggled. She was found a couple of days later when a man driving a JCB uncovered her body. You see, it was very tragic, but really had nothing to do with the crime that we're investigating. It takes a different mind altogether to think up the complicated scheme that we're looking at, from picking up a young woman and attacking her on a building site.'

'And did they ever find out who did it?'

'No. No one saw her getting into his car. No one reported them leaving the motorway. But then, who would notice? It was dusk and pouring with rain. The hostel where the group was staying was in a lane with no other houses near by. The police think it was an opportunist attack and are still trying to link it with other similar crimes.'

'If it was such an unpromising evening, why would he want to take her to an open piece of ground in a rainstorm?'

'I don't know. I doubt whether we'll ever know now, unless he's picked up for another crime and confesses to this one as well. But as I said, you can forget about Jenna Coates. I really believe she has nothing to do with our case. What we're interested in is missing books, not dead people.'

'If you say so.' And she finished her glass of mineral water and wondered about the relevance of a peony, if indeed she had heard Paul correctly, and whether he would be very cross with her if she rang him up and tried to find out more about the Jenna Coates case. It had always seemed to her that dead people were more important than missing property, however valuable, but doubtless Andrew would tell her that she lacked the proper perspective that a decent education in a venerable university gave you.

That night, she typed up her notes. There wasn't much to add, and all of it involved Jenna Coates. She had to put a question mark at the end of nearly every sentence.

# V

## *A Variation in the Narrative Form*

*I'm sorry I haven't seen any of your work for a few weeks, Viv. When you're feeling confident enough to show me some pages, I should very much like to see them.*

Isn't this the point in the narrative where I should change its form? I think I should give you some pages from my diary, or even copy in a few letters.

This first one isn't so much a letter, more a memo. It came from Harry.

*J: Meeting in my office, 5.00 tomorrow. H.*

And my reply ran as follows:

*H: I'll see you there. J.*

I don't know how other writers manage to produce pages of beautifully wrought descriptive prose that carries their story forward while varying the pace of the narrative. Perhaps they invent things. Personally, I have always found it more amusing to invent my life and to keep the truth for my fiction, so in the interest of that truth I shall give you an account of the meeting in Harry's office which is taken from the notes that I made at the time.

HARRY: Thank you for coming at such short notice, but I think you'll find it worthwhile when I tell you of my idea. We were speaking, if you remember, of the choice of product to sell on the international market and I believe that I have found just the thing for us to deal in.
   [*At this point Harry paused, doubtless for dramatic effect. He had our full attention.*]
HARRY: I'm sure you are all familiar with the Sensation novels of the nineteenth century – daughters, one might almost say, of the Gothick that preceded them. Even established novelists attempted to write them, notably Dickens in *Great Expectations* and *The Mystery of Edwin Drood*; Wilkie Collins, of course, in *The Woman in White* and *The Moonstone*; and Thomas Hardy's first published novel, *Desperate Remedies*, was an extraordinarily inept attempt, but with a title that sums up the whole genre. Even if you are not familiar with the novels I mention, I am sure that their very titles give you some indication of their contents. [*He consulted a piece of paper.*] *The Fatal Three*, *Dead Love has Chains*, *Sir Jasper's Tenant*, and my own favourite, *The Mystery: A Story of Domestic Life*. I'm sure you get the picture.
TOM: Fascinating as this background is, Harry, do you think you could get to the point?

*[Harry smiled. He had no intention, it seemed to
me, of shortening by one well-judged phrase this
introduction of his. Personally, I was rather
enjoying it.]*

HARRY: Bear with me, Tom, I'm sure you'll find it worthwhile. Where was I? Oh yes, Sensation. But as you
might imagine, the greatest exponents of the genre were
women. You have all heard of Mary Braddon?

*[We nodded. Tom, I am afraid to say, with his
now customary impatience.]*

TOM: Mary Braddon, Mrs Henry Wood, Eliza Baughn.
Yes, Harry, we've heard of them all. Second-raters, the
lot of them.

MYSELF: Women can never be authors. Fiction is about
truth, and what do women know of that? *(They filled
my life with their lies; they forced me to live them.)*

HARRY: But you can't just dismiss them. Think of the
rise, particularly in North America, of Women's Studies.
*[Groans from Tom.]* There are books to be written,
chairs to be had, on the backs (if you will pardon the
expression) of writers such as The Sisterhood of the
Veil.

MYSELF: Now, I have heard of them. Not only were they
a group of women writers united in their interest in the
Sensational, but they liked to think of themselves as
concerned in social issues of the time. Wilkie Collins
was a correspondent of theirs, even an admirer and,
like him, they eschewed marriage in favour of looser
connections, and spent much time in examining questions of social inequality. They even disagreed with cur-

rent views on the British Empire and insisted on regarding their Indian and African brethren as equals. A very radical and unpopular idea at the time, you understand. The Veil in their name refers to the fact that the veiled woman is a Sybil and a Seer – a Prophetess – so they were speaking of the social order that they believed was to come. They referred to themselves as the Veil, for short, and they supported each other emotionally and professionally, even financially when necessary, in the manner of sisters, rather than as competitors for the small number of marriageable men.

TOM: How politically correct of them!

HARRY: Precisely. Which is why eager young women with unshaven armpits, black leggings and heavy boots are pursuing their works all over the world. As I am sure you will appreciate, scholarly libraries in the nineteenth century, or even in the first three-quarters of the twentieth, were not keen to acquire stocks of these works. And these ladies—

TOM: Women, Harry, not ladies, surely.

HARRY: If you insist, these *women* then, were prolific. They produced illegitimate offspring by the dozen, and volumes by the gross. By the nineteen-thirties, when all academic libraries were finding that their book stacks were insufficient for their needs, they turfed out hundreds of the things, along with collections of women's fashion magazines, for example, which are now highly sought after.

TOM: We can hardly tout round the respectable university libraries of North America hoping to flog them our libraries' collections of Sensation novels, though, can we?

HARRY: Would I be so vulgar? I have looked through the Oxford catalogue to see what works of the Veil are sitting in obscure library cellars, and then I have looked at one specialist library in the States. In California, to be precise. There I found a small college at Santa Luisa, belonging to the University of California, which specializes in women's fiction of the eighteenth and nineteenth centuries. They have a wonderful run of the Veil books, but with just a few notable gaps. In particular, they are missing some of the Eliza Baughn works that just happen to be buried in . . .

*[And here Harry gave the name of the Oxford library where these works by Eliza Baughn could be found. I'm sorry, but really I can't put my colleagues' liberty at risk by revealing the actual name of the library.]*

TOM: Now, supposing that we could get our hands on these books, and cover our electronic tracks so that no one could follow us, can we really assume that the librarian at Santa Luisa would buy them, knowing them to be stolen?

MYSELF: How crudely you put it, Tom.

HARRY: Tom has raised some points which must be answered before we proceed, but let me remind you that we still have our expertise. I suggest that we first *borrow* one of the Eliza Baughn volumes that Santa Luisa might well be looking for. John can show us how he gets rid of the electronic footprints in the catalogue,

Tom can look at the various identifying marks in the volume and see whether they can be removed and replaced by others of our own devising. Luckily, there was very little in the way of rubber-stamping done in the nineteenth century, so little will have to be removed. I must say that I have already thought of a collection that these books might have come from: a collection put together by a Suffragette and Fabian during the latter part of the last century. We could write a letter purporting to come from the present, elderly, owner of the collection, offering one or two volumes for sale to the University at Santa Luisa, in the knowledge that they will find a suitable and happy resting place that is entirely in accordance with God's Own Providence (as dear Eliza would put it) and in fulfilment of their purchaser's wishes and beliefs.

TOM: What would you call this collection?

HARRY: The Iron Shoe.

MYSELF: The connotations escape me.

HARRY: But they won't escape any feminist nineteenth-century scholar. The Iron Shoes (and indeed the Red Shoes) refer to the unpleasant Grimm fairy story, Snow White. At the end of the story, the wicked Queen has to dance in red-hot iron shoes (hence red for both the glowing heat and the blood that came from the dying queen) at Snow White's wedding until she dies.

MYSELF: Where is the feminist message in that?

HARRY: It is seen as being the punishment for any woman who dares to escape from patriarchal authority and express herself in a creative manner. And Tom will

124

concentrate on the practicalities for us. And if you could think of turning your skills to a touch of forgery, Tom, so much the better.

TOM: Hardly forgery, Harry. I shall be inventing a new collection, not imitating an existing one. I shall be only too pleased to think about designs for their bookplates, for their rubber stamps, even for their letter heading and the literary style of their elderly keeper. And the constitution of their paper and ink ...

MYSELF: Wonderful, Tom. The rest of us can only marvel at your arcane knowledge.

HARRY: If all goes well with this first operation, I think we should consider setting up a perfectly proper book search agency. Libraries in need of a particular work could contact us and we could ascertain whereabouts the book was located. If we build up our contacts slowly and carefully, we will find out which librarians are willing to bend the rules a little to assist in this work of placing the right book on the right shelf.

MYSELF: We're all off to conferences this year, I suppose? Well, what could be better opportunities for meeting people and finding those who would see things our way? I'm sure that we could all start by making a list of two or three likely contacts in other libraries.

HARRY: We need a name to hide behind. We don't want to be identified if someone gets suspicious.

TOM: Oxford Bookfinders?

MYSELF: Too specific, don't you think? There's no reason why we should pinpoint the geographical location of our operation like that. How about Bookfinders Inter-

national? We could have a Post Office box as an
address and ...

TOM: Meanwhile, before we get too ambitious, let's get
back to Miss Baughn, shall we? Assuming that the
librarian takes the bait, which of us is going to
accompany *Dead – and Alive!* to Santa Luisa?

And that, dear reader, is how I came to board an aero-
plane for San Franscisco one day in spring, just after the
close of the Hilary term.

When I took over John Exton's life, when I carried on
living it for him after his death so that he would eventually
achieve the natural span that had been denied him by his
unfortunate accident, I did not entirely eliminate my own.
That would have been to kill myself off in his stead, and
although there were many aspects of my life that I was
happy to forget, I did not wish to erase myself entirely.
To some extent, I lived both our lives. Think of it, if you
like, as a bilingual child who keeps up both his languages
(though of course, as he gets older and more mature, it
becomes more onerous to keep up two languages in all
areas of knowledge). Just because I became John, I did
not renounce Vivian: that would have been a form of
suicide, and I cannot approve of that. No, I kept a corner
of my life as Vivian. I kept a bank account going – at
one of the large central branches where no one noticed
me or recognized me. I put money in, I took it out, I had
a cheque book, Connect and Visa cards, and I kept them
all active in a very low-key way so that no one could take

any notice of them. And I kept my passport – I even renewed it – and the driving licence that I had in Viv's name (I had to take a second test as John, and I'm ashamed to say that he failed first time and had to take it again a couple of months later).

So when I went to California that first time, it was as Vivian Moffatt. I had passport, driving licence, credit cards, and I bought my ticket (from a London travel agency) using a cheque on Viv's account. I didn't bother to change my appearance since I didn't expect to meet anyone I knew in Santa Luisa – there was no conference going on there at the time, and it is a small and obscure campus. I was looking forward to the trip: the slight apprehension that came from taking a risk added a little chilli sauce to the plain boiled rice of my existence.

*You see, Mrs Dolby, I am trying to express myself in a lively and individual manner, even though I am never going to show you these pages.*

I had several books with me in my overnight bag: the latest in fat paperbacks from the airport bookstore, and three volumes, in mint condition, of *Dead – and Alive!* by Eliza Baughn, with bookplates showing that they came from the Iron Shoe collection, and with the spidery autograph of Eleanor J. Westgate on the fly-leaf (courtesy of Tom), together with the date, November 1863. I also had, in writing, the authority of her great-niece, Miss Joan

Westgate (MA Oxon.), to negotiate the sale of other volumes in her collection that the University of California at Santa Luisa might be interested in.

It is a long flight to San Francisco, and the in-flight films were not to my taste, so in only mild curiosity, I have to admit, I put on a pair of clean white cotton gloves and started to read *Dead – and Alive!*.

I hope that my laughter didn't disturb my fellow-travellers, for within those dark-green, gold-printed boards, I found a story of two young men in love with the same young woman, a story of loss of identity, of duplicity and duplication, of a death reported and a life taken over by an outsider; a story of madness and murder, bigamy and blackmail. Hardly a character is introduced without his or her double also appearing on the following pages.

By the mid-point of the second volume I had lost my way in the plot, although the sheer exuberance of the writing kept me going. I am not sure that the irrepressible laughter with which I greeted each new implausibility in the story was quite what the author had intended.

The degree to which Miss Baughn used coincidence, or God's Own Providence as she called it, would hardly be tolerated in a modern thriller.

I stopped smiling at her outrageous implausibilities a few weeks later, when I was on a further trip, bringing yet more volumes for the Californian library. After I had caught the local flight to Santa Luisa and at last came out of the airport and into the Californian sunshine, I thought for a moment that my eyes must be dazzled by the brilliance of the light shining on white concrete, for I was sure that I had recognized a figure from Oxford. I blinked, I reached into my overnight case and found my sunglasses and put them on. Then I stepped back into the shadow of the building as I watched her approach a red Honda. Jenna. She was walking beside a young woman, and carrying a small case, and I imagine she had just been met by her friend at the airport, possibly off my own flight. I could only hope that she hadn't seen me, for I had told no one of my destination. Why hadn't I listened more closely to the girl's chatter? Doubtless she had been telling everyone over the past few weeks that she was spending her holiday in California. I was getting over-confident: everything had gone so well up to now, and the money was starting to flow into our accounts. It was really only Santa Luisa that was getting this personal service now, as our first and most respected client. For the rest, we used the ordinary post, for who would query packages of books franked by one university library and addressed to another?

Why had Jenna come to a small place like this, just a seaside town, with its Spanish-style buildings and blood-red flowers rioting in every garden and over every wall? I waited until the Honda drove away before getting into a cab and giving the name of my hotel. Well, Miss Baughn, let's hope that you aren't going to come up with too many more accurate prophecies from behind that veil of yours. I have to admit that I was rattled. What would I say if she asked me what I was doing in Santa Luisa, and why I hadn't mentioned it back in Oxford? Could I make up some story of an illicit liaison with a married woman?

Would Jenna believe me? Knowing me, would anyone?

Our operation was expanding nicely as university libraries heard about Bookfinders and its discreet worldwide service. The Iron Shoe, too, was contributing books to obscure little libraries all over the world, with its seemingly inexhaustible supply of early feminist works. We were branching out into other periods, other territories, and perhaps it was time to call a halt to the Santa Luisa operation. But then again, I thought about the huge budget controlled by their librarian, the eagerness with which she signed large cheques to obtain the books she needed to fill the holes in her collection, and I resolved to find a better solution.

# Chapter Five

The Toddler from Hell was in his pedal car, pursuing a cat, when Kate arrived home that evening. She was wondering why he was out on his own, unsupervised, when a voice behind her said something that sounded like "Ere!'

She turned round. It was Harley, Toadface's older brother. "Ere, miss! I've got the cones to put in the road for you to practise your reversing into a small space,' he said. 'Do you want a lesson tonight?'

'Can you give me a few minutes to recover from my day's work?' she asked.

'Better have your tea first,' said Harley, kindly. 'You might need your strength for this. And I've got Darren's brother Dossa to come and show you how to get into a locked car. It'll cost you just ten quid. Darren says he'll show you his own method for another fiver, but I should give it a miss if I was you, and don't offer him any money, whatever he promises.'

'Do I really need to know how to break into a locked car?'

'How many times have you locked your keys inside your Peugeot?'

'Only about twice. Or maybe three times.'

'There's your answer. I'll be round your place in half an hour, and I'll tell Darren to bring his brother round Sunday afternoon. OK?'

'OK,' said Kate, wondering what sub-culture she was being initiated into, and imagining Paul Taylor's disapproval. At least she wasn't being offered a course in hot-starting yet – probably because they thought her driving skills weren't good enough. She wasn't at all sure of her abilities to perform a normal emergency stop, let alone a handbrake turn.

As she let herself into her house, Toadface had caught the cat by its tail and was trying to haul it into the cab of his pedal car. He had succeeded in getting the hind, or blunt, end inside, but the sharp end was preparing teeth and claws for a counterattack. She left Harley to deal with him and went indoors.

She found a message waiting for her on her answering machine. It was Emma: she didn't want to be a nuisance, but would Kate ring her back when she had time to talk. Tomorrow, thought Kate. I'll ring her tomorrow. Or maybe the day after.

The phone rang. She wondered for a moment whether it was the persistent Emma, but gave it the benefit of the doubt and answered it. It was Andrew.

'How much longer it is going to take you at St Luke's?'

'Good evening, Andrew. How are you? How has your day been?'

'Yes, yes, all right. Good evening, Kate, and how are you this lovely evening?'

'I'm very well, and I've got two or three hours' cataloguing to do and half an hour or so to spend on writing the report. Say a morning's work. Why?'

'Charles has had a call from Kennedy House. They have been losing books, and now they think the thief is trying to cover his tracks by using the libraries' computer.'

'How did this come up?'

'It was an observation from Graham, one of the Security Team. He was doing some routine work there when he noticed something wrong. He reported to Charles, who wants you over at Kennedy House as soon as possible, because we think this may be our man.'

'And Charles, like God, needs an intermediary to stand between Himself and Woman.'

'Don't be facetious. Tomorrow I'll buy you a sandwich for your lunch and fill you in on what's happening. I must fix a meeting with Graham, too. You can show him that little trick you learned from Ennis (though I can't believe that he doesn't know it already) and he can tell you what he's found out at Kennedy. Then you'll be starting there as soon as possible.'

'I need more than a sandwich for my lunch: I shall be running eight miles before breakfast tomorrow, and that burns a lot of calories.'

'I'll pick you up at St Luke's lodge at twelve fifty.'

Kate drank a cup of herb tea and ate a slice of toast and strawberry jam, then changed into jeans and sweatshirt for her lesson in reversing into a small space. The lad had done her proud: he had found some red and white cones (Council property? Borrowed from the roadworks on the by-pass?) and gave her clear instructions on the angle at which she should be approaching the kerb. He made her repeat the operation until he was satisfied she had got it right.

'Not bad,' he said, finally, when he allowed her to go back indoors. 'See ya.' And he went off towards the Fridesley Road on his skateboard, carrying the three cones and with Kate's five-pound note in his back pocket.

Next day, Kate met Andrew as arranged outside St Luke's lodge. They went to an unpleasant pub, full of stale cigarette smoke, and in spite of Kate's complaints, into an eating area that was noisy and crowded. They ordered some sort of flat pasta layered with pulped beef and topped with a pungent cheese custard. It was served with chips and mushy peas by a waitress who was making it plain that she would rather have been doing some other job. As she disappeared through the swing doors into the kitchen, they could hear the sound of upraised voices arguing about weekend rotas.

'Kennedy House,' said Kate. 'I know very little about the place, so could you fill me in?'

'The Oxford Centre for North American Studies,' said Andrew, catching the waitress by one corner of a grubby frilled apron and saying, 'Two lagers, please, dear.'

'They're not getting me do a sodding extra Saturday,' was her response, but she wrote something on her pad, so presumably lagers would eventually appear.

'Kennedy House was founded in the nineteen-seventies,' said Andrew, 'as a reaction against the colonial attitude of the Bodleian Library. That's the trouble with these Americans – they lack a proper historical perspective. To an institution founded in the fifteenth century, of course America is just a former colony.'

'Andrew! Stop teasing.'

The waitress crashed two plates of food on the table in front of them, dropped a couple of forks, and said, 'We're out of black pepper,' before disappearing again. Andrew continued speaking as though he had noticed nothing.

'Very well then. It was endowed by some hugely wealthy American charitable foundation to provide the resources for the study in Oxford of North American history and literature. I imagine that they have vaults full of Congressional Papers, or whatever the things are called, and endless rows of novels by Chandler and McBain and people like that.'

'Here's your drinks,' said the waitress, slapping them down on the table. 'You'll have to pay me for them now. I can't put them on your food bill.'

Kate could see that Andrew was about to start an argument about this, so she quickly got a note out of her wallet and paid the girl. Then she speared a chip with her fork and listened as Andrew continued.

'The Kennedy Centre is well, even extravagantly, funded.' Which might explain why he was being so acid about it, thought Kate. 'And I believe that they have a comprehensive collection of American and Canadian children's literature of the nineteenth and twentieth centuries. There was some expert in children's literature and lore – rather like our own dear Opies – who left them her entire collection when she died, about ten years ago. It didn't really fit in with the rest of the Kennedy collection, but since she also left them a huge – well, quite obscenely large – sum of money to go with it, they built a small (but elegant) annexe and accepted gratefully. Apart from that, they concentrate on the serious materials that you would expect in a centre of excellence such as Oxford. The Kennedy Centre is very well staffed – eight full-time, and three or four part-timers, as well as the domestic staff and the porters. There are a couple of comfortable study-bedrooms, with microcomputers linked to the University network, for any visiting North American academics.'

'How many of the staff work in the library?' asked Kate, dipping a fork into the hard brown varnish on her pasta.

'Five full-time, two part-time. And they take a trainee most years, too.'

Kate stopped herself from asking whether Jenna had ever been their trainee. She could find that out easily enough once she got there.

'And what books have gone missing?' Kate gave up on her pasta and laid down her fork.

Andrew sighed. 'Some volumes of a complete set of Nancy Drew mysteries. They were part of the donation by the generous benefactor, and if it comes to light, her trustees will not be at all pleased with Kennedy.' And as Kate laughed, he called, 'Can we have the bill now, dear?'

The waitress appeared at their table without her frilly apron. 'I'm off duty really,' she said. 'And I've told them

I'm not doing any more overtime this week.' Andrew paid for lunch, but refused to leave her a tip.

'When do I start work at the Kennedy Centre?' asked Kate.

'You can have this afternoon off,' said Andrew. 'But be there at eight thirty tomorrow morning. I'll fix a meeting for the two of us and Graham as soon as I can, but I've got a Book Selection Committee meeting this afternoon that I really can't get out of. Ask for the Director when you get there tomorrow. He'll want to show you round and introduce you to the staff himself.'

'Detective Sergeant Taylor? This is Kate Ivory.' Thames Valley Police had found Paul Taylor for her and put her through.

'The undertaker's assistant?'

'That's the one. Undertaking is livelier than I expected. Do you think we could meet so that I could ask your advice on a little problem I've come up against?' She thought that this submissive approach would suit his engrained sexism.

'I don't trust you when you're not insulting me,' he said. 'But I would hate you to go to someone else for advice, and only come to my attention again when you were in deep trouble.'

Kate swallowed a sharp retort. 'How about lunch tomorrow?' she said sweetly. 'Or a drink after work?'

'I'm knocking off in the next half-an-hour and I'm ready for a square meal,' he replied. 'Will you join me?'

He means McDonald's, she thought, or an Indian curry

house. Yuck, but worth it if she learned more about Jenna than Andrew appeared to know.

'Wonderful,' she said. 'Where shall we meet?'

'Are you at home?'

'Yes.' Did he mean her to cook him a meal? There were limits to what she would do for a male chauvinist to find the answer to her problem.

'I'll pick you up and we'll go out to the pub at Cumnor, if that's all right with you.'

'We could take my car if you like.'

'I know you like to be in control of the situation, but if you want to pick my brains you'll have to indulge me. I'll drive.'

'Yes, fine.' He must have seen an example of her awful driving around Oxford some time. 'I'll see you in about three-quarters of an hour then.'

The pub was of the genuine low ceilings and beams variety and there were log fires which were agreeable on the chilly evening. Their table in the dining section was gently lit and the atmosphere was perhaps more appropriate for a romantic dinner *à deux*, rather than a working meal for a policeman and an amateur sleuth. It was, she had to admit, an improvement on the fast-food joint she had imagined, and on the nasty city pub where she had eaten her lunch, so that she was having to rethink some of her prejudices about Paul Taylor.

She waited until they had eaten their way through the first two courses before asking questions. She had been very witty up to now, or so she thought, on the subject of

Oxford college librarians while they ate their smoked trout, and she had concentrated on being a wonderful listener while Paul told her about the principles of cross-training if you wanted to compete in a triathlon, over the stir-fried duck. But after she had shaken her head sadly at the dessert trolley and settled for a decaffeinated coffee instead, she slid into the subject of Jenna.

'I'm just doing a little cataloguing in some University libraries,' she said. 'There's a small problem with a couple of lost records' – and she hoped she was making it sound properly unimportant and low-key – 'so I'm keeping my eyes open for any discrepancies.'

'And?' He didn't look as though she was fooling him for a moment.

'Very junior work, you understand,' she tried again, 'just to give me a little extra income while I'm working on my book.'

'Yes, that car of yours must cost you a fortune in insurance and repairs,' he said.

'Quite. Well, it just happens that I came across a reference to a trainee from last year who, um, you might say, um, well, got herself killed.'

'What was her name?' But she knew he knew what she was talking about.

'Jenna Coates. She had been working at St Luke's College, where I've been doing some cataloguing. I know she was murdered just outside Oxford, after she had been away for the weekend with some friends. It's assumed that she accepted a lift from a stranger in a car, and her body was found a couple of days later by a workman on a building site. That's all public knowledge, but I was hoping that you could give me a little more.' She tilted her head to one side and opened her eyes very wide in a manner designed to appeal to the average sexist policeman.

'The Oxford Exit,' said Paul, taking no notice of her ploy.

'What?'

'She was murdered on the Oxford Exit. There were some road improvements going on there at the time, and he must have driven along the track that the contractors were using until he was out of sight of the motorway and the slip-road. It was deserted at that time on a Sunday.'

'And are you sure she was killed by a man? How did she die?'

'She was strangled, using a pair of tights. It could have been done by a very strong woman, I suppose, but this form of murder is generally done by a man, and has sexual overtones.'

'Had she been raped?'

'How very direct you are. No, she hadn't. But there was considerable bruising on the body. Perhaps he hoped for a more compliant partner, and strangled her when she refused to go along with it.'

'After removing her tights?'

'Now that is one odd feature of her death. Jenna was wearing jeans, socks and trainers, not tights. She didn't have a skirt with her for the weekend, and so there is no reason to believe that she would have had a pair of tights with her, either. He must have taken them with him.'

'Is that usual?'

'Less than two per cent of cases of strangulation by ligature, using stockings or tights, are carried out using tights belonging to anyone other than the victim.'

'So it's rare, but not unheard of,' said Kate, wishing that he wouldn't talk like a police training manual.

'In layman's terms, yes.'

'But if he had taken a pair of tights with him, it means that he had planned the whole thing. It wasn't a stranger, and it wasn't opportunist.'

'You're making a lot of assumptions there. Maybe she had packed a pair of tights, after all. Maybe she hadn't, but his wife or girlfriend had left a pair in the car. Maybe he was a salesman with samples in a suitcase.'

'Do you believe any of that?'

'I keep an open mind. Would you like some cheese? No? More coffee?'

She shook her head. His account agreed largely with Andrew's, though she now had more details. She knew that there was something else she wanted to ask him, but it had slipped to the back of her mind for a moment. Perhaps it was because Paul Taylor had very regular features and grey-blue eyes, and darker lashes than usually went with that sandy hair. The Victorians thought that blue eyes were a mark of faithfulness, she thought, an idea that doubtless went back to medieval times and . . .

'I'll drive you home then,' he was saying.

They were just turning left off the Fridesley Road when she remembered the other thing she wanted to ask him about. She also remembered the half-bottle of fifteen-year-old single malt whisky that still remained in her kitchen cupboard.

'I can offer you a nightcap,' she said, then added quickly, 'a very small one, of course, well diluted with spring water.' Why did talking to a policeman always make her feel guilty?

He laughed and followed her into the house, then watched her pour out a small whisky for each of them. He sat on the pink sofa and she put some quiet music on the stereo player, then joined him on the sofa since it seemed both unfriendly and coy to sit on the opposite side of the room.

'You realize I'll have to stay until I've metabolized this lot,' he said.

'How long will that take?' she asked, startled.

'I'll let you know,' and he laughed at her again. 'Now tell me what else you've thought of to ask me.'

'When I met you on the tow path, and asked you whether you knew who Jenna was, you said something that sounded like "Dead girl with peony". What did you mean?'

'If I tell you, you must promise to keep it to yourself. It was one of those things that might well be the murderer's trademark, and we don't want it to get out or we could get copycat murders.'

'I promise.' It was a pity her own eyes weren't bluer, but he seemed to believe her anyway.

'She had been hidden in a shallow grave – or the murderer had just shovelled some loose earth over her perhaps so that she should not be immediately visible, but then he had placed a pink peony on top. It was faded, of course, but it was what drew the workman's attention to the spot. She might have stayed hidden much longer, otherwise.'

Kate shivered. 'And is it a trademark? Have you come across any other murders signed with a pink peony?'

'No. Not yet.'

'And there's another thing. Just how likely is it that she accepted a lift from a stranger? I wouldn't, I know. And she can't have been stupid. The girl was a graduate, after all.'

Paul Taylor gave her a look that made her realize just how little the police thought of women graduates. 'Girls do stupid things,' he said dismissively.

'The police don't seem to believe that women have brains at all, and this evening you're talking like a policeman.' She had started to raise her voice.

'I thought I was talking like a friend.'

That silenced her just for a moment. Then she said:

'Come on, we've all read about women hitchhikers being knocked off by male motorists.' She managed to make the word 'male' into an insult. 'I don't believe that she'd accept a lift from a man unless she knew who he was.'

'So you're saying that either it was a woman, or it was a man that she knew. Or, I suppose, a woman that she knew, come to that.'

'You've got it.'

'But you don't know how desperate she might have been to get back to Oxford. There wasn't another train for two hours. Maybe she had a date, or was expecting a phone call from her mother, or something.'

'Crap.'

'I don't like to hear words like that from a woman.'

'So you have a choice: stick with your ladylike friends, or get used to it.'

His lips tightened. He didn't like rude, foul-mouthed women. And she still needed his co-operation.

'OK, I'm sorry. I'll try to clean up my language when you're around. Tell me what else is on your mind.'

'Suppose you're right and she was killed by someone that she knew – man or woman. I don't want you to be the second victim. She was working in a succession of different libraries the way you are. Suppose she had noticed the same discrepancies that you have, and was asking the same questions. And why did she suddenly take time off work to fly off to visit a friend in California? She must have found something suspicious and she took the chance to follow it – or him – up.'

'I didn't know about California,' said Kate, wondering how she could wangle a trip to follow in Jenna's footsteps.

'Don't even think about following her. Do you understand me, Kate?'

'I understand that this probably wasn't a random killing, and that therefore it might well have something to do with the matter that I'm looking into for the Security Team. But really, I'm not asking any unusual questions at all.'

He laughed. 'I don't believe that. No way. You can't meet anyone, anywhere, without going straight for the outrageous question. It's your trademark. And it could get you into trouble. Well, look at you this evening: you've been asking me some very direct questions, and then you've invited me into your house when you hardly know me.'

'You think I'm taking a risk? But I hadn't got you down as a dangerous man.' Did he look a little disappointed at this? His was not a face that gave away his emotions.

'I think for your own safety you should tell me more about the job that this Security Team has got you doing.' In his voice was all the scorn of the professional for the amateur.

'It's confidential. They made me sign a paper.'

'And you think what I told you is common knowledge? I've signed pieces of paper, too, you know.'

As she still hesitated, he said: 'It's your safety I'm worried about. I don't want to trample all over your investigation, whatever it is. But neither do I want you to get into any sort of danger.'

She made a decision. 'Come and look at my notes, if you like. There's very little in them yet either to please the Security Team or to worry any possible book thieves.'

Downstairs in her workroom, Paul looked at her computer with approval. 'Nice fast machine,' he said. 'And I see you keep two sets of backup floppies in separate cases.'

'I am quite an organized person,' she said.

'But what do you want all these books for?' he asked, looking round the walls lined with shelves. She looked surprised: this was a small selection, a few hundred or so of her books, just the ones that she used frequently.

'They're so messy,' he said. 'Look at all those dog-eared markers sticking out of them.'

'That's because the books are used,' she answered. 'I read them, you see.'

'My sister has books,' he said. 'She gets them from a club, but she keeps them behind glass so that they don't get dusty.' He picked one out from the shelf and blew along the top: a thin stream of dust emerged and danced in the light from the table lamp.

'Yes, they are dusty, some of them. And some of them have been dropped in the bath, others have been spattered with tomato soup or splashed with coffee. Many have broken spines and torn dust jackets. One or two may be singed by the afternoon sun. I do not apologize for this. My books lead exciting lives. They leave their cellar home and venture into the outside world, where they meet temptation and occasionally disaster. And don't lose that bookmark, it is marking an important point, something that I wanted to refer to.'

'And that's another thing. Why have you got so many bookmarks? How can you read all those books at one time?'

'How can *you* work on so many cases? I hold more than one idea in my head simultaneously: it's a feminine characteristic.'

He looked at her without replying, but replaced the book on its shelf and picked up the three or four pages of typed notes that she gave him.

'There's nothing much here: just the reference to Jenna, which I think I've explained to you.'

She put the notes back in their file and they left the room. As they mounted the stairs, he said: 'And you'll keep me informed of what's happening in future?'

'Yes. How's your metabolism making out with the whisky?' She wanted to have the house to herself again.

'It needs another fifteen minutes.'

So she made more decaffeinated coffee and they sat and drank it sitting on the sofa. He had thick, springy hair, and if she sat and looked at it with her eyes half-closed, she could imagine that it was the rich, dark brown that she always found so attractive in a man.

'Is Jenna's case still being investigated?'

'Not actively. No murder case is closed and filed away until it is solved, but I'd have to say that this is on a back burner, waiting for some new evidence, or a case that replicates the details of Jenna's and that gives us a new lead. The details are on the computer, and if something replicating them crops up anywhere in the country, we'll tie the two cases in together, and Jenna's will be "live" again. But none of what you and I have talked about is official: my boss wouldn't want me to spend police time on something with such a small chance of success.'

'Poor Jenna. It looks as though her only hope of justice lies with me.'

She got another direct look from the blue eyes. 'I think you're over-dramatizing the situation.'

'Your fifteen minutes is up, Paul,' she said.

After he had gone, she thought about ringing back Emma, but decided that it was really too late, so she went downstairs to add to her notes on Jenna Coates. Paul had answered some of the questions she had typed in yesterday, but she didn't enjoy filling in the answers.

When she had finished, she went upstairs to bed and another stint with *Frankenstein*.

# vi

*Portrayal of Character*

There are some people who are so uncompromisingly
virtuous that they really have no place in this world of
ours (or so, perhaps, if I am honest, I argued afterwards).
Tell a story with a hint of exaggeration to make it funnier
and they interrupt you with 'Oh, but surely she wasn't
*juggling* with the mince pies . . .' or whatever little grace
note you had added to the basic line. Such literal truthful-
ness does not fit them to live in this world of ours. Not,
that is, if they wish to survive. And when I (and you too,
I imagine) sign out at lunch time, as the clock shows three
minutes to twelve, you put down 12.00, to simplify the
arithmetic later, while she, breathing earnestly down your
neck, follows you immediately with 11.55. She didn't seem
to like it when I said, 'It's quality time that counts, not
quantity.' I could see the frown of concentration that
meant that she was working herself up to some portentous
announcement about the nature of the contract between
employer and employed. It was another of Jenna's irritat-

149

ing characteristics, this unburdening of herself of everything, but *everything*, that was on her mind at the moment.
She had no idea of editing it, of shortening it, or even of
suppressing it entirely.

'John,' she said, with her earnestness escaping in small
pants from her thick, pale lips. 'There is something, something important, that I have to talk to you about.'

Such a pity for the stupid girl that on this occasion at
least she hadn't kept her ideas to herself.

I have always thought that it is the duty of the young
to be attractive, especially if they are female. Even if they
have few natural advantages in this respect, surely they
can make the most of those that they do have by dressing
becomingly, keeping their hair clean and sweet-smelling
and wearing cosmetics to make the most of themselves.
A young woman should not sit in a library with her hair
in greasy rats' tails, her thick body encased in baggy sweatshirt and tight black leggings, her large feet in heavy boots.
And above all she should *smile*. Such are the duties – not
onerous, surely? – of the feminine woman. And then, the
crowning glory of any woman should be her hair. Couldn't
she have let it grow? It wasn't a pretty colour, not the
reddish-brown that is the colour I love best, but she could
have done whatever it is that other young women do to
themselves to make it look thicker, wavier. Why couldn't
Jenna make some effort to be prettier? I'm sure I would
have reflected twice about her future if I had thought that
she had one of any significance.

Jenna had a heart of gold, they all said. Once she had
decided that you needed caring for, Jenna would do the

caring. Without hesitation or deviation. Not that she had ever got her claws into me, but dear old Robin, white-haired and scholarly, had been on the receiving end of her relentless charity. Admittedly, the old boy was getting a bit doddery, and maybe the rest of us didn't offer to help him to carry his piles of books as often as we might have done. But Jenna, with that sickly smile of hers, surely overdid it. Not that Robin seemed to notice. He treated her with the same old-world courtesy that he would have bestowed on a visiting Goth or Vandal.

'But he knows so much about the place,' gushed Jenna. 'Do you know that he's been here for forty-two years?'

'Yes, Jenna, I do,' I said, but she took no notice of me.

'He was telling me about the way the place was run years ago,' she said. 'Explaining the ins and outs of the system. It really is fascinating.'

'Fascinating,' I said, thinking hard. 'Not that they had much of a system in those days.'

'Oh yes they *did*,' said Jenna. 'All sorts of checks and double-checks to make sure that you could tell at any time exactly where a book could be found. I know these computers are wonderful, but in some ways I think that the old system was more foolproof. And then, Robin is, well, like a repository of the lore and history of the place. I felt that if I can learn it from him, then I will be able to pass it on.'

'Like a sacred trust?' I said.

'Exactly,' said Jenna, missing the irony and pleased that

I had taken her point at last. 'Of course, I make the time up,' she said virtuously. 'It wouldn't do to gossip on Library time, would it?'

'No,' I said. 'And speaking of which, Jenna, I really must be moving along.'

Jenna was right of course: Robin was a fund of anecdote and fable, and fascinating insights into the working of the establishment. And his health was failing, so that it was only a matter of weeks after this conversation that he took his retirement (to write a definitive bibliography of eighteenth-century something or other, of course), though he was not to enjoy his retirement for very long. No, don't look at me like that. It really had nothing to do with me, much more to do with clogged arteries and a schoolboy love of cream cakes.

At the time she first spoke to me, I went away and thought about it. Could the girl have an idea of what we were doing? It was possible that she had gone nosing into the old records of the library and found some discrepancies in the stock. If so, did she realize that it spread far beyond the bounds of her own institution?

I arranged to meet her in the staff common-room (in reality a nasty little cubbyhole where we made ourselves instant coffee and drank it black while cartons of milk solidified on the window-sill) at a time when no one else was likely to be there. I made us each a mug of coffee and invited her to sit down. She smiled at me. I have never found large teeth attractive.

'Well now, Jenna,' I said, at my most avuncular. 'I know that something has been worrying you, so do tell me about it. Maybe I can help.' I attempted a friendly smile, but I think it might have come out wrong.

'I believe that you've been stealing books,' she said in her crudely direct way. A lock of greasy hair fell across her forehead and she pushed it back with a stubby hand. Flakes of dandruff floated down on to her shoulders. 'Why don't you tell me the truth of the matter, and then we can go to the Director and confess it all to him.'

She took my breath away. Is this really how some people think: that one should go and present the truth, like a slab of meat – unseasoned, undressed, uncooked – to a superior? It was uncouth, immoral. Didn't she understand the corrosive, the corrupting effect of raw truth? Life could only continue in her expected way if we wrapped her nudity in a decent package of harmless lies to preserve her modesty and keep her from shaming herself and us.

'I'm sure you've got this wrong,' I said, trying to keep the smile on my face. 'What makes you think that I've . . . um . . . what you said?'

'Let me show you,' she said, and she got up, poured the rest of her coffee down the sink, washed up her mug (ignoring mine, I might say, in her unwomanly way), dried it and then led the way out of the room.

'You see,' she said, seating herself at her terminal, 'the management think that you can't delete someone else's records unless you are very senior indeed. More senior than me, certainly.' She logged into the system, typed in her identifying name and her password – so quickly that I was unable to see what it might be. Then she called a record – looking like a detailed catalogue card – on to her screen.

'This is one that I catalogued yesterday,' she said. The book it referred to still sat on the small trolley beside her desk. 'If I wanted to steal it, the theft would be discovered the first time that someone looked in the catalogue, found its shelf-mark and looked to find that it wasn't there. There would be no record of another borrower taking it, the thing would simply be missing. But the name of the library, my initials, and yesterday's date are there at the end of the Notes. So someone would come straight to me and ask me where it was.'

'Very good,' I said humorously. 'They'll have you on the Library Security Interest Group if you go on like this.'

She ignored me. 'But if I could remove the record, I could take the book and no one would be any the wiser. It might be months before someone remembered that we should have it, and then it would be very difficult indeed to trace what had happened to it – or even when.'

'If you could remove the record?' I said. I had a nasty feeling that I knew what would happen next.

'I can't delete this record, as you well know,' she said. 'But I can replace it with another. I've checked to see that no other library is using it to add details of their own copies with their accession numbers and shelf-marks. We're the only people so far to have a copy. So I bring another record in from an outside database. Let's say,' she said, lifting up another new book from her trolley, 'that I'm cataloguing this book, and I find that there is a record for it made by the Library of Congress.' She typed in a few more keystrokes and a catalogue record for the second book came up on the screen. 'There you are,' she said. 'Now, when I transfer this record from the other database into our catalogue, the system asks me whether I wish to replace an existing record. As you know, the answer is normally "No", but this time I tell it "Yes", I give it the Document Number of the book I want to steal,' and she typed rapidly: I have to say that the girl was good, 'I type "Yes" again and there you are; the original record has disappeared, replaced by the new one.'

The Oxford Exit. It was simple enough if you knew what you were doing. It was a pity that she had been chatting to Robin as well as improving her computing skills. She had much of the knowledge she needed to put the whole story together now.

'But you still have details of its accession number and shelf-mark,' I said, though I guessed she'd know the answer to that one.

'Simple. I have the authority to change them, so I replace them with the accession number and the shelf-mark of the second book.' She typed away and changed them as I watched.

'That's no kind of proof of theft,' I said, though I knew she knew I was bluffing.

'But there are other facts to add to that one,' she said. 'Once I got an idea of what might be happening, I rang a friend of mine who is doing a two-year exchange at the University Library at Santa Luisa in California. She told me about the exciting women's studies programme that they have, and how pleased they are to be offered just the books they wanted to complete their collection of the works of the Sisterhood of the Veil.'

She was nearly there. I found that I was holding my breath.

'And at that point I started putting things together because another friend of mine at' – and here she named the library that had supplied the Eliza Baughn volume – 'had mentioned that it was odd, but a reader had been looking at a book by Eliza Baughn, and when he came back a few weeks later to see it again, he couldn't find the shelf-mark in the on-line catalogue. In fact, he could find no record of the book at all. Perhaps shortsightedly, the librarian had destroyed the card catalogue as items from the stock were re-catalogued on to the computer. It was taking up valuable library space, she said.'

'And you think that I'm responsible?'

'Yes. Not on your own, I think. I have worked out that you probably have two colleagues, possibly more. I was wondering how you removed the books that you wished to steal from the library. You wouldn't do anything as obvious as putting them in your mac pocket and walking out through the front door, would you? No, I thought that the simplest way for one of us to take a book was to use the postal system. The internal mail, probably, with the book placed in a much recycled Jiffy bag so that it looked just like the other mail arriving on a colleague's desk. Perhaps you added some sort of sticker or identification mark to alert your opposite number.' (The girl was right: we stuck on an inconspicuous label with *Iron Shoe* printed on it). 'And I thought that, since you aren't particularly knowledgeable about books – not like Robin, for example – you would need someone to tell you which books to steal to make the crime worth the risk.'

'I don't like to hear you using the word "crime",' I said, to show her that she was being vulgar and insensitive, but she took no notice of my gentle rebuke.

'Don't you? Well, stealing is a crime, and you can't get away from it. I rang my friend in Santa Luisa again. She told me when the representative of the Iron Shoe Collection was expected to arrive from England with the next batch of books. It all fitted, but I wanted to be sure. Then I invited myself over to stay with Sharon, my friend. I would only have to find the fare, and I could get a reduction with my student card. When the Iron Shoe representative was due, Sharon drove me to the airport so that I could watch you arrive. I don't suppose you saw me, but I recognized *you*.'

'So you think you've caught me out in this complicated theft?'

'Yes. But we can do something about it.'

'What?' But I knew the girl would have no constructive suggestion to make.

'We have to go to the Director and tell him what you've been doing,' she said. Just like that.

I looked at the dandruff on the shoulders of her black sweatshirt. The girl would have to go.

'Give me time to think about it,' I said. 'I have to prepare myself, Jenna. Focus myself, you know.'

She seemed to understand what I meant better than I did, for she nodded and smiled. 'And you'll have to speak to your colleagues and persuade them to give up this scheme,' she said. 'I'll leave you to think about it until Monday morning. We'll go to see him together then, if you like.'

I had five days to work up a plan. I couldn't risk involving the others: they might not see things the way I did. Jenna would have to disappear, permanently, silently and without any incriminating evidence left behind. One further manifestation of the Oxford Exit, you might say.

# Chapter Six

The Centre for North American Studies at Kennedy House stood a little to the north of Rhodes House, on slightly higher ground, and rose thirty feet above it, so that it could look down over the leafy streets of North Oxford and feel superior to its dependent cousin. It had been built in its grassy setting at a time of architectural confidence, and its dome floated above the treetops, and its copper-coloured glass windows reflected back the sunlight in a bold and strident way that less financially well-endowed establishments liked to sneer at.

Very nice, thought Kate. I shall be working with proper up-lighting and clean air. They might even give me a desk and chair of the correct height so that I don't get backache.

'I have an appointment with the Director,' she said at the entrance desk. Even the porters seemed younger and more helpful than those further south.

'Give us a note of your car licence number and you can park out there in the car park while you're working here,' one of them said. And then there was discreet whispering into a telephone and only a couple of minutes later a tall, thin man appeared.

'Chris Johnston,' he said. His voice was a soft mid-Atlantic, as though he didn't want to commit himself to sounding either positively English or American.

His head poked forward on his thin neck, and when he turned to lead the way towards his office, his profile was of two unbroken straight lines, meeting at an angle of 130 degrees at the point of his nose. Some sort of bird, thought Kate. A very young duck, perhaps, whose bill has not yet fully grown.

'Take a seat, Miss Ivory,' he said.

'Won't you call me Kate?'

'That might be better if you're going to get to know the staff. Now, I gather that you're going to look at our stock and give us some idea what a retrospective conversion job would involve. That in itself will be very useful to us.'

Kate looked suitably helpful yet modest.

'And then, I gather from Charles that you will be able to find our book thief for us.'

Kate changed her expression to one of determination and sharp intelligence.

'I'll take you round and introduce you to the rest of the staff, and Angela Rugby, our Librarian, will show you where you'll be working. If there's anything else that I can do to help you in your work, just let me know, won't you. All my staff come to me with their problems, so you won't be unusual if you knock on my door at the end of the working day.' And the duck's bill nodded gently up and down while the lids nearly closed on the pale blue eyes.

'There is one point you might be able to help me over,' said Kate. 'Do you know who is in charge of the one-year library trainees?'

'That one's easy,' he said. 'I am.'

Sandy lashes blinked. His hair was fairish, greyish, receding. Did he look like a man who would attack a girl in his car and kill her on a slip-road on a wet Sunday evening? His hands were the usual soft well-cared-for librarian's hands; it was easy to imagine them writing neatly with a gold-nibbed fountain pen on a catalogue card, impossible to imagine them twisting a pair of tights around a girl's throat and pulling until her life was extinguished.

'I wonder, then, if you could tell me anything about Jenna Coates? She was on the training programme last year and she—'

'She was killed,' he said. There was suppressed anger in his voice. 'Murdered. Such a waste. Such a wicked, meaningless waste of a young life.'

'I'd like to know which libraries she had worked in,' said Kate. 'I know about St Luke's, but can you tell me where else she had been?'

'I'm not sure that I understand how this fits in with retrospective cataloguing, or with finding a book thief,' said Chris Johnston.

'Neither am I,' said Kate. 'But there are too many coincidences so far to convince me that her death is completely dissociated from the thefts. And I agree with you:

the death of a young person is a waste, and I would like to find out who did it and why, if it is at all possible.'

Chris Johnston didn't comment, but went across to a filing cabinet and pulled out a folder. 'She started work at the Bodleian,' he said. 'In their Cataloguing Department. She did two months there, learning the basics of on-line cataloguing. It made her quite useful when she went to other libraries. Then she moved on to Leicester College, where she worked on the book issue desk, learning about the duties of a library assistant: all that stamping and ticking-in of periodicals, and chasing of overdue books. She got on very well with the undergraduates, I believe, and she picked up a favourable report from Kevin Newton, their librarian.' Kate made a quick note of the name as Chris Johnston went on. 'After that, she returned to the Bodleian for a few weeks and then she came here to Kennedy House. I like to have the trainees here, even if only for a short time, so that I can have some personal contact with them and make sure that their progress is what it should be. She worked with our Conservation Officer, Susie Holbech. I believe they were going through the Kilworth Collection – that's the collection of American juvenile literature that was bequeathed to the Centre a few years ago – and Susie was teaching her about the day-to-day work of Conservation.'

Kate had a brief mental image of a room where white-coated assistants brewed up specialist jams, but dismissed it again as being too frivolous for a serious institution like Kennedy House. 'Can you tell me briefly what Conservation does?'

'A lot of the time, they mend books. They try to make sure that books are kept in the best conditions so that they don't get damaged in the first place. There is a rumour that Conservation Officers would like to take over their libraries, place all books in acid-free protective boxes and keep them in temperature-controlled, air-conditioned vaults. Their natural enemies are the Readers, people who want to get books off the shelves, handle them, open them and turn the pages, exposing them to the damaging rays of the sun.'

Kate thought guiltily of her own battle-scarred and careworn collection. She could see that she would be the natural enemy of a Conservation Officer, but she would have to meet this person soon and talk to her about Jenna Coates. It looked as though a large piece of the jigsaw puzzle was to be found here at Kennedy House. She was about to suggest that they move on to meet the rest of the staff when the Director added, 'And after leaving us, she took an unexpected holiday. She had the chance to go to California, it seems, and since she had been doing so well at her training programme, we allowed her to go. When she got back, she moved to St Luke's. She learned about ordering, doing the accounts and accessioning, and then Michael Ennis was showing her their Special Collections.'

'I believe that I saw one of them,' said Kate, remembering some startling illustrations. 'How many have they got?'

'I don't know. Not many, I should have thought. But I do know that Jenna was interested in nineteenth-century women writers, and they might well have had a small holding of such works.' He rose from his chair. 'Shall we go and meet the rest of the staff now?'

He led the way down a corridor carpeted in slate-grey, with soothing green-grey walls and lively yellow and gold abstract pictures. Then he knocked at a door and ushered Kate inside. 'Angela Rugby, our Librarian,' he said. 'And Angela, this is Kate Ivory, who will be doing some retrospective cataloguing for us.'

Kate saw a woman with white hair cut in a chin-length bob, and a smooth, tanned face that was too young to go with the white hair. She sat behind a desk with the ubiquitous microcomputer on it, doubtless linking her to the University network and thus to databases across the world. In front of the desk were packages of what were probably that morning's delivery of books.

'I'm giving Kate the rapid tour of the factory,' said Chris Johnston. 'I'll bring her back here again when I've finished, Angela.'

Again, a cool, assessing look from Angela Rugby and they were out in the corridor again and moving towards the back of the building.

'Conservation Office,' he said, opening a door and showing her in. 'And this is Susie Holbech, Kate.' Kate made a note to come back and talk to Susie about Jenna, but for the moment she just took in a slight figure in a white lab coat, with nondescript brown hair and spectacles. In front of her, on the bench, were some dull brown shapes and a lot of dirty balls of cotton wool. Susie Holbech smiled vaguely at her and then went on with her work.

'This is the reference desk,' said Chris Johnston, stopping at an expensive sweep of shining wood with the obligatory VDU. 'And one of our assistants, Martin L. Preston, over here on an exchange from the United States. He's indexing our official papers for us.'

'Call me Marty,' said the young man, and Kate smiled in return, for Marty was tall, broad-shouldered, black and very beautiful. Why didn't glamorous English people go in for being library assistants?

'And here we have the general office and cataloguing room,' said the Director, moving on and opening another door. 'We thought it would be friendlier and brighter to have one big room where everyone could work together, rather than divide it up into two little cubbyholes.'

Oh yes, thought Kate, very nice, as she was introduced to the Secretary, the Accountant, and the Housekeeper.

'And have you met Graham Kieler, from the Libraries' Security Team? Graham is here to make sure that we're taking normal precautions with our computers.'

'How do you do?' He wasn't very old, but he had a formal manner, and was wearing a dark grey suit and white shirt with a blue tie.

'I can't think that anyone wants to break into our computer!' said the Housekeeper. 'It's not as though there's anything very interesting or valuable in here.'

Graham Kieler pulled a face. 'That's what we're up against, Miss Ivory. Nobody wants to take security seriously until there's been a break-in and thousands of pounds' worth of records have been vandalized or lost.'

'Surely not,' said Kate, but realized that she was in the presence of an enthusiast.

'If a hacker finds a weak spot, he can get into your system and find out more about it, learn the names of people with higher authority levels, and gradually push his way into the centre, and then he can wreak havoc if he wants to. So make sure that your password is the full eight letters long and is a word that cannot be found in the dictionary.'

Kate could tell that this was an instruction that he had given a hundred times before.

'I use my Christian name,' said the Secretary. 'Then I can be sure of remembering it.'

'And it would be the first thing that any hacker would try, if he was attempting to get in under your identity,' said Kieler.

How could you stop people abusing the system, helping themselves to what they wanted, when you had attitudes like that? Kate and Chris Johnston left him to his thankless task and crossed to the other side of the large, sunny room to meet Fiona Bliss, the Kennedy Centre's cataloguer.

Fiona was young, tall and thin, with a small head perched on a long neck and a frizz of dark hair. She wore large round spectacles that gave her an intellectual air that was contradicted when she started to speak.

'You're a Bodleian cataloguer, I hear,' she said. She had very large teeth. 'I expect you know how to catalogue properly, then.' Kate made 'Well, um, I suppose so' noises, which Fiona ignored. 'We tend to do things our own way, here. Well, you have to, don't you? Victor's been here for yonks, and he's not going to change his cataloguing methods just because the Bodleian orders him to.'

Kate had no intention of getting into an argument over consistent cataloguing standards, so she just smiled sweetly in return. There was a yellow Post-it note stuck to the edge of Fiona's screen with the word 'doglead' written on it.

'My password,' said Fiona.

Kieler must have heard her for he was at their side immediately.

'Never leave your password on your screen,' he said.

'How would anybody guess what it was?'

'Don't worry, they'd guess.'

'Don't be so ridiculous! No one's interested in getting into my computer. Why does everyone always pick on me?'

A full-scale row was about to develop, and Chris Johnston said quickly: 'Your statistics are up this month, Fiona. You've catalogued a lot more books than usual.'

'I have?' She looked startled. 'I don't remember doing so, but statistics don't lie, do they?'

No, thought Kate. But they can tell little fibs. Someone else could have borrowed your password and altered records in your name. That would add to your totals. She caught Graham Kieler's eye. He would doubtless come to the same conclusion and check on her records.

She followed Chris Johnston back to Angela Rugby's office, where more packages of books had been delivered in the past hour, though Angela looked as collected as ever. Chris Johnston left them to go back to his own office. Before he went, Kate asked him who Victor was.

'Oh, Victor Southam. He's just a part-timer, now. You'll see him when he comes into lunch. He works here in the afternoon. He's been here since the place opened back in the seventies. He does a little cataloguing, and he's compiling a bibliography of some sort, I believe.'

'Have you seen any books yet?' asked Angela, when he had left the room. 'No? Then I'll show you our reading room and bookstack.'

And very nice they both were, with well-lighted desks, oak bookcases and a thick carpet underfoot to deaden the noise of people moving about. Oh, how different from our dear Bodleian Library, thought Kate disloyally. The bookstack was on a couple of floors underneath the reading room, and had moving bookcases and a lift to the upper floors.

'We can get books to readers within fifteen minutes,' said Angela. 'Faster, if they're really in a hurry.'

'And do you let your readers take books away to read?'

'No, like the Bodleian, we have only one copy of each work, so they are always kept on the premises. There is a card index system in the reading room which shows which books are out and being read at any given time.'

'So a book that is missing from the bookstack should have a corresponding card in a reading room?'

'Right. If it hasn't, it's either misplaced, or it's walked.'

They went on through the reading room, crossed a small quadrangle with a fountain and green plants and benches rather than the standard Oxford lawn, and entered a small modern building.

'This is where we have housed the collection of juvenile literature donated by our recent benefactor.' She didn't sound overwhelmed by the gift.

The building was again very pleasant, and empty of people. 'We shall be moving another part of our collection in here, but it makes sense to recatalogue on to the computer while we are relocating our stock. I'd be grateful if you would take a look through this collection of children's books and let me know how quick a task it will be: I don't want to take too much library time over it.'

'Hasn't Victor Southam been cataloguing some of it already?'

'I don't think he's made much headway. You'll see if you check the titles index on the computer which ones he's already converted.'

'I'll start here then, if you like,' said Kate. 'I can probably give you a good idea after three or four hours' work.'

'Fine. There's a live microcomputer in the office here, and if you don't mind being on your own for a while, it would be more convenient than carting books back to the main office.'

'I like being on my own,' said Kate. Especially with a view over grass and flowerbeds, with trees shading me from the road, and blocking out the noise of the traffic.

At Kennedy House the staff ate together in a staff dining-room, collecting their meals from a counter and sitting together at a long table.

If Andrew and Charles are right, thought Kate, one of these people is a book thief. It wasn't a comfortable thought. It was even less comfortable to think that she might unmask him, bringing his career to an end. What happened when you were caught at something like that? That is not your responsibility, said a voice inside her head. He or she should have thought of that before they started. But they're only *books*, said the awkward voice, and you're contemplating ruining somebody's life. Right and wrong, replied her other self. Justice. And perhaps the thief was responsible for the death of a young woman, and that was worth finding out about. There should be justice for a crime like that.

She realized that Susie Holbech, the Conservation Officer, was talking in her loud, gushing voice, asking her something, and that she had been staring for a long time at her red kidney bean and brown rice salad.

'Oh yes,' she said. 'That's right, I'm a writer. Where do I get my ideas from? I really don't know. They just seem to come to me if I sit down at my word-processor and concentrate.' She dug her fork into the rice and started to eat.

'Do you get to travel much?' persisted Susie. 'I've always wanted to travel, but I've never had the chance. I'd like to go to really exotic places and get away from it all.' Her loud voice and pale and insignificant face seemed incongruous when Kate placed them amid tropical vegetation.

'I thought I heard you were off on a tour of South American countries this autumn,' said Marty.

'Oh, well, I don't know about that,' said Susie, huffily. 'I didn't realize that people were gossiping about me like that.'

'I wouldn't want to travel,' put in someone else, a few places down and opposite to Kate. An elderly man, with a domed, bald head and sedentary figure. He must be Victor Southam. Why is it that librarians so frequently live down to your expectations of what they should look like, wondered Kate. She looked at herself surreptitiously: it was all right, her skirt was the shortest here.

'Just leave me alone with my books and my garden,' Victor Southam was saying. 'And my dog, of course. I'm very fond of my dog.'

Ho hum, thought Kate. If this is the level of conversation at lunch here, let me out of the place. She caught Marty's eye and saw the suspicion of a wink. Oh well, maybe she'd stick around after all.

After lunch, she walked briskly back into the centre of Oxford, whisked round the Covered Market and picked up the makings of a meal for the evening. She looked at the car park when she got back to Kennedy House: there were several free places and she would drive her car in to work tomorrow, she decided, though she had read only that week that Oxford's car parks were notorious for car theft. In fact, one of the cars was flashing its lights and blaring its horn in a corner of the tarmac, while no one inside the building took the slightest notice. Maybe it wasn't even audible behind all that thick plate glass. She decided to be helpful, and went in to report it to the porter at the reception desk.

'Car alarm?' said the porter. 'That'll be Mr Kieler's, I expect. The thing goes off if a sparrow farts within ten feet of it. I'll let the gentleman know.'

Kate returned to the Kennedy House annexe and filled a small trolley with a selection of books from the shelves.

A couple of hours later she had reached the Nancy Drew mysteries, and she checked down the titles index on the computer to see whether any of them were already recorded. Six of them were, and she started to go into the records to see how they had been catalogued, so that her own entries would fit in with the rest of the series. It took her only ten minutes to find the first three discrepancies.

She rang Andrew when she was sure what she had found. She wouldn't be disturbed in the office in the annexe.

'What I've seen is something very clumsy, Andrew. Five books are missing from the shelves, and are not accounted for by cards in the file in the reading room. Which means that, in the words of our Librarian, they've walked. Now, the cards from the old manual catalogue have been removed from the drawer, so that the only record of the books is on the computer. I found them straight away when I was checking the Nancy Drew series and looked to see who else had copies of them. Someone tried to cover his tracks by removing the Kennedy House copy records from the computer. But since theirs aren't the only copies, he hasn't been able to do so, and has merely removed the shelf-marks. If you look further into the records, you can see that the accession numbers are still there, and most ridiculous of all, he has left his fingerprints all over the record.'

'Fingerprints?'

'Well, his initials. As you leave a record and go into the detail of the copies, the machine automatically signs it with the short form of your library name, adds your initials and the date.'

'Yes, yes, I know all that. Tell me who it is.'

'The identification reads *ken.vs*, and the dates are all in the past month or two. Ken, as you can guess, is Kennedy House, and vs is Victor Southam.'

She felt sick as she said it. That pathetic old man with his garden and his scabby dog. What would he do now? What does anybody do when they are thrown out of a job in their sixties and have put even their pension at risk?

'I'll contact the Security Team. They'll check the records to make sure of what you're saying, and they'll send someone round to interview Southam. You won't be involved, Kate. Your name won't be mentioned.'

Which was a very minor compensation, it seemed to Kate.

She called in on Camilla on her way home.

'What's wrong with you?' asked Camilla.

'Nothing. I just don't like my job much today.'

'That happens to a lot of people. Why don't you go back to writing?'

Kate was wandering round the room, looking at Camilla's books. 'I can't afford to at the moment.'

'Go home, Kate, and get on with your book.'

The evening was overcast, and as Kate arrived back in Agatha Street, lights were going on in front rooms, illuminating the scenes inside like a peep show. As she walked up to her front door, Kate could see every detail of the Toadface family eating its evening meal. On the wall opposite her, a huge photograph of little Toadface scowled down on them, every fold, pouch and extrusion of its face in horrid close-up. Around this centrepiece crowded other photos of the Toadface family, staring at their originals as they forked food into their faces.

Kate found her key, opened her door and walked quickly into her house. Camilla was right. It was time that she got on with her book.

# vii

## *Extract from a Writer's Notebook*

It's amazing how a deadline concentrates your thoughts, isn't it, Mrs Dolby? I'm sure you've found that with your own writing. You sit there with all the time in the world, and the blank pages stare back at you. There is no reason to fill them this morning, so you go off and make yourself another cup of coffee, or go for a walk, or switch on the radio. A week later, and the same blank pages stretch through your notebook, and no new idea has popped into your mind.

But give yourself a deadline, and oh, how different things are. You open your notebook and a feverish activity takes over. You feel worried, unhappy, even frightened. But this tension produces ideas, and the words fall over themselves to get on to the page.

And so it was with my plan to get rid of Jenna. I became sensitive to everything happening around me, I listened for the first time to the gossip of the young women, and I strove to fit what I heard into a framework that I could use before the following Monday. I learned two things, minor in themselves, but which when put together I could make use of.

The first happened on the afternoon after our distressing conversation about the book disappearances. Jenna's voice came wailing down the room:

'I've lost my *Concise Oxford*!'

I imagine that she was referring to her copy of the single-volume dictionary, published by the Oxford University Press. I took no notice since I knew that it had nothing whatsoever to do with me.

A voice answered her: 'There's a copy on the shelf by the telephone. Why don't you use that one?'

'But I have my own copy. I keep it in the book trough on my desk, and now it's gone.'

'It'll turn up,' said someone else. 'Use the library copy until it does.'

But Jenna wouldn't give up. She started at one end of the room and examined every book on everyone's desk – and some people have a very large number of books heaped in random piles on their desks – until she had reached the other end of the room. She stood by the door, looking furiously at us all.

'Someone must have it,' she said. She had her hands on her hips in an unattractively belligerent way. I must say that I continued quietly with the work that I was being paid to undertake.

'Try the room next door,' suggested someone. 'I'm sure they're a light-fingered lot in there.' Jenna duly disappeared, and we could hear her raised voice questioning every unfortunate member of staff in the adjoining office. There were giggles and sniggers in our room and references to loopiness.

Jenna spent the entire afternoon searching for her dictionary, and was still there, working her way along the shelves of books that lined the walls and were waiting to be catalogued, when the rest of us left at the end of the day.

'It must be here somewhere,' she was muttering. 'I'm going to find it. I can't bear losing things, it leaves me feeling jumpy and frustrated until I find them again.'

I believe that she finally ran the thing to earth on a bar-coder's trolley in the bookstack: the dictionary had somehow got mixed up with a pile of catalogued books, and was waiting to have a shelf-mark stuck on it and a barcode affixed. If she had been patient until the next morning, someone would have seen that it was not a library book and returned it to her. Silly girl. (In the circumstances, *very* silly girl.)

The other piece of information that I needed was given to me during coffee break the next morning. I was sitting on my own at a table, eating a plain biscuit, pretending to read a book while my brain struggled with my overriding problem. At the next table were seated a gaggle of young girls, all with skirts and hair too short, voices too loud. When I heard Jenna's, I tuned in and started to listen to what they were saying.

'We'll be staying at this hostel,' said Jenna.

'Any likely men in the group?' asked one of the others.

'That isn't the point of the weekend,' said Jenna, primly.

'But yes, it is a mixed group, though we are all going because we are interested in singing Christian music in the folk tradition.'

I tried not to shudder. But I needed to know: was she talking about this coming weekend?

'It looks as though the weather will be good for you,' said a blonde girl, confirming my supposition. 'Though there is rain forecast for Sunday afternoon.'

'How are you getting there?'

'By train. It isn't far, just north of Charlbury. I'm taking Friday afternoon off so we can get the two thirty-five train. We can walk the two miles from the station.'

There was laughter and groans from her friends. I made up my mind to check the location of this hostel on an Ordnance Survey map in Blackwell's travel book shop. I would check, too, the times of likely trains back to Oxford, since Jenna and her friends were finishing their coffee and returning to their work without giving me the information.

Have you noticed how, after writing a thousand words, you need to take a short break? Or is it that professional writers can train themselves to write, say, five thousand words at a stretch? I took a break just now, going out into my garden for some peace and a little fresh air, but I was distracted by the abominable woman next door. She had done the laundry for her family and hung it up on her washing line, stretching it right across her garden and in my full view. Today it is all white: knickers of all sizes and genders are blowing in the breeze; bulbous, ballooning shirts wave anxious arms at the sky; merry pants and vests flap lasciviously at me. It is not to be borne.

I would not bear it. I gathered up some dry stalks and crumpled newspapers. It took me half a box of matches to get a fire going, but I fed it with some sticks that were sitting in my garden shed, and once it was blazing, I damped the whole thing down with grass cuttings, green twigs and leaves from my compost heap. The effect was magical: thick, dark smoke swirled and climbed over the low wall that divides our properties and then wiped its ghostly grey fingers all down that woman's washing. My bonfire was out by the time she came back from her shopping trip, but she stood at the wall and stared over into my garden, hoping to catch me in the act.

No one catches me in the act.

I came back inside to continue with my writing, but I do believe that she has hacked off the branches of my buddleia that lean over into her garden. Never mind, I shall go out tonight and cut all her pink roses. The woman doesn't deserve them.

I'm sorry that we can't have these conversations in reality, Mrs Dolby. There is so much that I would like to talk to you about, on this fascinating subject of writing. But I'm sure you would understand how impossible it would be for me to share these experiences with you, though of course I talk to you constantly inside my head.

Well now, there I was on Thursday of that unforgettable week, with the outline of a plan in my head. You will not be surprised when I tell you that I filled in the details of my plan quite meticulously, checking on train times, visiting the hostel (not that the residents were aware of my visit), and preparing the inside of my car so that any traces of Sunday's event would be removable. I also planned, at a date some two or three months after this, to sell the car in part exchange for a new one, so that a thorough cleaning, inside and out, would seem quite appropriate and arouse no suspicion. I believe that I have already mentioned that I was wearing my shell-suit. Not, as you might imagine, my usual style of dress, but I managed to find one in a subdued colour that would not stay in the memory of anyone who might see me wearing it.

I wasn't going to write about this, but I'm afraid that I'm being watched.

A stranger came into the office while I was out, and I can't discover why. Why are they keeping it from me? Are they starting to suspect what I've been doing? No, that isn't possible: I've covered my tracks too well. Since Jenna went, I have been even more careful about the security of our operation.

But I have to confess that this is an interesting feeling, and I should like to write about it. All the time, I want to look over my shoulder, as though if I turned quickly enough, I might catch sight of the person who has been following me. And everything that I do seems open to a second, guilty interpretation. Is this how an innocent person feels and acts when they are being persecuted?

Isn't it odd how, once you become a writer, any happening in your everyday life can be twisted and turned into material for your fiction? And vice versa, of course. You

are opening my eyes to all sorts of possibilities, Mrs Dolby.
I do look forward to our next lesson.

# Chapter Seven

Chris Johnston called Kate into his office and introduced her to Graham Kieler.

'We've already met,' said Kate.

'I've just seen a copy of your report to the Team. I gather you've come across the same piece of pilfering that was worrying me,' said Kieler. He looked quite animated, with spots of colour in his pale cheeks. Just like the class sneak, back in her junior school, thought Kate.

'How did you find it?' she asked.

'I was here one lunch time when Victor came in to work. It was one of those surprisingly hot spring days, with a cloudless blue sky and no rain forecast all week. But Victor Southam was wearing a heavyweight Barbour.'

'One of those green waxed jackets? So what? They're very practical garments.'

'He was sweating in the heat: they really are uncomfortable in hot weather, especially if it isn't raining. And apart from being waterproof, the great thing about them is the number of pockets. They have patch pockets in front, they have hand-warming pockets in the sides, and they have more, roomy pockets inside. They are a shoplifter's dream.'

'And did you see Victor lifting books? Did you catch him in the act?' She couldn't help preferring the rather pathetic Victor to the sharp Graham.

'If I had, he wouldn't be here now. But I did watch him leave, with the hem of his jacket sagging and bulges at knee level. But without more evidence than that, I could hardly ask for him to empty out his pockets.'

'Certainly not,' put in Chris Johnston. 'The Kennedy doesn't treat its staff like that.'

'But I did think it was worth keeping an eye on him,' went on Graham, as though nothing had been said. 'Which is why I put in the report that Charles and Andrew read and acted on.' He smiled at Kate. She had to be on his side.

'It seems such a sordid little crime to have found,' she said. 'A poor old man who has a thing about Nancy Drew mystery stories. What a way to lose your reputation!'

'He should have been more careful,' said Graham, and seeing Kate's expression, he added: 'To stay honest, of course. He only has himself to blame.'

Chris Johnston turned to Kate. 'We have already confronted him, and he has confessed to taking the books. He swears that this was the only time he has done it, and that there was no one else involved.'

'Well, he would, wouldn't he?' said Graham Kieler unsympathetically.

'And what will happen to him now?'

'He's been sent home, and he will be suspended on full pay while there is an inquiry. I'm speaking to the rest of the staff about it, and asking everyone to keep quiet until the results of the inquiry are known.'

A sour look came over Kieler's face, as though he wanted nothing less than Victor's public dishonour and humiliation. Kate said: 'Did Andrew tell you that the library assistant at St Luke's showed me how to zap a record without leaving a trace?' She just wanted to take the triumph at Victor's disgrace away from Kieler.

'I expect I know how it's done,' he said in a superior way. 'But show me anyway.'

They sat at Johnston's computer and Kate showed him the method that Mick Ennis had shown her.

'That's neat,' said Chris Johnston. 'I hadn't thought of doing that.'

'Well of course we've always known that it was possible,' said Kieler, dismissively. 'We just assumed that no responsible cataloguer would ever do it.'

'But if Victor had thought of it, we wouldn't have caught him yet, would we?' said Chris Johnston. 'Not unless we had started searching all the staff when they left the premises.'

Kate was pleased to see that Graham Kieler looked uncomfortable. She didn't think that his idea of security included standing by a staff entrance and looking through people's shopping bags and coat pockets, let alone listening to their sarcastic comments as he did so.

When Kieler had left to make his report to the Security Team, Chris Johnston said: 'Don't worry too much about Victor. He's worked at this place since it was first opened, and had an unblemished record up till now. He will probably be asked to take retirement instead of staying on as a part-timer, but no one wants any fuss or publicity.' He laughed ruefully. 'I expect we'll be lucky if we even get our Nancy Drews back.'

Kate was glad to leave the Kennedy Centre and make for home at five thirty. She walked the two or three miles to try and clear her head from the concentrated hours in front of the computer screen. A dull ache was settling in behind her eyes, and the thought of writing a thousand words of her book, or even reading a chapter of someone else's, was unattractive. When she reached Agatha Street, she saw that there was someone at her front door.

'What's up?' she asked from the pavement, as a figure in a dark green waxed coat beat on her front door with the handle of his umbrella. The man turned to face her and she saw that it was Victor Southam. She found herself staring at the large baggy pockets in his coat, and imagined them stuffed with stolen books. With an effort she raised her eyes to his face.

'You!' he shouted. 'Coming into the Kennedy, snooping around. Who wanted you there? No one! Why couldn't you mind your own business?' The hand not holding the umbrella was full of a solid-looking brick and he was looking around wildly, as though for something else to attack. Kate feared for her windows, and was glad that her computer was well out of harm's way in the back of the house. There were dents and chips in the paintwork on her front door where Victor Southam had been hammering at it.

'You've ruined my life!' he was shouting, spittle gathering in bubbles at the corners of his mouth. He came towards her. Kate stepped smartly to the side. 'Stupid little busybody! Interfering cow! Bitch!' He caught her in the ribs with a sharp elbow. This wasn't as bad as being attacked in a derelict house, but it was pretty bad. The aggression was coming out of the man in waves and crashing against her like breakers against the rocks.

Curtains were twitching at front windows the length of the street by this time, and Kate was wondering how she could get rid of him without involving herself in a brawl. Keeping his eyes on her, he shuffled across to her car.

'Is this one yours?' He prodded it with his umbrella and Kate saw a flake of paint come off on the ferrule. When she failed to answer, he moved on to Ken Toadface's immaculate white Ford Escort. 'Or this one, maybe?' He lifted the hand holding the brick and eyed the gleaming windscreen.

'No!' she shouted, as the pointed end of Victor's umbrella jabbed close to perfect paintwork. Seeing her look of alarm, he drew his elbow back for a double attack with real power behind it.

' 'Ere! Geroff that car!' It was Harley, riding his skateboard, closely followed by Shayla and little Toadface. He was travelling at considerable speed by the time he hit Victor Southam at mid-shin, and his close-cropped bullet head thumped into Southam's chest. Kate winced in sympathy as the two of them landed on the pavement in confusion, Southam's umbrella still waving dangerously, but the brick, at least, rolling harmlessly clear. For a moment the only sound was that of the wheels of Harley's upturned skateboard, still turning and whirring. She considered weighing in with the Toadface faction, but Victor did appear to be heavily outnumbered now.

'Bloody kids! I'll get you!' he started shouting, but little Shayla, in spite of her pink ruffled dress, was beating him about the ears with her fists, and young Toadface had grabbed hold of the hand with the umbrella and had sunk his fangs into it.

'Bastard!' Shayla was shouting. 'What the fuck you doing with our motor, then? Me Dad'll string you up if he catches you, and not by the neck, neither.'

Victor Southam had risen so that he was kneeling now, but this meant that Shayla could kick him in the thighs with her black patent-leather strapped shoes, while Harley grabbed his hair and little Toadface rammed him with his pedal car.

It was several minutes before Victor Southam scrambled clear and rose to his feet again.

'You'd better leave now,' Kate said to him. 'I was only doing my job, and you can't blame me if you were caught stealing books.' The man hadn't denied it, anyway, she noted. 'And don't try to come back here, because I have plenty more friends in the neighbourhood, I can assure you.'

'You're wasting your time,' said Southam, bitterly. 'There's crime enough going on in that place, but you haven't begun to understand what it is yet, have you? You and that oaf Kieler, you haven't got a clue!' The hectic colour had left his face, except for two bright spots on his cheekbones, scarlet against the grey of his skin. He raised his arms away from his body as though at any moment he might bestow a blessing upon them, and spoke with an intensity that was more impressive than his previous shouting. 'They came in, those computer pedlars, with nothing on their minds except cost-effectiveness. Money. They swept aside the old men, the ones who loved books and cared for them, men who had dedicated their lives to accuracy and scholarship, and they imposed their new regime with its modern jargon, its bastardized English and its obsession with speed and deadlines. They have no moral sense, no respect for people or tradition. They are taking over all the departments, all the libraries, and no one can stop them. What can you expect now but theft – and worse. Go back to your romances, Kate Ivory, it's safer there. And at least you were doing no harm when you were writing.'

He drew himself up so that, in spite of the dust on his knees and the hair hanging over his face, he had a dignity and a stature that he had lacked before. Behind Kate, the children had fallen back and stood silently watching and listening.

'Take a look at the empire building and the power structures in that library system,' he said. 'You think it's funny, seeing librarians locked in a power struggle. But consider what sort of budgets we're talking about, how much money in total these people are handling, and think again. Cataloguing may bore you, but these computer people see it as a way of taking charge. They'll be running all the libraries, deciding what the money is spent on, and the rest of you won't have a word to say about it.'

He started to walk off down the road towards the city centre, while the Toadface children stood and watched. Then he stopped again and turned, ignoring the children, and spoke to Kate.

'If you do find out what's been happening, you'll need more than a gang of kids to protect you,' he said. 'You'll get your come-uppance then, Kate Ivory, I promise you.'

'Wanker!' shouted Shayla, as he set off again and disappeared round the corner, but the insult lacked her former exuberance.

'That's enough,' said Kate, starting to feel ashamed at what had happened. 'But thanks for your help. Can I get you all an ice-cream at Mrs Clack's?' She felt in need of one herself after that, or even a stiff whisky. This sort of thing never seemed to happen to Reg Wexford or Adam Dalgleish after they had solved a mystery. She must be doing something wrong. But then, I don't think you have solved a mystery yet, a voice inside her head insisted on saying.

It was a good meal, involving trout wrapped in lettuce leaves and baked on a bed of puréed sorrel and coriander, and the bottle of wine that Kate and Liam shared put them into a mellow mood as they sprawled on the sofa. Even the music fitted in instead of jarring against her own tastes.

Liam reached out a long arm in a rust-coloured sleeve and pulled her nearer. 'We could make an early night of it,' he said.

She didn't say that this wasn't early for her, for she knew that he often didn't get to bed until well after midnight, and anyway, she felt in need of some tender care after her confrontation with Victor Southam. She started to tell Liam about it.

'Well, what did you expect?' he said, unsympathetically. 'A vote of thanks? I know you were doing your job, but you can't expect your victims to like you afterwards. And your trouble is that you don't look like someone from Security.'

'Why not?'

'You're female, you're young, you're good looking. It goes against all the stereotypes.'

'Tough luck. I'm not going to look like a battleaxe just to live up to people's expectations.'

'So you'll just have to grow some thicker skin if you're going to catch any more criminals, and get used to the occasional mouthful of abuse.'

'I think I'd rather be a writer.'

'Yeah, well, wouldn't we all?' He yawned and stretched. 'Time to clean your teeth, Miss Marple.'

Next morning her alarm went off at ten to five, as usual. She prised her eyelids apart and wished that she had drunk a pint of water before going to bed: this was not going to be a productive session on her book, she could tell. She knew the benefit of regular work though, and she wasn't going to let that thought put her off going down to the basement and calling up her word-processor. She was out of bed and half into track-suit and trainers and thinking about her current chapter before she remembered Liam. The alarm, swiftly silenced, hadn't woken him, and he sprawled across her bed, moving to fill the entire space in the way of men as soon as she shifted out of the way. She felt a mild twinge of irritation, suppressed it, and went into the bathroom to splash cold water on her face. The lavatory seat was standing upright, and she felt a wave of unreasonable resentment about the way Liam was invading her house. She lowered the seat again before going downstairs to make coffee to take with her into her workroom. She was glad at least that Liam wouldn't be under her feet for the next hour or two. After an hour on her book, she turned to her *Notes* file and started to write up the events of the previous day. It was the most productive session yet, from the book-thefts point of view, but she didn't enjoy going over the humiliating scenes of the afternoon.

1. Centre for North American Studies at Kennedy House. Books have been stolen from the children's collection, and someone has tried to doctor the records, but unsuccessfully. The culprit was found to be Victor Southam, a man nearing retirement who has a hatred of the computerized catalogue.

She shied away from describing the brawl in Agatha Street, and decided that the bald statement would have to do.

2. Jenna Coates worked here for a couple of months

or so and all the staff at Kennedy House must
have known her. These include:

3. Chris Johnston, the Director. A bit stuffy, but I
   liked him, and he appeared to be very upset at
   Jenna's death. I mustn't allow my liking to
   obscure the fact that he has to be on the list of
   suspects. He also has the cataloguing authority to
   doctor records more effectively than Victor
   Southam, as indeed do both the librarian and the
   head of cataloguing.

4. Angela Rugby, Librarian. Looks sharp and
   intelligent, and too busy to be involved in crime.
   Another subjective judgement, I'm afraid.

5. Fiona Bliss, Head of Cataloguing. She has to be
   on the list of possibles, and I shall have to go
   back and speak to her, if indeed anyone at
   Kennedy House will speak to me after my
   unmasking of Victor Southam. I can't believe she
   has the brains to take part in this crime, though.

6. Graham Kieler, from the Security Team. Another
   boring man, keen on computers, keener on
   computer security. He was on my original list of
   thirteen possibles, but that is redundant since
   Mick Ennis showed me how anyone could zap a
   record if they worked out how. Anyway, what
   does Kieler know about books, and has he even
   got the imagination of a grasshopper?

7. Susie Holbech, Conservation Officer. Jenna was
   working with her during her time at Kennedy
   House, and they were working on the collection

of juvenile literature that Victor Southam was pillaging. Did Jenna see what Victor was doing, confront him and then get killed? I've seen for myself what an aggressive man he can be. But could he overpower a strong young woman like Jenna? Did her death have nothing to do with the disappearance of books from the catalogue after all? Damn, I'm back to where I started.

8. Martin Preston, indexer of US official papers. I would hate to think he was responsible for anything more serious than raising the blood pressure of female staff. Anyway, he wasn't in England last year. (Was he? How can I be so sure? Bother, I'll have to check.)

9. There are a lot of questions unanswered about Kennedy House. Life is not going to be easy for me there when they discover that I was responsible for getting Victor the sack, but I've got to make an attempt to answer some of them.

She saved the file and switched off her computer, and then she put on her running shoes and went out for a twenty-minute jog around the back streets of Fridesley.

There was a postcard on her mat when she got back and opened the door. Delivered by hand.

*I was just passing and wanted to tell you to watch it and keep safe. Paul.*

She had received the occasional passionate love letter in

her past, and elegantly expressed missives from young men who were intent on impressing her with their literary style, but this card, short and to the point, seemed to go along with candid blue eyes and a policeman's mind. She wasn't sure how she felt about it. The caring part gave her a comfortable, warm feeling, but her head told her to watch out for the restraints and the restrictions that might be attached to it. It was still true that if you wanted to achieve anything in the creative field, you had to be free. But it was hard to get rid of the image of his blue-grey eyes. Pity about the colour of his hair, though.

She poured boiling water on to ground coffee, cut bread for toast and went upstairs to call Liam.

Kate and Andrew were sitting in the restaurant part of the wine bar, and he had ordered an expensive bottle of burgundy and the largest steaks on the menu. He must want something more than usually irksome from her.

Kate took an exploratory swallow of wine. It was very good. 'Put me out of my misery, Andrew. Tell me what it is that you want me to do for you.'

'Don't you want to wait until you've wrapped yourself round some of your steak?'

'No. Get on with it or I'll suffer from terminal indigestion.'

'It's information I'm passing on, Kate dear. Really, there's nothing difficult that I want you to do.'

'No more confrontations with book thieves on my front doorstep?'

'Pity about that. Well, the essence of it is that we've

194

found out that Jenna went on holiday to California over the Easter before she died, and from what she said, it looks as though our mystery has a Stateside connection.'

'Where do you learn these phrases? And so what? A holiday in California might have been more exciting than a Christian Librarians for Folk Song weekend at a youth hostel, but it doesn't appear to relate directly to our problem.'

Kate didn't repeat to him the conversation she had had with Paul and the conclusions she had come to then. 'But she sent postcards to her friends, and one has just come to light. She sent it to a fellow trainee at the Bodleian. Apparently they had a relationship through the electronic mail, so no one noticed that they were friendly.'

'Sounds painful.'

'Stop being facetious.' He paused for a moment to allow the waitress to put down their plates. 'Yes, thank you, the very rare one is for me. My friend likes hers cremated.'

'Medium rare is not cremated. And by the way, did you know that you've got sawdust all over the sleeve of your nice dark jacket? And no, you may not help yourself to my chips while I'm talking.'

'How mean of you. Well, anyway, take a look at this.'

' "Dear Iz," ' Kate read. ' "Having a great time, but guess who I saw going into one of the libraries on the Santa Luisa campus this morning! Looking *so* suave, relaxed and un-Oxford. I thought I must be mistaken, but I followed him in and watched him using the catalogue – he obviously can't keep away from the things, even when he's on holiday! And I can't help thinking that it all links up together. I have to find out what he's doing. Oh bother, no room to tell you more. See you next week, and we'll talk it over. Luv, Jenna." '

'Now I can't believe that these Nancy Drew things that you've found missing account for all that, so you've got to keep looking for more discrepancies. Preferably with an American connection.'

'You know what my current book's about, don't you, Andrew?'

'I haven't the slightest idea.'

'Thanks for the interest. Well, it's set in California during the last century, at the time of the Gold Rush, and it's about—'

'How fascinating. But how is that relevant to our present case?'

'What I need to do at this point is to travel to California – San Francisco, even – and do a little on-the-spot research. I shall get the feel of the place, the smell . . .'

'The look of those contemporary motor cars, you mean? The smell of diesel, the twentieth-century plumbing—'

'Don't be negative. The hills are still there, the ocean, the . . . well, the quality of the light, perhaps. I shall drink them all in and they will form part of the background of the story. And if I do that, I shall be able to claim my fare back on my income tax.'

'What fare?' Andrew could sound very sharp when he tried. 'You don't need to spend five hundred pounds to write a couple of sentences on the quality of the light in San Francisco. And I can't think that it would convince your tax inspector, either. What makes you think that you need to go there?'

'To find out what Jenna was doing, to see the people she saw, hopefully to find out who the Oxford librarian was that she bumped into.'

'To get yourself killed too, if you're not careful.'

'Oh, phooey. Stop being such an old woman. The trouble is that you want to find out who's stealing which books, while I want to find out who killed Jenna.'

'Why?'

'Because . . .' She paused. 'Because people are more important than books,' she continued more slowly. 'And I want to know what happened to her. Complete her story, if you like. At the moment there are three or four chapters and a lot of blank pages. No one's life should end as indeterminately as that.' She couldn't explain that once she started following Jenna's trail around the libraries, she didn't want to leave it. And she was sure that the Californian end was important to the story.

'You're getting an attack of the Omnipotent Author disease again, Kate.'

'Rubbish. And could you get me some English mustard, do you think?'

'Oh, right.' Andrew really was very good at catching the eye of a passing waitress. 'Satisfied now, are we? Good.'

'And show me the postcard again, Andrew, before I attack you with this steak knife.'

'It's a pity young Jenna had such large handwriting,' said Andrew, 'or our problem might be over.'

'Who's Iz, for goodness' sake. Not—'

'You've met Isabel, yes.'

'And she mentioned her friend Jenna, now that I remember. Why didn't you tell me about this postcard before?'

'Isabel kept it on the mantelpiece in her, um, well, not in her sitting-room,' said Andrew. 'It hadn't occurred to her that it might have any significance for us, and it wasn't until I saw it, and the name Jenna struck me as unusual, that I asked her about it.'

'And did Jenna ever come back and discuss it with Isabel? Did you ask her while you were in her, um, not her sitting-room?'

'Don't be vulgar, Kate. It comes out sounding like jealousy, and that wouldn't suit you at all. In answer to your question, unfortunately, when Jenna got back from San Francisco, Isabel had just left on a holiday of her own. Doubtless they would have got together and discussed what Jenna had seen and what her conclusions were, but that was the May when Jenna died.'

'And you still think it was a coincidence?'

'I do. I wouldn't have let you follow in her footsteps like this if I thought there was any danger. I think that Jenna went off with her frightful folk-singing friends – and thank goodness that Isabel never got mixed up in anything like that – missed her train, accepted a lift and was killed by a sex maniac.'

'Paul isn't so sure about that.'

'Paul? Your little detective sergeant? I don't suppose he knows anything.'

'Watch it, Andrew. You're sounding jealous, and that

just wouldn't be your style now, would it?'

'Look, Kate, we're talking about computer crime here. Nice, white-collar, middle-class stuff. Well-brought-up men who don't go around strangling girls with their tights.'

'I'm not sure about that. You should see the people I've met in the past week or so.'

'Stop being unkind about my distinguished Bodleian colleagues, and tell me you're not going to go to California.'

'As a matter of fact, I've always wanted to go to California, and San Francisco in particular. So yes, I shall be going, just as soon as I can book myself a seat on a plane.'

'Well, if you are going to go, you'd better hire a car and drive down to Santa Luisa, as well.'

'Is it far?'

'Not more than fifty miles, I believe. And while you're in San Francisco, I'll fix for you to stay with some friends of mine: they have a lovely house overlooking the Bay and they owe me a small favour.'

'Why do I distrust your co-operation more than your acquiescence?'

'Why do you use such long words to a simple man?'

'Let me see that postcard again.' She took the card and turned it over. It had a picture of a Spanish-style house, painted a cream colour and smothered in scarlet bougainvillaea. Geraniums and hibiscus spilled out of terracotta pots and the sky was an amazing blue. *Welcome to Santa Luisa* it shouted across the corner of the picture.

'I've seen a card like this somewhere before,' she said.

'I expect Jenna sent a dozen or so to her friends. And

then, she isn't the only person to go there. It could have been a coincidence.'

'I expect you're right. Does Isabel know any more about Jenna? From what I've heard of the girl, I didn't think she and Isabel would have much in common.'

'I don't believe she knows anything useful. And I don't want you upsetting her, or being rude to her.' He looked at Kate anxiously.

'It's all right, Andrew. I'll be as sweet as fudge cake with her. Just give me her phone number and I won't even have to embarrass you by going to visit her.'

'Oh, very well then. She's visiting her parents in Shropshire for the next few days, so you'll have to get in touch on your return from America. I shall be glad when you've left for Santa Luisa. What with getting involved in street fights—'

'Don't provoke me, Andrew. I'll be charming to Isabel, delightful to your San Francisco chums, cool and efficient down in Santa Luisa, and I'll write to you every evening to tell you what I've been doing. Stop worrying. Can I drive on my British licence while I'm there, by the way?'

Andrew shuddered. 'Officially, yes. Unofficially, Kate, only with extreme caution.'

'I'll book myself a flight and a hire car tomorrow morning.'

'And you must promise to keep in touch every day.'

'Yes, Andrew. Of course, Andrew. Are you going to pay for a proportion of my expenses? No? Oh, well. And now pour me out another glass of the burgundy since I'm not driving myself home.'

Back in Agatha Street, Kate was swept along by a tide of burgundy-induced good intentions, and telephoned Emma.

'Emma? I'm ringing about the writing class.'

'I knew you'd change your mind. It's such a challenge, Kate, and I know you can't resist one of those. And did I tell you that it's organized by the University Extra-Mural Department? It's the best writing class in Oxford.'

'How many writing classes does a city of a hundred and thirty thousand people have?'

'Maybe just the one in Central Oxford. But all so interesting, really. And such a high standard of work. Mostly, anyway.'

'Uh, well, actually, Emma, I was ringing to say that I'd love to take it on, but I've got to go to the States for a while. How long? Oh, I'm not quite sure, but at least a couple of weeks, I should say. I'm really sorry about it. Otherwise, you know, I would have been proud to take it on. Yes, I'm really sorry to miss the opportunity. Have I been out to a good dinner? How did you guess? Yes, of course I'll give you another ring when I get back from the States. You know I like to be of help to my friends.'

She looked at the phone for a moment. Was that an exaggeration? How much time did she make for her friends and their problems? She really was getting to be a selfish cow.

'Of course, when I get back from California, I'll give you a hand, I promise,' she said, to make herself feel better about it.

'Shall we make a date before we forget?' said Emma, quickly.

Oh well, she wouldn't be able to get out of it now, and Kate reached for her diary.

Afterwards, she went out to the kitchen, poured herself a pint of cold water, drank it and went upstairs to bed.

On Sunday afternoon, Kate was lying back on her sofa, the Sunday newspapers strewn across the floor, drinking lemon verbena tea and pretending to read the colour supplement. Something tuneful from the late sixties was playing on the music system. Even the neighbours were quiet. This was the first time she had managed to relax all week, and her life would become hectic again on Monday morning when she did enough work on her computer to see her through a couple of weeks' holiday, and then threw her suitcase together and left for California.

The doorbell rang.

''Ere!' said the figure on her doorstep. 'You forgot our agreement, then?'

'No, Harley,' fibbed Kate, hurling the colour supplement on to the floor behind her, pushing her hands through her hair and opening her eyes very wide so that they should get the message that she wanted them to stay that way instead of drifting shut again. She pushed her bare feet into a handy pair of shoes and followed Harley out on to the pavement.

Two of his friends stood there, presumably Darren and Dossa, in baseball boots and shell-suits plastered with all the right labels. Their hair was worn clipped very short to above the ears, then longish and dyed white-blond on top.

'This your car, then?' asked the one who had identified himself as Dossa. He had decorated his nose with steel studs.

Kate saw nothing to apologize for in the cream Peugeot, even if it was in need of a wash and polish.

'Quite nice car, this,' said Dossa, 'and if ever you need to get into one, you do it like this, see.'

He delved into a bright blue nylon pack and brought out a hand-operated drill with a half-inch bit fitted to it.

'This is it,' he said, indicating a spot a couple of inches to the left of the lock on the driver's door. 'You drill here—

'Stop!' shouted Kate. 'I get the picture. Really, I have a very good imagination, there's no need to demonstrate the technique, I assure you.'

Dossa looked disappointed. 'All right then,' he said. 'But when you've got your hole, you can operate your lock with a screwdriver like this one,' he held it up to show Kate, 'and then, you're in. Thirty seconds max if you're good. OK?'

That appeared to be it. Ten quids' worth of instruction that she would have to hide from her respectable friends. She had been expecting something tricky with hairpins, at least. She had hoped to be introduced to a crafty set of picklocks, which she envisaged as consisting of a neat row of steel hooks, like very fine crochet hooks, cosily embedded in a velvet-lined fruitwood case. This was what happened to detectives in crime novels, and she felt cheated by Dossa's quick and simple hole-drilling. Still, a bargain was a bargain and she dug out two five-pound notes and then paused before handing them over.

'I'm not sure I'd want to use it on my own car,' she said. 'Wasn't there an alternative way that Darren was going to show me?' Oxford, she had read somewhere, was the car crime capital of Europe, and so she was hoping to learn the tricks of the canniest tradesmen around.

'You sure?' said Harley. ''Ere! Darren! Show the lady how you do it, then.'

Darren had a pinched old man's face, with black circles round his eyes. He was not as articulate as his brother, apparently. 'Gotta find a skip,' he mumbled.

There was one, filled with builders' rubble and an old mattress, some twenty yards down the road. Somehow there always was a skip in every street in Fridesley. Kate put it down to the craze for home improvements that every resident except herself appeared to suffer from.

'Trust Darren,' said Dossa, with a quick nod.

'Always a skip,' confirmed Darren. He lifted the leaking mattress and scrabbled underneath it, coming up with a rock some twelve inches across and weighing several pounds. He carried it back to Kate's car.

'What are you going to do with that?' asked Kate, not wanting to believe the obvious.

'You frow it frew the windscreen,' said Darren, and looked hopefully at Kate.

'Thanks, Darren,' said Kate. 'But no. I'm sure it works: it has an elegant simplicity to it that I am sure is most effective.' Darren looked blankly back at her. 'Put the rock down, Darren,' she said gently. 'And thank you for your time and trouble.' She found another couple of pounds in her purse and handed it to Darren, who had apparently delivered himself of his daily quota of words.

'What should I do if I want to deter people from breaking into my car?' she asked Dossa, wanting to get her full ten pounds' worth from the boy.

'You don't worry about that,' he said. 'You're safe enough with this at the moment. The lads is all out practising on Montegos at the moment. You need a crowbar if you want to get their steering locks off,' he added helpfully. 'You got one in your boot?'

'Not yet,' said Kate. 'I've managed to get through life without one so far, but I can see that if I keep on with the amateur sleuthing I shall have to get myself some more equipment.'

'The lads are moving on to Sierras when they've cracked Montegos,' said Harley. 'So you're safe with your Peugeot for the next couple of weeks.'

'I could let you have some videos,' said Dossa. 'Special material. Special prices.' He looked hopefully at Kate, but she worked out what he was talking about and shook her head.

As she stood by her front door, the last she saw of the boys was three figures skateboarding off down the road and round the corner.

# viii

## *Practical Exercise: The Oxford Exit*

Is she watching? Can she see me, is she looking over my shoulder and reading what I am writing? Have you noticed that the presence of an audience, especially one that is judging what you have written, alters and edits your work? Even before the pen touches the paper and makes its marks, the mind has interposed a veil, so that the quick, bright thoughts evaporate and the nib stutters to a halt. So what is the answer? The answer, Mrs Dolby, is to keep silence in your class, to confess that I have not completed my week's exercise, but to write in secret.

The light, you see, is low, the curtains are drawn close, the telephone jack pulled out of the wall so that there will be no interruptions. And now I can begin.

I was woken by the cry of the trumpet, and soon the chords were crashing through my body until I felt myself shuddering in response. A few testy taps of the drumsticks reminded me where I was and what I should be doing.

We dance by moonlight on the terrace, a strange, slow waltz. She has reddish-brown hair, waving close to her head and falling to just above her shoulders, its colour turned to copper by the light. Her shoulders are matt white satin, her eyes obsidian, her lips scarlet enamel. She wears a black silk dress that clings and moves with her to the music. At the edge of the terrace are terracotta pots of flowering shrubs. This must be early summer, then. The moonlight turns the blooms to grey and silver and black, and their scent is cinnamon and samphire on the warm air. Heavy as dead doves, they look at me with their blind eyes and their empty hearts. The woman's feet are dragging with the slow woodwind and we circle to a stop. I look down into her black eyes and I see in their blank pupils that she does not love me, that she will not obey me. It can only be her own fault if I have to kill her. My hands circle her throat until she rests against the balustrade, totally submissive. I lay her gently on the marble floor where she lies, a whiter marble still. The flowers drop their grey petals on to her lifeless face.

I wish it had been like that.

I suppose it would have made sense to kill her in Oxford: a quick mugging as she took a short cut across the churchyard of St Giles's church, perhaps. But then, I would never again be able to pass the place without remembering what had occurred there. The city would be spoiled for me for ever. I would have to change my job and my home, and if I did that I might as well give in to Jenna and visit the

Director with her on Monday morning.

It was late spring and the evenings were getting longer, so I drove out that Thursday evening to see the place where Jenna's group was to meet.

I took the back road out of Oxford, swinging fast round the series of roundabouts, past Blenheim, through Woodstock and on to the flat ploughed plain that lies beyond. It was some miles before the countryside became more rolling and the road dipped down into hidden hollows before swooping up little rounded hills. This was secretive country; this was what I was looking for. The hostel, when I got there, was set well apart from its neighbours, with a large garden and tall shrubs screening it from their view. It had a steeply pitched roof and large, dark-framed windows at first-storey level like watchful, wide-open eyes. I was wearing my new dark green shell-suit, with a hat pulled over my hair, so there was little risk of being recognized by a casual observer, and I believe I was nearly invisible as I made my way round the house, through the shrubbery, to the back. Here, the house leaned against the side of the hill, and the windows were small and frosted, doubtless belonging to the bathrooms and kitchen. There was a back door and a boot scraper, and a small porch where people had left their boots and wellingtons and wet anoraks.

At this moment I heard footsteps approaching from the centre of the house, and I moved quickly back into the shelter of the shrubbery.

I had to wait until Sunday to carry it out, but I knew now what I was going to do.

* * *

On Sunday afternoon, I was again concealed in the thick dark bushes of the shrubbery, keeping a watch on the back door of the hostel. My car was hidden a couple of hundred yards away, on a farm track, out of sight.

The young people had been out for a walk after lunch, and now they returned, singing one of their wholesome songs, boots loud on the metalled road, unaware of anyone other than themselves, alert to none but their own concerns. I stood still and I watched them.

They entered the building through the back door, as I would have expected, removing their muddy boots in the lobby, hanging up their anoraks on the hooks provided. Obviously as children they had never walked their dirty shoes across carpets or thrown their clothes on the floor, expecting some parent to pick up after them. My observation of Jenna had paid off: I expected nothing less of the girl and her friends.

The young people moved on into the hostel, and I heard feet and voices move upstairs, presumably to pack their belongings ready for the train that left the station – a two-mile hike away, if you remember – in an hour's time, just after six o'clock.

When the rear of the house was again silent, I emerged from my hiding place and crept into the lobby. I had observed Jenna as she removed her boots, and I knew approximately where she had placed them, but the dear girl had made my work perfectly simple by marking them in thick black ink with her name, COATES, just inside the cuff. It was the work of a moment to pick them up and to retreat with them to my shrubbery.

It was some fifteen minutes later that the young people reappeared, carrying backpacks, to reclaim their boots and anoraks, and only a minute or so after that that a loud, familiar voice said: 'Has anyone seen my boots? I *know* I left them out here. I didn't want to walk mud into the house.'

Oh yes, that was Jenna. I could hear other voices, arguing half-heartedly with her. Poor things had had two and a half days of Jenna being positive about things and now they weren't prepared to miss the train back to Oxford just because Jenna thought she had put her boots somewhere where they plainly weren't.

Within ten minutes the voices and their feet disappeared: they would have to step out briskly to get to the station in time. Jenna walked up and down outside the house, looking round corners, while I crouched deeper into my bush. Then she disappeared indoors, and I could hear her unmistakably heavy tread going up stairs and along corridors. The house sounded emptier than it had before. The others were tramping down to the railway station, and sure enough I heard their shouts: 'Come on, Jenna! You must have packed them already. You'll miss the train if you don't come now.' I hoped and believed that dear Jenna would value her walking boots even more highly than she did her *Concise Oxford Dictionary*. I waited for what seemed like a long time, and still I could hear her heavy footsteps and her loud voice as it moved all over the hostel. I looked at my watch: she would have to be able to run better than seven-minute miles, and over a distance of two, to catch the train now. I crept out of my hiding place and put the boots outside the back door and a little to one side. And then I sprinted for the car. I got in and started the engine. I was pointing away from the railway station, and I drove slowly towards the hostel, but still out of sight, my side window rolled down ready to hail Jenna when I saw her.

'Here they are!' came a triumphant shout from just ahead of me, and a stoutly shod and bobble-hatted Jenna appeared from the side of the house, waving her boots at her long-departed companions.

'Oh,' she said, on a low, dejected note. I waited until she had turned back to pick up the rest of her belongings before driving the few remaining yards towards the house. The road was narrow and it was natural to slow down for a pedestrian coming towards me. As I drew level, I stopped the car and called out of the window.

'Jenna!' I shouted. 'Isn't that Jenna Coates? What on earth are you doing here?'

'I'm just on my way back to Oxford,' she said. 'But I think I've missed my train. And there isn't another for two hours.'

'What a lucky meeting, then,' I said, with my most open and friendly smile. 'Hop in and I'll give you a lift back.'

The motorway stretched ahead of us, a grey shining ribbon in the rain, split by the lights of the oncoming cars. In the glove compartment in front of my passenger was a pair of tights, removed from their packet but new, unworn. They were rather a pretty, delicate colour, like wood smoke. I put a cassette into the player. It was Mahler, I remember, his fifth symphony.

Jenna was speaking.

'What was that you said?' There was a drumming from the wheels of the car on the concrete of the road and her voice came from a long way away. Ahead of us was nothing but grey road and greyer sky, and the yellow lights of the cars' headlights, breaking and hazing on the windscreen.

'You have to take the next left,' she was saying. She spoke too loudly as if I were deaf or stupid or a very great distance from her.

'Are you sure?'

'Oh yes,' said Jenna, in her self-confident, ugly voice. 'Didn't you see the signpost back there?'

'No.' How could you distinguish words when everything in the world was grey?

'Next left,' said Jenna. 'We have to take the Oxford Exit.'

You're going to tell me that you want more action in this scene, aren't you, Mrs Dolby? Short, vivid sentences. Strong, lively verbs. Well then, if you want action, you shall have it. And climax.

But I can't write you a pretty piece about death, because death isn't pretty. Not real death. You should only ever see it in black and white: by moonlight, perhaps; or caught in the photographer's flashlight. What you don't want to see is death in colour, in all its glistening shades of purple and red. If I were you, I would stick with the poetic

212

description I gave you at the beginning. The police, the ambulance staff and the pathologist, they see what it is like, but they have denatured words to cover the ugliness, to distance themselves from the reality.

When it was over, I remember that the cassette player was still playing inside the car. It had reached the *Adagietto*. Such a heart-breakingly beautiful movement. Perhaps it was the music that prompted me to leave the peonies on her grave.

I wish I could sleep. I wish I could forget. Do you think that now I've written it all down, I will finally be rid of it?

I'm sorry, Mrs Dolby, but this is one assignment that I can never allow you to see. Put me down as absent.

# Chapter Eight

San Francisco,
Thursday.

Dear Andrew,

The good thing about the ladies' rest room at San Francisco airport is its dim lighting. Someone has super-glued my eyelids open and my eyeballs are full of grit after the journey through twelve hours of brilliant sunshine. And still it is only four o'clock in the afternoon, and the sun outside is shining relentlessly out of a clear and cloudless blue sky and means to do so for a couple of hours yet, as far as I can tell. If ever the super-glue wears off, my eyelids will click shut and I will not be able to prise them apart again for at least another fourteen hours. So, before that happens, here is my first report.

Shall I tell you about this place? In spite of the notices everywhere written in English, it is definitely abroad. People keep smiling at me instead of scowling, and seem concerned that I should enjoy myself. But even the simplest gadgets, the ones you take for granted, work in a different and confusing way. I tried to flush the loo, but there was nothing obvious to pull or push, and after a battle with levers which I lifted, pushed, pulled and twisted, some obscure combination worked and the thing flushed. Across to the hand basin to wash my hands, and my tired brain refused to work out which metallic orifice would dispense liquid soap, which would eventually gush with water to remove it.

You think I am going on a bit about it all? You want to know how I am getting on with my investigation. You are wondering why I am not hastening to the library to find out what Jenna discovered. Well, if you remember, this trip is being paid for out of my earnings as a writer, set off against my taxable income, so a bit of writing is what you are going to get, Andrew dear, whether you like it or not. (Oh, and Andrew, do you think you could keep these letters? They could come in handy for background material some time. Thanks.)

Outside, the sky is huge and transparently blue, dazzling my tired eyes with its reflection from the white concrete. And in my nose the smell of California, so different from that of England: a smell of drought and of a huge population. Dry smells, unlike the damp, vegetable smell of England. And Andrew, the cars! I was expecting great gas-guzzling shiny things like you see in the movies (I'm learning the language, you see), but they're not: nearly every one a Honda, the rest European or other sorts of

Japanese; the occasional Dodge or Lincoln stands out like an elephant among gazelles.

All right, I will put this piece of lyrical writing in the post and get some sleep. Your friends met me at the airport and drove me to their house (and Andrew, this place is built on a positive *cliff*) and have fed me and left me in peace to make up the missing sleep. I promise you I will make more sense tomorrow.

> With love,
> Kate

> San Francisco,
> Friday.

Dear Andrew,

I've been to the library here at Berkeley to check on the University's holdings of Sensation novels, and I have found something odd, and possibly significant.

But first, did you get the letter I posted yesterday? The mailboxes here are most peculiar: big metal bins with a sliding top that scoops in your letter and swallows it into its bowels. I wondered when the blue envelope disappeared whether it would be sent to England, or just to the municipal tip. I hear you sighing over the amount of local colour I'm giving you, but please hang on to these letters, since I'm sure I can recycle them in some useful way in the future.

This place is a paradise for writers. I woke up even earlier than usual to find the mist sitting outside my window, blocking out sound, swaying gently like muslin to give occasional glimpses of trees and houses. I padded quietly around the garden, to say good morning to the plants, then settled down in the enveloping silence to write pages in my notebook. I sketched out a whole chapter of my book before the rest of the household awoke and came down to breakfast.

Your friend Sally (who sends you her best wishes, by the way) is being wonderfully hospitable. After taking the children to school, she drove me over to the Berkeley campus so that I could check on their holdings of Sensation novels. There are the usual holes in their collection, as you would expect, with one notable exception. Santa Luisa. They have unexpectedly unbroken runs of the works of the Veil. It looks as though everyone is clean as far as we are concerned, except for this one place. So I shall have to go and investigate Santa Luisa. I shall be hiring myself a car, in spite of your unkind comments, and driving down there in the next day or two.

Be happy, Andy baby,<br>Kate

San Francisco,<br>Saturday.

Dear Andrew,

I will try to cut down on the descriptive passages and stick to the business in hand today. I thought you would like more detail about what I found in the library at Berkeley.

I looked up in the on-line catalogue all the Veil books that we had on our list and yes, the University of California at Santa Luisa has copies of *all* of them in its library. It is impossible to tell from the entry here how long they have had them, so that is one of the things I shall be looking for when I get there. The campus at Santa Luisa is quite a small one, and I'm hoping that they'll be really impressed by that nice identity card that the Bodleian gave me, even if it has got the photograph of some blonde criminal on it.

With love,

Kate

Santa Luisa,
Monday.

Dear Andrew,

I could go for this place in a big way: blue skies and blue ocean with a frilling of white foam against tasteful blond sand; Spanish architecture, bougainvillaea cascading over rustic walls, and plenty of swillable Californian Chardonnay. And, of course, the university campus.

This morning I went for a very early walk along the beach. Five miles of silver-grey sand, and just me, a few sea birds and a couple of joggers. The sky was a brilliant cloudless blue, but there was a stiff breeze and the bay was covered with white-capped waves. Off to my right stood a row of brown grainy hills, like dark wholemeal dough that someone has kneaded into peaks and pockets. The buildings are made of weathered timber, like large, architect-designed garden sheds.

Santa Luisa is tiny compared with Berkeley, and they've kept the Spanish feel with stuccoed walls and red-tiled roofs (and the aforementioned bougain-villaea, still cascading in scarlet profusion). The librarian is a most pleasant and co-operative person and showed me (proudly, and with good reason) their collection of Sensation novels – and in particular those of the Veiled Sisterhood. I hadn't realized just how prolific these Victorian women were. Mary Eliza-beth Braddon wrote eighty-five of the things – and produced five illegitimate children as well. How did they do it, Andrew? We're not talking novellas here – none of your fifty thousand words – but the full three-volume touch. But more of this when I get back to England. For the moment I'll stick with their recent acquisitions of the Veil.

I took a good look at these, under a strong light, and with surreptitious use of my magnifying glass. I couldn't see anything to indicate that they had ever belonged to an Oxford library, I must say. They did have bookplates – presumably inserted by the insti-tution that Santa Luisa bought them from – and they looked as though they had been in place for a long time – at least since the end of the last century, I would say, though as you will remind me, I am no expert. The name on the bookplate was Iron Shoe, and they had once belonged to an Eleanor J. Westgate, back in 1863. Proof, I am sure you will agree, that if it's a phoney there's a librarian (or two) at the bottom of it. Do you know anything about this Iron Shoe collection, or institution? And about Eleanor J. Westgate, if it comes to that?

It's time I wrote another draft chapter of my book, don't you think? I will get back to libraries and Sensation novels in my letter tomorrow.

With love,
Kate

Santa Luisa,
Tuesday.

Dear Andrew,

What do you mean, how lucky I am to be able to pick up all this local colour while I'm also working for you? As I remember it, I paid my own fare, and have taken unpaid holiday to follow up this important lead for you.

You notice, I hope, that I'm getting stroppy at the patriarchal fictions that you are imposing on my female imagination. I could get used to this place, and the way that women are treated *seriously* in this culture.

I had a chance to read, too, the missing Baughn (not that I'm sure that it *is* the missing Baughn: there was no evidence to show that it might have been).

Another rollicking good read, I have to say, though I wish that they hadn't felt they had to write in three volumes – but then I suppose that was at the demand of their male publishers (who paid them and therefore dictated the terms). Back to *Dead—and Alive!*. I have to say as a fellow-writer that Miss Baughn does rely somewhat too heavily on *coincidence* – or the Hand of Destiny, as I am learning to call it – to move her plot along, and I can't say that I go for her heroine all that much, either. Here is the passage where she first appears:

He saw her first in a mirror, so that she was not aware that she was observed, and thus he was at leisure to stare at the wonders of that clear, innocent face, a face of oval perfection, with a slender, aquiline nose and eyes of some dark colour that might have been brown or yet green, he could not tell in the gentle light from the taper. Her head was inclin'd as she bent to her needlework, and the slenderness of her neck seemed to him too delicate to support its weight, like the stem of the harebell. But it was her hair, lit from behind, and surrounding her head like a halo that enthralled him in its massy net. It seemed to move and sway like a wave around her head – hair of a rich reddish-brown colour, but fine as unspun silk and full of the movement of the sea, and seeming as bountiful and as endless. It was with difficulty that he stopped himself from walking through the mirror to grasp its rich tresses in his hands, and claim her for his own.

Poor old Marianna (restrained, perhaps by that impossible head of hair?) has little to do in the story except wait passively, and faithfully, for the return of her lover.

You are doubtless wondering why I am digressing so far in my pursuit of your missing books, Andrew. Well, I have to wonder, if indeed they *are* your books, whether they have not found a happier resting place than the cellars and attics of your Oxford libraries.

> With love,
> Kate

> Santa Luisa,
> Friday.

Dear Andrew,

I hope that before you telephone me again, you will grasp somewhat more accurately the time difference between Santa Luisa and Oxford. I am not at my best at that hour, and it is therefore your own fault if you did not receive coherent answers to your questions.

What do you mean, you don't think much of the change in my writing style since I've been reading the Veil novels? I have read just the one, Andrew, and I have to confess that I skimmed it somewhat, as it was possible to get the gist of the story by reading about one page in three, and that at a rate of knots.

You asked somewhat curtly about the progress of my investigations, which I feel is most unfair of you since I have been speaking again to the lovely Ms Corinna Marques, and persuading her to show me the correspondence that she had with the Iron Shoe. I have to say that it looks pretty genuine to me: the right sort of thick creamy writing paper, with the solid black letter heading, and just the style you would expect from an elderly, educated woman of Fabian extraction. But as you would say, what did I expect? Perhaps it proves that the books are genuine, and not ours, perhaps it merely reinforces our belief that we are dealing with high-class thieves here, Andrew. I have been trying to put a price on the works that Santa Luisa has acquired from the Iron Shoe, but it is obviously difficult for me to ask too directly without implying to Ms Marques that she is the recipient of stolen goods. She thinks there's something a little iffy about me already, in spite of the highly creative cover story that I fed her on our first meeting. Perhaps you're right, and my imaginative gifts are ebbing away with advancing years and distance from my homeland. You wish me to return to the point? Well, I think so far at Santa Luisa we are talking thousands, not hundreds, and sterling not dollars. I'm sorry, if that's still too vague for you, but I cannot get any nearer without straying well over the bounds of that courtesy which is due from guest to host. (I see what you mean about the influence of the Veil. Perhaps it is time I returned to the diesel fumes of the Oxford air and the snappier style of yesteryear.)

                                    With love,
                                    Kate

                                    Santa Luisa,
                                    Monday.

Dear Andrew,

I have had a brainwave before leaving this delightful place. This morning I paid one last visit to Ms Marques, ostensibly to say goodbye and thank her for all her help. Now comes the subtle bit, Andrew.

'By the way,' I said, 'can you tell me about the representative from the Iron Shoe collection who originally came to see you in person?'

'Yes?' she queried, raising a perfect arc of a black eyebrow. She wasn't going to give anything away to this suspicious character from across the water.

'Was he not one of my library colleagues from Oxford?'

'I think not,' she said. 'He told me that he worked for Miss Westgate, the current keeper of the collection.' I was still giving her my winsomely innocent smile, and at last she gave in and added, 'Though he did mention that he had previously been employed by Oxford University's Bodleian Library.'

'My own employer!' I exclaimed joyously. 'I wonder whether it is possible that I should know the gentleman?'

'You want his name?' she asked, extraneously I thought, in the circumstances.

'I would hate to miss hailing a fellow enthusiast when I return to my Alma Mater,' I gushed.

She looked less than convinced by my performance, I have to admit, but she said, 'His name was Vivian Moffatt. Do you know him?'

'No.' Damn, I've never heard of the man. Have you, Andrew? 'Are you sure that was his real name, Ms Marques? Did you see any sort of identification?'

She sighed, and the perfect black arcs nearly disappeared into her hairline. 'I'm not a fool, Ms Ivory. When someone whom I do not know turns up and offers me just the books that I need to complete one of my collections, I examine his letter of recommendation and I ask for identification. Mr Moffatt showed me his passport. It contained a clear and recent colour photograph of the man who stood before me. Does that answer your question?'

'Unfortunately, yes. And thank you so much for your co-operation.' I meant it. Why should the lovely Ms Marques co-operate in proving that her recent acquisitions were hot Oxford property?

Can you look for a Mr Vivian Moffatt, Andrew? Just because I haven't come across him doesn't mean that he doesn't exist in the University libraries system somewhere. Though I have to admit that I've never seen his name on the electronic list of users when I've mailed a message to my friend Jo Morgan at the Bodleian.

> Yours despondently,
> Kate

*Fax from Andrew Grove, Oxford, to Kate Ivory, Santa Luisa, CA.*

Dear Kate,

I've checked on your Mr Moffatt and I'm afraid you're right: no one of that name has used the staff side of the on-line catalogue since it came into operation in September, 1988. I've also checked through Charles, who has access to files that I can't get my hands on, that he hasn't been employed by the University in any capacity in the past ten years. I thought we had drawn a complete blank, but when I mentioned his name in the canteen at coffee this morning, Ian (that rather unpleasant young man from the office upstairs) said:

'I was at school with a kid called Vivian. He hated it because everyone teased him about having a girl's name. He was a funny little kid. He lived with foster parents, well a house full of old ladies I think they were, and this odd-looking woman used to turn up to collect him from school every day. I suppose we made his life a misery: no one was friendly with him, because he was different from us. Lousy things kids are, aren't they?'

I have to say, Kate, that in my opinion, this Ian character is a real slimeball: hair greased back from his spotty face, denim jeans a size too small, thinks too much of himself by a mile. But I endeavoured to be pleasant to the man.

'What school was this?' I asked.

'The local primary school in Jericho,' he said. 'We

moved away from the area when I was nine, and I don't suppose I've thought about Viv from that day to this.'

Now, it strikes me, Kate, that there are two possibilities. One is that the Vivian that Ian was talking about is the one that we are looking for – remote, I grant you, since you really can't rely on that sort of coincidence, even in a town the size of Oxford. The second possibility is that our Viv is a different person, but one who met the same problems as Ian's school chum and decided to do something about it when he grew up. I mean, just in case you aren't following me, that he CHANGED HIS NAME! (Your beastly Veil writers are having a bad influence on my style, too, you notice.) Unfortunately, I didn't find a reference to any Moffatts with different Christian names, but it occurs to me that if it was Ian's Vivian, and if he was fostered, then at some stage he might have changed his surname, too. But he would still have his original birth certificate, and could apply for a passport in his original name.

No? Too far-fetched? You may well be right.

Yours,<br>Andrew

Santa Luisa,<br>Tuesday.

Dear Emma,

Hope you like the picture: this place really is just as picturesque as it looks on the postcard. I'll see you when I get back and we'll fix when and how I'm going to take over the writing class. By the way, you never did tell me why you had to give it up before the end of the year. See you soon, Luv, Kate.

Tuesday evening,
Santa Luisa.

Dear Andrew,

This is a postscript to my last letter and will probably reach you after I get back to England, but I thought it was worth noting, anyway.

As I was leaving the Santa Luisa library, I was followed to the door by a young woman who introduced herself as Sharon White. She was English, working here on an exchange. She had previously worked at the Bodleian, where she had become friendly with Jenna Coates. And it was Sharon who invited Jenna to come and stay with her last year – on Jenna's own suggestion – and who was with her at the airport when she recognized Vivian Moffatt.

So there we have confirmation of what we had suspected. Jenna told Sharon that she knew Mr Moffatt from Oxford, where he worked for the University. She became very quiet and reserved, apparently, and when Sharon questioned her about it, she said it confirmed suspicions she already had, but she didn't want to talk about it before confronting the person concerned. It might be that he had a complete explanation for his appearance at Santa Luisa, under a different name, and she did not feel that she should gossip about him, or spread rumours about his possible dishonesty without good reason. She was, unfortunately, a very high-principled young woman: the rest of us would have had great pleasure in gossiping and postulating explanations for his behaviour to all and sundry.

But she did hint to her friend that she thought there might be some major fraud or theft under way here, and she had to think it all out before talking about it to anyone.

Nothing very new or very revealing here, but it is a further affirmation that the two crimes – Jenna's death and the theft of the books – are connected. And before you deny it again, I would remind you that it was only a few weeks after this that Jenna's body was found buried off the motorway. You can't tell me it was a coincidence any longer, we're not living in a Sensation novel here, Andrew.

With love,

Kate

*On the plane from San Francisco to Heathrow.* This is a very good opportunity to think about the things that have been happening and sort out the people I have met. Every crime novel I have read does this at some time. A couple of characters sit down with pens and paper and go through the possibilities. It's a pity there's only one of me to do it, and I had better forget the fact that I am not usually very good at compiling lists – somehow I always manage to miss off the one vital item, or else I simply lose the final product – and just get on with it.

I think I shall tackle this chronologically, and since I could never work out a timetable of alibis, I shall do it by listing the people I have met and treating them as though they were characters in a novel that I was writing. (OK, Andrew, I know you think I treat everyone I meet as though they were a character in a novel, but this time it's for real.)

Perhaps I should start by stating what the investigation is about, since that is an area that has shifted since I began.

A. An unidentified number of books have disappeared from Oxford academic libraries. Not only the books, but the computer records for them have been deleted.
B. A trainee librarian, Jenna Coates, who almost certainly stumbled on the thefts and their cover-up, was murdered a year ago. No one is interested in this death any more, since it appears that she was killed when hitchhiking by a man who picked her up in a car, and the only clue is the peony that the killer left to mark her grave.

1. Andrew Grove. Old friend. Not a suspect.
   Couldn't possibly be. Works at the Bodleian
   and is a good source of information and
   gossip, except for the items that he wishes
   to keep to himself, for political rather than
   sinister reasons.

2. Isabel Ryan. Andrew's girlfriend (all right,
   Kate, stop grinding your teeth and
   remember that you didn't want him as more
   than a friend anyway). Where is she
   working now? (Check with Andrew.) A year
   ago she was working as a trainee at the
   Bodleian, where she became friendly with
   Jenna Coates (q.v.) and received a postcard
   from her when Jenna was on holiday in
   California. Go back and find out what else
   Isabel knows: maybe Jenna was killed by a
   jealous boyfriend and her death has nothing
   to do with the present investigation. But
   after my conversations with Ms Marques
   and Sharon White, I can't believe that. Jenna
   Coates was killed because she knew who
   was behind the book thefts.

3. Charles Trim. Director of the Libraries
   Computer Security Team. An unpleasant
   man. Oh how lovely it would be to find that
   he was behind everything, but I am afraid
   that it is unlikely. He has the authority level
   to do more or less what he likes with the
   cataloguing system: he could slither in and

out of it, deleting, adding, changing, and without even leaving any fingerprints. On the other hand, does he have access to the books he needs? Wouldn't libraries notice if he walked in, inspected their stock, fiddled with their computer and then walked out with a carton of their best books? He would need at least one partner, probably more. No, regretfully, I shall have to leave him to one side.

(Whatever is that film they're showing? Oh, it's that thing that I went to see in Magdalen Street a couple of weeks ago, minus the sex and bad language, I suppose. I might as well get on with this list, though it is soon going to be so long that it won't be of any practical use.)

4. Francis Tabbot, Librarian of St Luke's College. Another man I didn't like and didn't trust. He didn't seem bright enough about computers to be able to doctor the records, but I do think he may have had more valuable books hidden away in that locked room of his than I was allowed to see. I think perhaps that he got out the Phi material for me so that I wouldn't ask any more awkward questions. And he was right, I didn't. Hmm.

5. Mick Ennis, Library Assistant at St Luke's. Not my favourite person, but a definite improvement on Charles and Tabbot. (Is this just going to be a statement of your prejudices, Kate? Try and remember that this isn't actually one of your books, but real life.) He has the know-how to change the records, but he didn't strike me as having enough initiative to market the books, even if he had the courage to walk out of the place with them. It's a pity these libraries can't afford proper security, with a porter checking bags and briefcases when readers leave the library. Is there collusion between him and Tabbot? Between them they have the skills and knowledge necessary for the thefts. And there was something shifty about the man. If he was quite innocent, why was he chewing at his fingers in that disgusting way? (Come on, Kate, I'm sure you've got some anti-social habits, but they don't make you into a criminal.) What was obvious was that he and Tabbot didn't like or respect one another, and it is difficult to imagine them collaborating in anything. But maybe that was an act put on for my benefit.

(This detecting game is more difficult than I had imagined. And why is it that in books there is a small, restricted number of suspects? In this case, everyone I meet is suspect, and it seems that just about everyone in the University library system could be on my list. This isn't fair.)

6.  The Centre for North American Studies at Kennedy House. Bugger this, there's a whole lot more suspects, even if I discount Victor Southam. This crowd didn't seem to be so bad: the worst I could accuse most of them of being was boring. And I'm not even sure I could remember all their names. OK, try harder, Kate.

    *i.* The director, Chris Johnston. He seemed to be a nice bloke, and he was practically the only person I've met so far who knew Jenna and cared about her death. And I suppose that makes him a suspect. Yes.

    *ii.* The librarian, Angela Rugby. Efficient woman with grey hair and a young face. I don't remember much else about her. She's an unlikely candidate, simply because she's a woman, and Paul Taylor said that it was most likely that Jenna was killed by a man. And the Vivian Moffatt who turned up in Santa Luisa was a man. OK, delete Angela Rugby, and the other women.

    *iii.* Susie Holbech, the Conservation Officer. Female, therefore out of the frame. (But just a moment, didn't Chris Johnston say that she was working with Jenna when J. was at Kennedy House? She was such a colourless woman that I forgot to check whether she remembered anything about Jenna. And they were working on the American juvenile literature, so is there a connection with Victor Southam?)

*iv.* Marty Preston, the beautiful indexer of US official papers. I can't believe he'd be involved in any of this, and anyway, he wasn't in England in the spring of last year. (Are you sure, Kate? Aren't you allowing appearances to cloud your judgement again? Whereabouts in America does he come from? Could it be California? Perhaps he was running the selling end of the operation. You'd better go back and check on him, hadn't you? Come to think of it, I can just imagine those lovely broad shoulders leaning back against a whitewashed wall, and that handsome face framed in scarlet bougainvillaea. *Welcome to Santa Luisa.*)

(I've just remembered where I saw that other postcard: in the Conservation department at the Bodleian, pinned to the board in the office of the man who tried to chat me up, Slimeball Ian Maltby.

And isn't he the man who told Andrew that he was at school with a child called Vivian? And if it's the same Vivian, what does it mean? Could Ian Maltby even *be* Vivian? I am not doing very well at this game. Maybe I need a bit of a sleep. I might wake up brighter and smarter.)

'Thank you, I'd love another drink. Make it a brandy, with lots of soda water to combat the dehydration.'

Ten minutes later Kate pulled down the blind, switched off her reading light and allowed the brandy to take effect.

She woke up to find her mouth full of evil-tasting fur: when she stumbled along to the toilets, she found a long queue, so she went back to her seat and paddled through her hand luggage until she found a damp flannel, which she used to scrub at her face, and then she flagged a passing stewardess and was served with a couple of beakers of water. These emergency measures improved matters, but not a lot.

She leafed through the pages of notes she had made during the night. After years of word-processing, she had the most awful handwriting, and she found it difficult to read what she had scrawled down. The list served only to remind her of how much she didn't know. Then she turned to a fresh page, found her pen, and tried to compile a new, much shorter list.

1. Get in touch with Isabel and ask her about Jenna.
2. Go and see Ian Maltby at the Bodleian and ask

if you can look at his postcard from Santa Luisa.

3. Chat up Marty Preston (mmm!) and find out where he comes from and what he was doing before he came to Oxford.

She remembered now that someone sensible had once said that no list of things to do should contain more than three items. This latest list of hers was obviously a perfect example of the genre. Then she remembered that she should go back and talk to Suzy Holbech at Kennedy about Jenna, so she added a fourth point, then, before she could think of anything else, she closed her notebook, replaced it in her bag and went to join the queue for the lavatories.

# ix

*Statement of Major Themes*

They say there are only two subjects for a serious writer to address, Love and Death, so that is what you are getting here, Mrs Dolby. Love and Death. Neither of them is very pretty when you get close, I am afraid.

Has this been exciting enough for you? Has it got enough action in it yet? When it comes to a climax, there really is nothing like a violent death, is there, Mrs Dolby?

I have to admit now that I wasn't very fond of Jenna when she was alive. She lacked the fineness of feature of the women that I admire, the gentle voice, the submission to a superior intellect. I would have agreed with anyone who wanted to point out her shortcomings. But now that she is dead, somehow, I feel responsible for her. People who have saved a life say this: the life they have saved is in their hands, so perhaps it is irrational for one who has taken a life to say the same thing. But that is the way it is. That at least is the way that I feel.

I haven't hidden Jenna behind a pseudonym, the way I have the other characters you have met on these pages. I haven't changed her gender. I have described her the way she was, or at least, the way that I saw her, as accurately as I can. I have a duty to her that I cannot escape. As long as I live, I carry her life along with my own, as though something remained on my fingers: not hair, or skin or sweat, nothing that could be seen under your electron microscopes or identified by your DNA testing, but rather the vestiges of what I must call Jenna's soul.

That's ridiculous, isn't it? For if there is such a thing as a soul – and I am not convinced that there is – then that is just the part of the human being that goes flying off to heaven. Or to hell. But hers stayed here, like a cobweb, sticking to my fingers, and however hard I try to rid myself of the silvery filaments, they remain, immovable, immutable. I try to tell my story, but it is *her* story that I tell, for the two are now as intertwined as the spider's web and the peony bush.

I carry both of them with me now, like invisible companions: John Exton and Jenna Coates.

I went in to work this morning and there was a stranger there. I saw her walk out through the door into the brilliant daylight. She was outlined against the sun, a slight figure, about medium height, with hair so fair that it seemed nearly transparent, standing up from her head like some young boy's and shining like pale gold in the sunlight. I don't know who she was, but she moved out through the door and I watched her turn left and walk towards Oxford, and she had the carriage and the stride of a woman who knows what she wants out of life. She behaved as though she belonged here: who is she and what is she doing?

I've seen her again. This morning she was wearing a navy blue skirt, just a little too short for my taste, and a long linen jacket in a deep shade of gold. Today I saw her face: grey eyes, rather round and with a candidness that I didn't quite believe; dark, rather thick eyebrows; a narrow nose, with just the suggestion of a hook; a determined mouth; her hair still standing on end, as though she had just been woken up. Good muscle tone. But she'd look prettier if she grew her hair and wore some make-up. I like a woman to make the best of herself. Around her neck she had looped a long, flimsy scarf, made of some chiffon-like material, and when she turned away from me, I saw that one end of it floated down her back. Such a temptation.

Today, I went to see Harry about a business transaction we had going. And there she was. *Who is she and what is she doing?* I didn't mention it to Harry, since his nerve isn't as good as mine, and if one of us starts to panic we shall all be lost. The fact to hold on to is that our operation is professional. I suppose that someone might have missed one of the books that we had removed, but we have left no traces, there is no proof. That is what I have to remember.

Tomorrow, if I see her again, I will try to talk to her and find out what she is doing.

This morning we met at last. I watched her mouth smiling and talking while her eyes assessed me as coolly as she would a dead fish on the marble slab at the fishmonger's. I have never seen eyes so grey, like a light stroke of charcoal on textured white paper; there is no hint of blue or green in the colour. Wood smoke, that's what they reminded me of.

They say that she is a writer, and that she has taken a temporary job, going round the various libraries giving advice on how to change their catalogues from card indexes to fully-automated, computerized records. What a useful woman. She will make our task so much easier, and we will be able to expand faster than we had hoped.

On the other hand, I don't like the way she is asking so many questions, and some of them about Jenna. And if she is only a simple cataloguer, what is she doing with Andrew Grove, Senior Assistant Librarian at the Bodleian Library and member of the Libraries Computer Security Committee?

# Chapter Nine

'Hallo, Kate, Andrew here.'

He sounded unusually formal, and issued no invitation to the wine bar or pub. They had met and discussed Kate's trip to California the previous week. Andrew had been less impressed with her findings than she had hoped. 'Charles is a tiny bit concerned about the last report I handed in to him, and he'd like to see us both this afternoon.'

'We're being summoned to the headmaster's study, are we?'

'He wants us – well, *you* really – to explain what we've been spending his money on and what our priorities are.'

'You'll be talking about cost-effective investigation in a minute.'

'Well, what's wrong with that? Look, Kate, can you wear that nice navy blue suit of yours, do you think? And meet me outside the Taylorian Institute at five to four.' He didn't leave time for her to answer, but just said a slightly nervous 'Goodbye' and put down the phone.

\* \* \*

'I thought it had a longer skirt.'

'Navy blue suit, you said, and that's what I'm wearing.'

She had been feeling uncooperative when she had exchanged the usual respectable skirt of her suit for the short tight one she had bought in Little Clarendon Street. Then she had put on her new, shiny, deep scarlet lipstick and had to agree with her image in the mirror that the effect was slightly tarty, which was what she had been aiming for. She hadn't forgotten how much she had disliked Charles on first meeting and although she hadn't actually completed the analysis of the investigation and the list of suspects that she had started on the plane back from San Francisco, she did remember that Charles had been up there as one of her favourites for the role of rapist and murderer.

Andrew had thrown a heavy silence and was walking beside her making a point of not speaking. He stopped in front of the door in St Giles'. The same tinny voice hailed them and challenged their identity before letting them in with a buzz and a cloud of dry-rot spores.

'Sit down, both of you,' said Charles, just like the headmaster of Kate's imagination. 'And explain to me just what Kate Ivory has been doing for these past few weeks.' He didn't pause for either of them to answer, but carried straight on, 'I was under the impression that she was being paid – and at an unreasonably elevated rate – to find out how the computerized library catalogue was being utilized to steal books from the participating libraries. In addition, and if possible, she was to identify the perpetrators.'

That's the first time I've ever heard anyone use that

word in speech, thought Kate, looking at Charles with greater dislike than ever.

'I gather that Miss Ivory gave up the cataloguing task that we had assigned to her, and the search for the book thieves, to go off on holiday in California. Some sort of fool's errand of her own, I believe.'

'But we aren't only dealing with book theft,' she began in reply.

'Oh yes we are,' said Charles. 'We're dealing with the potential loss of millions of pounds' worth of goods.'

'Books, you're talking about *books*. Those inanimate objects that sit around on shelves and gather dust. Me, I'm talking about *people*. At least, one person, a living person.'

'Except that she isn't,' said Charles coldly.

'Exactly. And I want to know who is responsible, and how and why he did it. And I want to see him pay for it.'

'They've abolished hanging,' said Andrew.

'They haven't abolished trial by jury and life imprisonment. And they haven't, yet, got rid of over-crowded cells, slopping out and banging-up of prisoners for twenty-three hours a day. They'll fill my idea of justice for the bastard nicely, thank you.'

'You're getting too emotional, Kate,' said Andrew.

'She wasn't even very attractive,' said Charles. 'A little, plump, rather spotty girl, as I remember her.'

'So you did know her? I thought you'd never met.'

'Not really. I'm sweeping through the dead leaves of my memory here.'

'And do women only count if they're attractive to men?' Kate's voice was rising in the way that Andrew hated.

'The plain ones can be murdered with impunity, can they? You stick with your books, I'll keep searching for Jenna's killer.'

'But we can dictate what you do, since we are paying your salary,' said Charles.

'For cataloguing books, I believe. Well, I shall continue to catalogue the beastly things, so you can carry on paying my wages.'

For a moment they sat there, the two men glaring at Kate, Kate scowling in return. Charles picked up an expensive-looking fat black fountain pen and tapped it on his blotting pad. His hands were long and thin, with papery dry skin. Kate spoke before he could launch another attack on her.

'You did know Jenna, then?' She wanted to ask when, where, how well, how long for, but she thought Charles might throw her out of his office if she tried them all.

'As I've already told you, I didn't know her in any meaningful sense of the word. One doesn't know people like that.'

'But when we spoke before you gave the impression that you had never met her, never heard of her.'

'Andrew, your little friend is repeating herself in a very boring way. She is taking her detecting game far too seriously. And she has failed to convince me that we should continue to pay her an inflated salary merely to go round and insult senior members of this university.'

Kate was still watching his hands: the white, smooth-skinned librarian's hands with their well-manicured nails. But strong, she thought. She could see that under the unblemished skin were sinews and muscles that could catch a girl and twist a stocking around her neck and then pull it very tight. The tapping of the pen was louder and more rapid now. She lifted her eyes to his face. Charles was furious, but whether with Andrew, her, or Jenna, she really couldn't tell.

'Well, we could review the situation,' said Andrew. 'But I must point out that Miss Ivory's contract gives her the right to a calendar month's notice, if you really do wish to terminate her employment.'

'Is this interview over?' Kate said. 'I should like to leave now.'

'Take your friend out of here, Andrew,' said Charles.

As they walked back down St Giles', Kate was silent for a while. Then she said:

'And how about you, Andrew? Did you know Jenna, too? Have you been concealing things from me?'

'No, Kate. I didn't know Jenna. She was Isabel's friend, not mine, and she died before I met Izzie. And to answer your second question, yes, of course I conceal things from you. Any sane person would.'

'Well, before you go off to bury some more evidence, perhaps you'd let me have Isabel's phone number.'

'Why?'

'Because I want to ring her up and check on something she told me.'

'You're not to upset her.'

'It's only men like Charles who bring out my claws and fangs. With your Isabel I'll be boringly kind and lovely.'

'Very well then.' He wrote a telephone number in his

neat library hand on a scrap of paper. 'I don't know why I humour you like this. You behaved abominably rudely to Charles just now.'

'Yes I did, didn't I? And no, Isabel's not on my list of suspects, but Charles has just talked himself to the top of it.'

'Oh my God. What have I done to deserve you?' And Andrew strode away towards the Radcliffe Camera.

'Thanks, Kate. This is really letting me off the hook without closing my options for next year,' said Emma.

They were sitting in Emma's untidy sitting-room, on her huge, sagging sofa with the cat-shredded upholstery. Kate had removed a plastic tub of clothes awaiting the iron from one end of the seat and cleared a small space on the cluttered table in front of her. The mess made her skin itch. She didn't know how Emma could get any work done in a place like this. Her own brain would be in a permanent tangle, though Emma managed to produce a modest series of children's stories, and people spoke well of her writing class. Ah, said a voice inside Kate's head, but just think what she might achieve if she ever cleared this lot up and introduced some order and discipline into her life.

Emma's reason for giving up the writing class was only too obvious now that Kate was sitting next to her.

'Well, you should have told me before that you were expecting another child,' said Kate. How many did this make? Three? Four? 'It must be awful to feel so sick and have to face a class of would-be writers. When's it due?'

'Another two and a half months. But they're a bit worried about my blood pressure. I'm supposed to be taking things easy.'

Once she had seen how pregnant Emma was, Kate couldn't refuse to take over the class. 'Well, tell me what to do with these budding writers of yours.'

'Here's my folder on the course,' said Emma, handing her a manila folder with Income Tax written in big black letters across the top. 'Take no notice of the label, I believe in recycling.'

'So do I,' said Kate. 'But I relabel, too.'

'Here's a list of students,' said Emma. 'You get them to tick their names off each week and make sure it goes to the Department of Extra-Mural Studies at the end of term so that we get paid.'

'Right, I understand that bit. There are instructions printed at the bottom of the page.'

'And here are my notes on what we should be covering for the rest of the term: suggestions for reading, for group exercises, for homework for those who want to do it. There's no compulsion to turn in homework, and some of them are very private about their work, but others of them push in thousands of words for me to look at every week. I'm afraid I've really got behind on that part, and I'd be really grateful if you could whip through these outstanding assignments and let them have your comments. Be positive and encouraging, then give them some constructive criticism. I'm afraid there aren't too many potential winners here.'

'Keeps the competition down,' said Kate. She picked

up another typewritten sheaf of papers. 'What's this?'

'Didn't I give it back to him? It's a piece by one of the students. I think he writes a lot, but he's very secretive about it on the whole and only gives me in a piece to read a couple of times a term. He's got quite a gift for vivid description, if only he could get his imagination under control and keep his stories believable. Have a look through it, if you like, see what you think.'

'Right,' said Kate, her heart sinking at the thought of ploughing through all the thousands of words that Emma's students had set down on paper. Should they really be encouraging the destruction of so many trees to so little purpose?

'Oh, the other odd thing about this one,' said Emma, 'is that he uses a pseudonym. It's as though he can throw off his everyday, boring self, and become this great romancer – but only if he changes his name.'

'It doesn't seem so odd to me,' said Kate. 'Think of all those writers of romantic tales who hide behind pseudonyms. It's mostly because they put their own fantasies down on paper, and which of us would like to have their fantasy life nailed like that, signed with our own names?'

'You may be right. It certainly works here. Oh, give me back that folder a sec, I do believe there's a large section missing. I wonder where I put it.' And Emma got heavily to her feet and starting moving piles of things from one place to another. 'I bet it was one of the kids,' she muttered. 'Look, leave it with me for the moment, Kate. I'll find the rest this evening and drop it in on you tomorrow.'

'Yes, fine,' said Kate, groaning inwardly. She could see

that Emma would never be able to find anything in this house. 'Do the punters know that they're getting a new teacher, by the way?'

'I told them about it during the last class. They're all looking forward to meeting you.'

'Right, I'll take this lot of manuscripts off with me, and see you tomorrow for the rest,' she said, getting to her feet.

'You're sure you wouldn't like a cup of tea or something?'

Kate shuddered at the thought of Emma's kitchen. 'I haven't time, I'm afraid. I'll be off now.'

Outside, she gulped in fresh air and promised herself she would turn out yet another cupboard next weekend, just so that she was never tempted to get to Emma's state of sluttery.

When she got home, she rang Isabel.

'Oh, hallo, Kate. I was wondering when you'd ask me about Jenna. No one else seems to be very interested in her, do they?'

'Would you like to come round to my place? I can open a bottle of wine and cook us an omelette and throw a salad together.'

'With the lovely fresh basil dressing that Andrew told me about?'

'If you like.'

'I'll see you in half an hour.'


Kate was glad to see that Isabel was enjoying her salad, but she wished that she would stop eating for long enough to tell her what she wanted to know. She poured them both another glass of Australian Semillon Chardonnay and told herself to enjoy the meal and the wine and stop being impatient.

'Could you explain a couple of things to me, Isabel?' she said, as she poured near-boiling water on to coffee grounds. 'First of all, what were you doing at the Bodleian, being a trainee librarian? And second, how come you were a close friend of Jenna's? From everything I've heard about her, the two of you wouldn't have much in common.'

'I wasn't a proper trainee – not a graduate like Jenna, aiming to go on to library school. I was just a very junior library assistant, working in one of the reading rooms. I spent a lot of my time filing index cards and putting books back on shelves, things like that. And I wasn't so sophisticated then, you know.'

Isabel might be sophisticated on the outside, but Kate wasn't so sure about what went on inside her head.

'And Jenna wasn't the sort of girl that appealed to young men much – they didn't appreciate her qualities – but she was liked by all the other young female staff. All of us under twenty-five or so used to have our coffee together in the canteen, have a good laugh, eat chockie bars, that sort of thing.'

It sounded innocent enough, certainly.

'And was the postcard I saw, the one from Santa Luisa, the only one that she sent you from California?'

'I'm afraid so. She may have sent cards to some of the other girls, but I don't suppose they've kept them: you don't keep postcards for more than a year usually, do you?'

'And did she ever talk to you about some dishonesty that she suspected in the libraries?' Kate gently pushed the plunger down and poured out two cups of coffee. 'Cream? Sugar?'

'Cream, please. And four sugars.'

'She didn't say anything definite, she wasn't that sort of person. She said it wasn't fair to destroy someone's reputation by gossiping before you had proper proof. I think she would have confronted the person if she had been sure, and then gone to the librarian or someone even higher up to make a report. She was a very direct, very honest person.'

Very stupid, thought Kate. First of all she warned him, then she accepted a lift in his car and was never seen alive again. But she was jumping to conclusions.

'Did she even indicate which library was involved?'

'She did say something about its involving several libraries, but that she had only really tumbled to it while she was at her last place. She had seen something at Santa Luisa, I think, then something or someone at Leicester gave her the final piece of the puzzle.'

'Leicester? Leicester College?'

'Yes, it's one of the places where she worked. Have you got some more coffee, Kate?'

Kate poured coffee and found the remains of a box of chocolate mints (brought as a present long ago by Andrew, she remembered).

'Oh, choccies, how yummy. Don't you want one?'

'I'm not a chocolate person. Tell me more about Jenna at Leicester.'

'Well, she was working in the library there. It's quite a small one, just the usual undergraduate set-up, with a librarian and an assistant.'

Like St Luke's, thought Kate. I must get over there and meet these people.

'There was something else she said once, only I wasn't listening very carefully. It was about cheating on a large scale, she said. And she said something about needing various sorts of expert knowledge, and if you looked around in the different libraries, you could see that it was all there, but scattered among different people. Does that make sense?'

'Sort of. Did she mention any specific expertise?'

'No, but she did comment that the skills that you need for conservation must be very similar to those that you need for forgery.'

'Now that *is* something to think about.' Slimeball Ian Maltby from the Bodleian, she thought. And Susie Holbech from Kennedy. Potential forgers, both of them.

After that, Isabel had nothing more to add to her knowledge of Jenna, Kate found.

'Just tell me, though,' she said, 'what made you leave the Bodleian, and what you do now.'

'Oh, I don't think I was really a Bodley person,' said Isabel. 'I couldn't take all those old books nearly seriously enough: the readers used to make such a silly fuss if the wrong ones turned up, when I couldn't see what difference it made, and you've no idea how rude people can be, just because you're working behind a counter. They think you must be stupid or something.'

'How awful.'

'And then I saw this notice in the window of a really nice dress shop in the High Street, and I went in on an impulse, and they offered me the job. I'm Assistant Manager now,' she said. 'And I earn more than three times what the Bodleian paid me.'

'I can well believe it.'

'I'd better be going now, I suppose. Thanks awfully for the meal, Kate. And the choccies. I promised I'd call in on Andrew if I wasn't too late.'

'You'll tell him that I didn't bully you, won't you? I think he was a bit worried about it.'

'Oh, you're not nearly such a bully as he is, Kate. You're as nice as anything, really.'

When Isabel had left, Kate went down to write up her notes on the day's investigation. At least she could add some facts to her usual sequence of question marks. When she had summarized what Isabel had just told her in a couple of points, she added:

3. Meeting at the Security Team office with Charles Trim and Andrew Grove. Nothing helpful for my investigation, just a warning that I should stick with the book thefts and forget about the murder of the girl. That man is a *pig*. Oh how would I love to pin the whole thing on to one of the members of the Security Team, preferably

the aforesaid CHARLES TRIM. Especially
since I now know that he knew Jenna. (And why
did he keep quiet about it before?)

She read it through. She had to admit that it was just
another of her subjective, emotional outpourings, and
probably had nothing to do with either the books or the
murder of Jenna Coates.

She got out her list of things to do. She could cross off
item number one (*Get in touch with Isabel and ask her
about Jenna*), which made her feel good, especially since
it reduced the items to three instead of four. Then she
remembered that she had to add a visit to Leicester College to her list, which brought it up to four again, and
also reminded her that she hadn't heard from Liam, or
contacted him herself, since she got back from San Francisco. He might even admire her slight sun tan. She would
ring him the next morning to find out what he knew about
the Leicester College library. God, she was getting to be
a real cow: she never contacted anyone these days unless
she wanted something from them. When this thing was
over, she would invite a whole lot of people over for a
meal, just to be sociable, and she wouldn't have a hidden
motive, or ask them a single intrusive question. On the
other hand, maybe it would have to wait until she had
finished the first draft of her current manuscript.

She looked at the list again: she had to talk to Marty
Preston and Susie Holbech at Kennedy House, so if she
did that on the following morning, she would have tackled
two jobs at once. And she must go back to the Bodleian

to see Ian Maltby and read his postcard from California. Pleased with this solution, she worked at her book for an hour or two before going to bed. To her surprise, she had managed to keep up with her average of a thousand words a day, in spite of all the other distractions in her life.

Now that she had finished *Frankenstein*, she was looking for something lightweight to read to get her mind off the day's happenings so that she could get to sleep, when she remembered the typescripts that Emma had given her to comment on. She had opened a new file in her cabinet, *Creative Writing Class*, and she fetched it out of its clean new folder and settled down under her duvet, with her shoulders propped against a pile of pillows.

*My neighbour has done me proud: the peonies have a colour so amazing that it can only have one of those vivid names like heliotrope or indigo, magenta, lavender or cardinal. Plain pink, the colour of blancmange and of old ladies' knickers, just won't do to describe it. I choose a single bloom to throw down on to the domed lid of the coffin. The flowerhead bursts as it strikes polished mahogany and petals drift across the shining surface and lie there, like little pleading hands.*

At the bottom of the page he had typed The End, and added his name and the date. Vivian Moffatt, it said. *Vivian Moffatt*. While she had travelled across the world to find him, he had been waiting for her here in Emma's writing class.

It was a wonder she had even read the piece: Emma had already done so, apparently, and her comments (positive and encouraging, and offering constructive criticism) were written in red biro at the end. And then she remembered what else Emma had said about this man: he could only write if he used a pseudonym. So now she needed two things, his real name, and his address. She looked at her clock. It was too late to ring Emma now, but first thing in the morning she would be on the phone to her, and she would ransack that messy house from top to bottom if necessary to find the rest of the material on the writing class.

# X

## Short Piece on the Subject of Magpies

They say that magpies are black and white, but they're wrong. In certain lights, anyway, their feathers are an iridescent green, like a peacock's tail. Black lies, white truth; white lies, black truth; or flashing, iridescent green in the shifting sunlight. You'll have to make up your own mind.

Don't you wish you could fly? Using a long tail as a rudder? Glancing, zigzagging after flying insects, catching them, open-beaked, on the wing. Flight, chase, death: all my dreams of life are there.

I love heights. To stand suspended over an abyss, to sway, to know that at any moment I can give in and give up, that I can float and fly for a few moments like a bird before the pain, blood and death. Is it control? Is it my need to demonstrate superiority over those who know only fear in looking down into the void? Whatever its origins, it is why I love working in this gallery, climbing to the top of the building and sitting here with my head near the clouds, my feet a step away from the empty spaces and the concrete far below, and my mind on the Gallery opposite.

I look through the glass walls and I can see to the heart of Oxford. The tops of the trees stretch beneath me like a meadow, with the spires of churches rising up through the surface. It belongs to me. I own it all. Play the last movement of the symphony. Let the hammer blows fall. Here I am master of the city and no one can defeat me.

There is a very interesting collection just on the other side of the central well, but it is reached by a separate staircase and kept locked. I could find a reason to ask for permission to consult it, but it would be remembered and I would be regarded with suspicion when eventually the volumes were missed. Such a short distance between the wooden railings. Four feet? I'm sure I could jump it. But then again, even a librarian might notice a figure flying, arms outstretched like a magpie's wings, across from one side to another. There seem to be two alternatives, both of which involve lying, hiding, flying.

# Chapter Ten

'Sam?'

She was trying to keep the urgency out of her voice. The last thing that Sam and Emma needed to know at this time was that there was a murderer loose in Emma's writing class.

'Sam, I need to speak to Emma. Is she there?'

'No she's not. She's in the John Radcliffe.'

'In hospital. What's happened?'

'Her blood pressure has reached a dangerous level, and they're keeping her in bed until the baby is born.'

'I'm sorry. It sounds serious, Sam.'

'It is. So whatever you need to know from Emma, I'm afraid it's going to have to wait.'

'How long for?'

'A couple of months.'

'Oh. In that case, can I go and see her today? I need the folder that she was going to give me, the one with the stuff for the creative writing class.'

'Sorry, Kate. I'm not having her disturbed for something like that.'

'It's important.'

'So are my wife and baby.' She had never heard Sam sound so fierce. He was usually an easy-going, woolly mammoth of a man. You'd have to be, she thought, to live with Emma. 'Keep away from Emma, Kate,' he said. 'I've heard about the sort of things that you get mixed up in, and they belong in the pages of a crime novel, not in a quiet suburban street. If you've got problems, leave them to the professionals, you're just an amateur.'

It wasn't worth saying that the professionals were showing no interest in the case, so she said: 'Well, could I come to the house and look for the file I need?'

'I don't think there's much point. You see, we had a break-in yesterday evening, while we were all out at the hospital. I didn't notice it for a bit, I mean to say he had turned our stuff over, but—'

'Yes, I see, Sam.' No one would notice in Emma's house if all the contents of all the drawers and cupboards were tipped out on to the floor and then sorted out by a team of gorillas. 'Was much taken?'

'That's the odd thing. All he took were some papers of Em's. I remember that she had that Income Tax folder of hers out on the table ready for you to take, and she was looking out some more material to add to it, but this morning it isn't here.'

'Are you absolutely sure?'

'Well, pretty sure.' As sure as anyone could be in Emma's house that something was, or was not, there, she supposed.

'Well, thanks for your help, Sam. And don't worry about

the folder. I'm sure I'll manage somehow. You just concentrate on looking after Emma. And give her my love next time you see her.'

Emma had said that she had told her class that week that Kate would be taking over from her. What were the chances that one of that class had recognized her name and had removed the folder from Emma's house? She didn't think it would take much professional expertise to break into Emma and Sam's place: she couldn't imagine that they had much in the way of security, in fact she was willing to bet that they were the sort of people who rushed off to the hospital, piling all the children into the car and leaving their back door open.

Sod it, that was her best clue so far, and it had been snatched away from her by the shortcomings of female biology – and not even her own. Frustrating as it was, she would have to think of another way of finding Vivian Moffatt. She didn't think, somehow, that he would be sitting there in the front row of her class when she took over next week. And if he had bothered to steal Emma's file, it must be because he knew it was incriminating and that she was on his trail. She made a phone call.

An hour or so later, a metallic blue car stopped outside her house. It was shiningly clean, with dazzling chrome and a windscreen clear of insect smears. The driver indicated, and backed, in one smooth movement, so that he was parked, four inches away from the kerb and parallel to it, in a space that it would have taken Kate half the morning to get into, even after Harley's instructions. She knew only one person who could manage that, and she went to open the door.

'Hallo, Paul.'

He was looking away from her, apparently having a polite conversation with Toadface. She didn't even bother to enquire whether he had pulled faces at the child: she knew it wouldn't have occurred to him.

'Interesting looking child,' he said, as he followed her into the sitting-room.

'Hmph,' she said. 'Can I get you a coffee, or some mineral water?' There was no point in offering the remains of the bottle of Bulgarian red that was beckoning from the kitchen to someone like Paul at this time in the morning.

'Thanks. Instant will be fine. Milk, three sugars.'

By the time she had made the coffee she couldn't keep her news to herself any longer.

'I've found him,' she said.

'Found who?'

'Our murderer. The man with the peonies.'

'Oh yes?'

Why didn't he sound more enthusiastic? 'Look at this,' she said, pushing Vivian Moffatt's writing exercise into his hands. 'Here, towards the end. First of all there's the bit where he goes to the theatre – well, pantomime more likely by the sound of it. And then there's this bit at his aunt's funeral, when he throws the flower down on to the coffin. Read it, Paul.'

He read quite slowly, with no noticeable reaction. 'Yes. So? You say this is an exercise from a creative writing class? Well, that's just what it is, isn't it? Something made up for the teacher. An invention.'

'But not entirely, surely.'

'Lies, the lot of it,' said Paul. 'Did you ever go to anything like that at the theatre when you were a kid? I don't believe it, not unless he's a man of seventy or eighty by now. And what was he doing being fostered by those peculiar women? Social Services Department would never have worn it, would they? Then there's the way he steals the flowers and goes to the funeral: well, life's just not like that, is it? And—'

'Yes, what's your concluding argument, then?'

'Just tell me whereabouts in the Covered Market you can buy horse meat to feed to your cats.'

'Well, some of it's made up, I grant you.'

'The whole thing is, Kate. You spend so much time inventing those stories of yours that you can't tell the difference between them and real life. I bet you this Vivian Moffatt is some poor old bloke, married to a bully of a wife, who just escapes once a week to his evening class. Hasn't even got much of a story to it, has it?'

'You've got no imagination.'

'And I thank God for it.'

'There was a break-in at Emma Dolby's house last night, and the file with Vivian Moffatt's address in it was stolen. I suppose you'll say that was a coincidence.'

'It does sound like it.'

'Well, what are the chances of finding whoever broke into their house?'

'Have you any idea just how many break-ins there have

been in Oxford in the past twenty-four hours? And this wasn't exactly serious, was it? Nothing valuable taken, no one hurt, I'm sure the uniformed branch is looking into it, but—'

'But no one actually gives a toss.'

'I don't like to hear you talk like that.'

'And I don't like it when you won't take me seriously. Why did you come round to see me?'

Paul had finished his coffee and now picked up his cup and saucer, and hers, and took them out to the kitchen and put them neatly on the draining-board. 'I was just going off shift when you rang and I thought I'd pop in and see how you were getting on, just check to see that you were all right.'

'I'm fine. My investigation is proceeding really well. And I do not want anyone fussing around me. I am not made of porcelain, and I am not in need of protection. I can look after myself.'

'I get the message. I've upset you by showing that you have no evidence whatsoever to connect this Vivian Moffatt with any sort of crime, and now you're telling me to piss off.'

Paul Taylor never used language like that in front of a woman. What was wrong with him? 'Absolutely right. You're a dull, unimaginative plod who can't see the most obvious thing. So just leave me alone.'

'I'm sorry if I've upset you, but you're behaving like the worst sort of amateur. And since you don't want me around, I'll be going now.'

As he drove his clean car out of Agatha Street as neatly

as he had arrived, Toadface gave him a beaming smile from the front window next door, and waved to him as he pulled away. But then, the child had no taste in men whatsoever.

Kate dressed in the ladylike version of her navy suit and got into her car. She swung out into Agatha Street a lot less neatly than Paul Taylor had done, and set off up the Fridesley Road towards North Oxford at a speed greater than the statutory thirty miles an hour. Minutes later she pulled into the car park of Kennedy House. She didn't care whether they all hated her or not, she was going to find out what they individually and collectively knew about the death of Jenna Coates.

Over in one corner, a red car was emitting periodic howls and flashing its headlights at her. No one took any notice. Graham Kieler must be visiting the place again, she thought. The man should get his car alarm fixed, especially if he's such a technical wizard.

The sun was shining at last, perhaps not out of such a cloudless sky as that over California, but enough to bring the new leaves on the trees to life, and reflect dazzlingly from the roofs and windscreens of the cars around her. As she walked past an ordinary black Fiesta, the sunlight caught a manila folder lying on the front passenger seat and thick black letters shouted at her: *Income Tax*. She stopped and peered in at it. Yes: pink folder, floridly handwritten title. Surely Emma was the only person who would keep her tax papers in a pink folder.

Whose car was this, anyway? She didn't recognize it

and there was nothing to indicate who it belonged to, but she knew it had to be Vivian Moffatt.

You're not going to come out while I'm here, are you, Viv? And you know me, though I don't know you. You're probably looking out of one of those copper-coloured windows right at this moment, watching me.

A shiver ran the length of her spine and she shook her head angrily.

Right, Viv Moffatt, Little Vivvy boy, I'm not going to give in.

She wished that she had a hand drill with her, fitted with a half-inch bit. In future she would make sure that she always had one in the boot of her car. But then she remembered the inarticulate Darren. Sure enough, there by the road was the ubiquitous skip full of rubble, and she walked across and chose herself a rock the size and shape of the one that Darren had used, then over to the black Fiesta. She looked around: no one in sight. She drew her arm back in the approved style and crashed the rock into the side window of the Fiesta. It worked a treat.

There were now two cars screeching in syncopation in the car park, and Kate reached through the shattered window, grabbed the file and walked quickly back to her own car. She didn't want to be seen with the folder in her possession by Vivian Moffatt, or whoever had stolen it, so she stowed it in the boot, where it was hidden from casual view, and walked into the building, looking back with disapproval at the two cars with the defective car alarms.

* * *

She strode up to the Reception desk. 'Who does that black Fiesta belong to?' she demanded.

'Not one of ours,' said the man behind the desk. 'Must be a visitor.' He checked a list. 'What's the registration number?' She told him. 'Not here. I'll look into it.'

The phone rang and he turned away to answer it.

'I'll be back in a few minutes,' said Kate, and went to tackle Martin Preston.

He was a foreigner and an outsider and might not dislike her quite so much as the rest of the staff for fingering Victor Southam. She found him at his desk, surrounded by heaps of dull-looking congressional papers.

'Hi, Marty!' she said, brightly.

'Hallo, Kate,' he replied, with what she could describe as a certain reserve.

'Do you mind if I ask you a couple of questions?'

'That depends on what they're about.' She was sure now that he wasn't as forthcoming as the last time she had been here, and his smile offered only the smallest gleam of white teeth. But at least he had stopped looking at his pile of official papers and was focusing somewhere behind her left ear.

'Where were you working before you came here to Kennedy House?'

He relaxed just a little, but there was still a wariness behind the brown velvet eyes. 'At the Library of Congress.'

Thank God it wasn't the University of California or Santa Luisa.

'What made you want to come to work here in Oxford? I should have thought that that was the top of the heap as far as library work was concerned.'

He stretched back in his chair. 'I kept hearing what a great place this was to live. You run across a lot of interesting guys at conferences, and it seemed like a lot of them were working here in Oxford. When this job came up, one of them sent me the details over the electronic mail. I applied, and I got it. It was that simple.'

She could relax. There was nothing in his history to connect him with Jenna Coates or the theft of books from libraries. Martin L. Preston was obviously the straightforward, honest man that he appeared to be from the first.

'Why the questions?' he asked. 'Are you working for the Security Team?'

'Just on one small project. There's the suspicion that books are missing from a few college libraries and that it's an organized ring that's stealing them.'

'Colleges? The only scam I'd heard of was Mick Ennis and his colour Xeroxes of historical pornographic material. Seemed pretty mild to me, but I gather he was making a few bucks at it.'

'Thanks, Marty. If that checks out, I owe you a drink.'

So that would explain the air of unease at St Luke's library and the expensive Xerox machine she had put her pot plant on. But was Ennis also mixed up in something more sinister than dirty books?

She had only two things to do from her original list: talk to Susie Holbech, the Conservation Officer at Kennedy House, and ask Slimeball Ian at the Bodleian about his postcard from Santa Luisa. On the whole she thought she could cope better with Ian Maltby, but since she was already standing in Kennedy House, she really should go and visit Susie Holbech.

She knocked on the door marked Conservation Officer and went in. Susie raised her forgettable face with its frame of mousey hair and scowled at her.

'I hope you're not here with more accusations,' she started, speaking too loudly and taking breath to continue.

'No, not at all,' said Kate, quickly. 'Do you think I could sit down and talk to you?'

'Must you? I'm very busy. And I already have a visitor.'

And then Kate noticed that Graham Kieler was in the room, standing in the corner, leafing through a leather-bound book. He looked shifty when he caught Kate's eye.

'Oh, hallo,' she said. 'Your car alarm's going off again for no good reason. It's probably flattened your battery by now.' That ought to move him out of the room. If he hadn't been so bloodless, she'd have suspected him of fancying Susie, and even of chatting her up.

'It can't be mine,' he said. 'My car's being serviced today, so it must be someone else's. But do carry on, I was just leaving anyway. And don't forget what I told you about choosing a password that can't be found in the dictionary, Susie.' But Kate didn't believe that that was what they had been talking about before she interrupted them.

'Do you mind if I sit down?' she asked, when Graham had left.

'If you must. Is this going to take long?'

'No.'

'And if you're looking for more evidence to hang poor

old Victor, you can leave right now.'

'No.' This interrogation was going less than well, she had to admit. She took a breath and launched into the middle of her subject. 'I know that Jenna Coates was working with you last year, and I wonder what you can tell me about her.'

She saw that she really had surprised Susie. 'Why on earth do you want to know about Jenna?'

How much should she explain to this woman who was looking at her impatiently, wishing that she would go? 'She's a friend of a friend, and there does seem to be some mystery about her death, doesn't there?'

'Since she was murdered and her killer was never caught, you could say so, yes.'

She wasn't making much progress. 'So, what can you tell me? What was your impression of her?'

'A rather dull child, I thought. Well intentioned, painfully honest, unattractive. Once she had hold of an idea she would never let it go, however erroneous it was shown to be, and on top of all that, she was a little busybody.'

'Not your favourite person?'

'I like people to be more adaptable, more subtle.'

'And you have no idea why she was killed?'

'I thought she hitched a ride and was killed by some sex maniac.'

'Not necessarily.'

'Well in that case I imagine that she poked her nose into other people's business just once too often. She could be very irritating.'

'So that's all you can tell me.'

'She and I were working through the Kilworth collection of children's literature, to see whether there were any repairs to be done before they were catalogued and made available to the public. It wasn't very exciting work, I'm afraid, but it introduced her to the principles of conservation work.'

'Thanks. I won't take up any more of your time.' She got up to go and had reached the door when Susie said:

'You could try asking Ian Maltby at the Bodleian if he knows anything. I think he was trying to chat her up for a while. God knows why.'

Kate called at Reception again on her way out. 'Any news on that black Fiesta?'

'No one's admitted owning it. It must be some unauthorized person using our car park.'

He followed her outside. The alarms had stopped shrieking and the black Fiesta had gone.

Kate wanted to drive away fast from Kennedy House to some quiet place where she could examine the Income Tax folder hidden in the boot of her car. (What would she do if it contained just what it said, she wondered. Oh well, presumably no one really minded losing their tax details; it wasn't as though they were love letters, or the manuscript of a novel, or anything important.) She looked at her watch. On the other hand, she just had time to get down to the centre of town, find somewhere to park, and get into the Bodleian to talk to Ian Maltby before he left for home or went off on evening duty. An extra hour wouldn't make any difference to the Creative Writing

Course file, she decided, and started the engine. She had the depressing feeling that Vivian Moffatt had removed any useful information from the folder before leaving it for her to find.

Ian Maltby was in his office when she put her head round the door. When he saw her, he smoothed down his already smooth hair and gave her his Number One smile. Nauseating, she thought.

'Can you spare a minute?' she asked, with her own winsome version of a smile.

'Any time,' he said, and moved across the room to stand too close to her.

'I wanted to ask whether you remember Jenna Coates,' she said, aware of his onion-scented breath close to her right ear.

'I didn't know her that well,' he answered. 'And she wasn't a patch on you, I promise.'

'No, really, Ian, I'm not jealous. I'm just interested in what Jenna may have found out while she was in California.'

'I was hoping you'd come and eat a pizza with me this evening.' Onion-flavoured, presumably.

'I'd love to, but I'm afraid I've got something else on.'

'Tomorrow then.'

'Tomorrow I have to give a course on creative writing for a friend of mine.' And she'd better go home and get some notes made, she thought, or she'd be standing up in front of twenty people with nothing to say.

'Do you mind if I look at that postcard over there?' It

273

wasn't subtle, but it might at least move her out of range of the onion breath.

'If you like, but I can't think why.'

He removed the drawing pin and handed her the card. Yes, on the front it had the same picture of a Spanish-style building covered with scrambling scarlet flowers, and the name *Santa Luisa* printed across the corner. She turned it over.

*Tom: There may be something we can use in the Gallery.*

There was no indication of who had written it, and it hadn't been sent through the post, so there was no address. It could be from anyone and about anything, but on the other hand it might just have been left over from Viv's trip to California, and he was using it to send a message to one of his fellow conspirators. The handwriting was not Jenna's – or at least it was different from the writing on Isabel's card.

'Do you know who the recipient was?' queried Kate.

'I've no idea who Tom is, but Susie Holbech dropped it when she was visiting one day – we do talk to other Conservation Officers, you know – and I stuck it up on the board to remind myself to give it back to her.'

'How long has it been there?'

'Some time. I'm afraid I'd forgotten all about it. You don't see things after they've been on a notice board for more than a week or two, do you? Still, it can't have been very important. Cheerful picture, though, isn't it?'

'I suppose so.'

'Well, how about that pizza? If we made it Saturday, we could go to a film afterwards.'

'Thanks, but I'm really booked up for the next week or so.'

There was nothing more to be learned here, and she couldn't wait to get away to examine her Income Tax folder. It was just possible that she'd find that Vivian Moffatt's real name was Ian Maltby.

It was the right file. There were the notes that Emma had prepared for the term's lessons, and some oddments of badly typed scripts with Emma's red biro comments on them. But there was no list of students with their home addresses and phone numbers.

The class register, she thought. Emma showed it to me when I visited her at her house. It should still be here. She leafed through the papers again a couple of times, but it wasn't there. She had known when she first saw the folder sitting on the passenger seat that someone would have been through it to remove anything incriminating, but there had been just an outside chance that there would still be something useful forgotten in the mess that Emma had left. Maybe Vivian Moffatt had been about to return it to her, and she need not even have broken into his car. She wished now that she had hung around until someone had come out to the black Fiesta, but the feeling had been so strong that she was being watched that she was sure that he wouldn't have allowed her to catch him.

She ran over the notes for the next evening's class: at least she wouldn't be standing there like a lemon, wondering what to say. Then her eyes fell on a short typewritten piece. The font and format looked familiar.

*I love working in this library, climbing to the top of the building and sitting here with my head near the clouds, my feet a step away from the empty spaces and the concrete far below, and my mind on the Gallery opposite.*

Gallery. 'There may be something we can use in the Gallery.' And the card was dropped by Susie Holbech. Susie was a Conservation Officer. She could probably forge bookplates and nineteenth-century handwriting. And she worked with Jenna when she had been at Kennedy House, and had not been very forthcoming when Kate had asked for information.

She thought back over the libraries she had visited, but she couldn't remember anything that could be described as a gallery. But there was another possibility. She went to the telephone.

'Liam? Yes, I'm fine. How are you? Good. Yes, you're right, we must get together again soon. How about tomorrow? No, not the evening, I'm not free then, either. I was thinking about the afternoon. And what I'd really like you to do is show me over the college library and introduce me to the staff. Half-past two? Yes, that's great. Thanks.'

She had the strange feeling, though, that she was being led through her enquiries by a controlling hand. Someone was feeding her just the pieces of information that he wanted her to find, in the order that he had determined.

She shook her head. This was fanciful. She was completely in command of herself, her life and her investigation. No question about it. But how did Vivian Moffatt guess that she was afraid of heights?

After eating her supper and going through Emma's notes in detail she decided on an early night and the first chapter of *Wuthering Heights*.

# xi

Don't you think that in the final chapter there should be a confrontation between the two protagonists? Good and evil, set up in opposition.

The problem is knowing which is which, don't you think? Did I do wrong when I decided to take my chance at a good life in Oxford? I stole nothing from John Exton, I gave him seventeen years of life after his death. I took nothing – I gave more than he could hope for.

Oh, Jenna. You're going to talk to me about Jenna, aren't you? That wasn't my fault. It was hers. She should have kept away from us, she should have listened to me. Or if she had made the slightest effort to be *pleasant*, to ingratiate herself, I might have thought twice about it. If, for instance, she had washed her hair that day, and brushed it, and put on some bright lipstick and made her piggy little eyes sparkle with something other than self-righteousness. Until the last moment, I would have let her go, but she made the decision herself.

'Take the Oxford Exit,' she said. She said that herself.

And so I did. You really can't blame me for what happened next.

And now we have this new woman, this Kate Ivory. She's been poking into our secrets, she's been asking questions. She's supposed to be a writer, though. So what the hell is she doing here? Why doesn't she go home and *write*. The Angel in the Home, that's what she should be, what every woman should be. They come out here and they try to tell us what to do, and they become monsters. *Monsters*.

She thinks she's finding out what's making the books disappear, and where they're going to. She's even been over to Santa Luisa. Good luck to her. Their collection of the Veil novels is complete now, thanks to us, and until they want to write large cheques for something else, our business with them is over.

We've expanded all over the place, and even if she stops one of us, there are twenty more to carry on the business of Bookfinders International. Once they hooked us up to their lovely networks, we realized the potential. And on our travels around the world to all the various librarians' conferences, we recruited, carefully, oh so very carefully, new members for the Company.

Like Luther (as I shall call him), our expert on the Library of Congress. That man has increased our profits by two hundred and fifty per cent in the past nine months, and I don't think that little Miss Ivory is likely to tumble to *him*. Or to . . . But I must stop gossiping or I shall be as indiscreet as dear Jenna if I'm not careful.

And anyway, it's time I went and changed into my dark green shell-suit (the colour of magpies' wings, did I mention?) for the last act.

# Chapter Eleven

Leicester College library had a light and well-proportioned eighteenth-century reading room and then, when in the twentieth century this had become too small to house its books and its students, it had built itself a tall circular tower to take the overflow of books and people. It was made mostly of glass, and had won some architectural award or other, but to Kate it was a nightmare. She could usually control her fear of heights, but when she had to walk up a spiral staircase with open treads and look out through glass walls as she did so, she felt herself floating and swaying so that she had to grab hold of the banister.

'It's worth it when you get to the top,' said Liam. 'And I believe that the floor is quite solid, really.'

He was right, and once there was a ceiling sitting a reasonable distance above her head, Kate didn't feel so unsafe. She even managed to lean against the broad wooden balustrade and look down the well at the ground floor far below. Concrete. Why hadn't they carpeted it?

'What is across there?'

On the other side of the gap there was a section of the library which they couldn't reach.

'Oh, it's a special collection of particularly valuable books. The librarian likes to keep them away from the general readers. They're not for undergraduate use, and you can only look at them if you ask the librarian for the key to the other staircase.'

'Do you know what the books are?'

'I'm afraid not. All I know is that there's no music there. I'll take you down to meet the Librarian and you can ask him about it if you want to know more.'

'Has the collection got a name?'

'We just call it the Gallery. Rather unimaginative of us, isn't it?'

'How wide do you think this gap is?'

'About four feet. Maybe less. I believe that there is a tradition of undergraduates getting legless and daring each other to leap across it. I hope that the story is apocryphal. It's a jump you would only want to do when quite sober, I should have thought.'

'It's a jump I wouldn't want to do at all.'

'I'll take you down to meet the Librarian, then we can find ourselves a cup of tea, if you like. We haven't had a chance to talk to one another for ages.'

'No, we haven't.'

For Kate, going down the stairs was more difficult than climbing up, but they made it to the ground floor at last and found a door marked *Librarian. Private. No Entrance.* Kate felt that the Librarian had wanted to add *Go away.* They knocked.

A woman who reminded Kate strongly of a small furry animal, a hamster perhaps, opened the door a few inches, ventured out a round, shiny nose and said: 'Yes?'

'We'd like to see the Librarian,' said Liam.

'Oh, I'm not sure he'd like that,' said the hamster, shaking her auburn head.

'Do you think you could ask him?' persevered Liam. 'Tell him it's Dr Ross and a guest from the Bodleian.'

The hamster opened the door a little wider and beckoned them in. They had to step over a barrier of bulging Marks & Spencer green and white plastic bags to get into the room.

'Who is it, Barbara?' asked a spidery creature sitting at a desk in the corner.

'He says he's Dr Ross and that she's from the Bodleian.' She sounded dubious, but Liam and Kate walked across the room anyway and stood in front of the desk.

'Kate, this is Kevin Newton, our Librarian,' said Liam.

'Can I help you over anything?' asked the Librarian, avoiding Kate's eyes and looking over her right shoulder. 'Not that we can offer to find books for you on a Wednesday afternoon, you know. Barbara has to go to her Italian lesson, and I can't leave my desk. No, no books.'

Kate tried to imagine this man bounding up the spiral stairs, sitting on top of the wooden balustrade, gazing out over Oxford, dangling his feet over the abyss and dreaming of flying over to the Gallery. It was, unfortunately, too great a feat of imagination. A pity, really, since she had really thought last night that she had tracked down Vivian Moffatt.

'And if there's nothing more that you need . . .' the Librarian was saying.

'No, of course not,' said Kate, wondering what the man did all day behind his *Keep off* notices and barricade of plastic bags. 'Except that I wondered whether you remembered Jenna Coates, the library trainee. She worked here last year.'

'Yes, that's right,' said Kevin Newton. 'I don't believe that I spoke to her, though. You dealt with her, didn't you, Barbara?'

'Yes,' said the hamster. 'I showed her how to type and file index cards and shelve books. I don't believe in trainees, really. You don't want them interfering in your work, do you?'

Poor kid, thought Kate, who couldn't imagine anything drearier than days spent filing index cards.

'And can you tell me what books you keep in the Gallery?' she asked.

'No, I can't. And why do you want to know?'

Private. No entry. Go away.

'I was just wondering,' said Kate.

'Well, they're not for general use,' said Kevin Newton.

And I wonder whether you would even know whether someone had been helping themselves to your collection, if you never leave this room.

But she said: 'Thanks for your help,' and she and Liam left the room.

Liam moved ahead of her towards the door. 'Oh, hallo, Olivia,' he was saying to a tall, slim, blonde woman. 'Yes, we're coming over to the common-room for tea now. Have

I introduced you to my friend, Kate Ivory?'

There was frost in the air, but Kate didn't know why, and it was a stiff tea party in the senior common-room, with no opportunity to talk to Liam on his own.

'I hear we may have succeeded in poaching the dessert chef from one of the top London restaurants,' said Olivia.

'Can you afford him? I thought you were going round with the begging bowl, pleading with old members for funds for student accommodation,' said Kate.

'That's different,' said Olivia. 'It's a question of priorities.'

When it was over, she left Liam talking to Olivia. 'I just want to take another look at that gallery of yours,' she said.

For someone who hated heights, it was too far to jump. But for someone tall, young and athletic, it was probably just a long step with a bit of a bounce to it. You would have to stand up on top of the balustrade, of course, which she would find quite impossible.

'Do you fancy the jump, then?'

It was Francis Tabbot from St Luke's library. He was, she thought, tall and thin, even if not particularly athletic looking. He could probably cross the gap with ease.

'You look like someone who doesn't like heights,' he said. 'If you were trapped by fire at the top of a staircase like this, you would have no means of escape, would you?' He was smiling at her in a way that made her step back a pace, and she thought about how he handled the porno-graphic works in his senior library.

'I don't like heights much,' she said. 'And I shall have to leave now. I'm expected in the seminar room at Kennedy House, to give a course on creative writing, and if I don't get out into the Oxford traffic in the next five minutes, I'll never make it on time.'

'I'll accompany you back downstairs, then. I wouldn't like to think of you tripping on those awkward open treads.'

'No, really, it isn't necessary.'

'I'm on my way to Kennedy House too, Kate, to visit a colleague.'

'Really, I prefer to go on my own. I'm a very independent person you know, Mr Tabbot.'

'But there's such a long drop, and on to concrete at the bottom. You must let me take your arm, it would be dreadful if we had another accident.'

'I don't know what you're talking about.' The library had emptied, as students gathered up their books and went down to the bar before dinner. She didn't think that Kevin Newton would come out of his office, even if she screamed. She was caught with a long, lethal drop between her and the ground, and she was increasingly nervous of Francis Tabbot. She had another ten feet in which to retreat, then she would be trapped against the wall. Tabbot didn't bother to come any closer: he knew she could sum up her position as well as he could.

She had three options. If she tried to push past Tabbot, shout at him, make a fuss, she would have to run down that long spiral staircase, closely pursued by a probable murderer, with no one around to help. She didn't rate her chances of beating him in a race, or of reaching the ground floor in one piece. She could continue to edge round the wall, but after another ten feet the solid surface was replaced by glass, and Oxford would float and sway below her. She would have to close her eyes and move crabwise so that she was never looking directly downwards. And all the time there would be the compulsion to jump that came to her in high places, as though the only way to break the tension that built up inside her was to submit to the pull of gravity and fall: out through the glass, flying like a bird for a few seconds before crashing on to the paving stones below.

There is a third option, she thought. If I can face it. If there is a key or a bolt on this side of the door.

'Come along, Kate. You'll be late for your class. And you know you have to come with me. You have no choice.' He stood well out of grabbing distance, between her and the top of the stairs. But terror was no excuse for inaction. She took the only choice that was open to her, fast, before she gave herself time to think about it. You could do anything if you took it at a sprint, if you were young and physically fit.

She vaulted up on to the broad surface of the balustrade, stood upright for less than a second and then sprang across the gap, landing with one foot on the opposite balustrade and carried forward by her momentum. She scrambled down and ran for the door in the corner. Behind her she heard Tabbot shouting, but she just prayed that door was not locked.

It opened, she banged it shut behind her, not waiting

to see if she could bolt it, and hurled herself down the stairs she found in front of her. These were not for public view and so they were comfortingly enclosed, with solid walls on each side, and she could take them two at a time and look out for a door through which she could escape.

There was no door until she reached what she knew by its solidity must be the ground floor. Locked. Liam had said that it would be. But just to the right, on a hook, a key. A sensible precaution in case some senior member of the college was locked in by an over-officious porter. She thanked Kevin Newton's cautious, spidery mind, and opened the door.

She heard Tabbot's feet coming down the spiral staircase in the centre of the library, and his voice shouting something unintelligible. She left the key in the door and came out. Her blood was still pumping from fear and exhaustion, and she felt as though her brain was working five times faster than usual. She moved quickly along the passage towards the main library door. As she reached it, it opened, and a voice said, 'I asked Francis to bring you down to the main door for me. I wasn't expecting quite such an athletic display. But never mind, you're here now, that's the important thing.'

Vivian Moffatt. Kate's brain stopped working altogether.

He had hold of her arm above the elbow, and he was wearing a dark green shell-suit and thin rubber gloves. His grip was hard and he pulled her close to his side, so that she knew that he must feel the way her heart was thumping and see the sweat pouring down her forehead.

'Did you leave your car outside?' His thumb dug painfully into the soft flesh of her upper arm.

'Let go of me!'

He stopped for a moment in the shadow of an archway and showed her his right hand. It held a knife. The sort she used at home in her kitchen to cut meat into thin strips.

'I don't like using a knife, but I will if I have to. Now walk.'

They were crossing the quadrangle and coming into the lodge. 'I asked you where you'd left your car.'

You didn't argue with a knife. 'It's in the parking bay in Parks Road.' They both sounded quite normal.

Kate looked round for Liam. Even Francis Tabbot would feel like an ally at this point, but she saw no one. Surely it wasn't possible to kidnap someone in broad daylight in the middle of an Oxford college?

And was this really Vivian Moffatt? She hadn't dared ask him, in case he wasn't sure whether she had guessed his identity or not. But I know the child you once were, she thought, and the man you have become. Once you start talking, I shall recognize you.

In front of them stood her cream Peugeot. Safety.

'Give me your keys.'

He made her get in on the passenger's side, then slide across to the driver's seat. He stayed within knifing distance all the time.

'Now drive.'

'Where to?'

'You're giving a writing lesson, aren't you? Drive to Kennedy House.'

Maybe everything was going to be all right. Maybe he was going to let her go. She drove slowly north down Parks Road, then turned right into the Banbury Road. Her knees felt like jelly and she could feel her foot shaking on the clutch when she tried to change gear. Other drivers were giving her amused looks at the noise her car was making as she crashed the gears.

She felt a knife point probe the soft gap between two ribs. 'Don't stall the engine. That would be stupid.'

'I'm not a very good driver when I'm nervous.'

'I've watched you. You're never a very good driver.'

She turned left and ahead of them the evening sunlight turned the copper glass of Kennedy House to molten gold.

'Pull in over there,' and Vivian Moffatt indicated a space on the far side of the car park.

When she had stopped, she could hear that a large blue car next to them was shrieking its alarm into the quiet of North Oxford.

'I asked them to fix it,' he said. 'But they told me that the car thieves are all stealing Montegos at the moment, and it needed to stay sensitive to marauders.'

'Yes,' said Kate. 'I'd heard that too.' It was a relief not to have to drive. Vivian leaned across her and removed the car keys from the ignition. Vivian Moffatt, or Graham Kieler. Whichever he was.

He had hold of her arm again. 'Get out of the car, but very slowly. I'm right behind you, and I still have the knife.' He transferred it to his left hand and brought out his car keys with his right, but the point of the knife was still resting against the space between her ribs and she didn't dare to make a run for it.

The alarm stopped.

'Not a black Fiesta, then,' she said. 'I thought it was your car I broke into.'

'No, that was the loan car from the garage when my own was being serviced. I watched you smash my side window. It cost me a lot of money when I returned the car. But then, that doesn't really matter to someone like me.'

'I knew someone was watching me. And I suppose, too, that I knew that I wouldn't find anything useful in the file when I opened it. Why did you leave it for me to find?'

'You thought you were being so clever, didn't you? You made me laugh. I dictated everything you did.'

Mad, the man was mad.

'Get into the car. Slide across the seat like you did before,' he said.

'But what about my writing class?'

'Your car will be found here in the car park, but you will have disappeared.'

'Francis Tabbot knows that I left Leicester College with you.'

'I shouldn't rely on him to rescue you, or even report what he knows to the authorities. Harry has a strong sense of self-preservation.'

'Harry?'

'Just a name I have for him. It's kids' stuff, I suppose, but we have different names for each other so that outsiders don't know who we're talking about if we're overheard.'

She thought about it. 'And Tom? Is that another code name?'

'Yes.'

'Who is Tom? Is it Susie Holbech? Or Ian Maltby?'

'Do you really want to know? You do realize there is only one set of circumstances where I would voluntarily let you into all our fascinating secrets, don't you? But since you insist, I'll tell you: it's Susie Holbech.' The knife moved again. 'We can't stay here. Someone might see us. Start the engine.'

'But I've never driven a car like this.'

'You'll learn. Start the engine.'

She moved carefully out of the parking space and headed for the road.

'Take the next right.'

'Where are we going?'

'The traffic's solid in town, so we'll take the bypass.'

She was driving slowly, but she was beginning to get the feel of the car. She must try to make friends with her abductor. She must talk.

'How did you get into Security, Graham? Have you always been a computer wizard?'

'No. I started as an assistant librarian at the Bodleian. Then I moved into one of the dependent libraries, and across into a faculty. It's only in the past couple of years that I've moved to Security. It seemed such an appropriate job for me, don't you think?'

'If you say so.' Could she get him on to more personal ground?

'Follow the signs for the motorway at the next round-about,' he said.

She concentrated on steering the big car and not hitting

anyone else. It might draw attention to them if she did, but she didn't believe that Graham would leave her alive to answer police questions. The concrete road beneath their tyres was noisy but Graham raised his voice.

'We're in the same business, you and I,' he said.

'What's that?'

'The making of fiction. You write it. I live it. Which is the more powerful?'

'You write, too. Why didn't you stay with the words on the page? Why did you have to translate them into action?'

'Haven't you ever been tempted to do it? Is the act of putting the words on the paper really enough for you?'

'Yes. It is. I live my life and I write my books. The two are separate.'

'I don't believe you. You look inside yourself, just as an actor does, to find an emotion that you want one of your characters to express. The two things, Art and Life, are linked.'

'And this, what we're doing now, which is it? Art or Life? Is it fiction, and if so, which of us is the author?'

'Oh, I think I'm writing this one, don't you? I'm in control here and you're just a character in an incident on a page.'

'Not necessarily,' said Kate. 'I definitely want to write the ending of this story, if you don't mind.'

Ahead of them there were signposts, but Kate was concentrating too hard on keeping control of the conversation to read them.

'You can take the next turning.' Graham had raised his voice.

Kate indicated left and pulled off the motorway. Into the sudden silence she asked:

'What about Victor Southam? Is he one of yours?'

'Stupid woman! Do you really think our operation is about stealing a few kids' books and creeping out of the library with them tucked into the pockets of our macs?' His voice had changed. Was this Viv or Graham? And which of them was more dangerous? 'We're big now. We don't even depend on a handful of key people. You could catch up with one or two members of the Company if you were smart, but you'd never trace them all. They're spread across the country, across the whole world now. You might close down one corner of our operation, but it's too big and too diffuse to comprehend. Especially since we brought in our American friend, Luther.'

Luther? Martin L. Preston, perhaps? Was that why he had left the Library of Congress? Was it Vivian who had sent him the details of the job at Kennedy Centre? She remembered Marty's eyes and the way he had looked at her with a hint of amusement. He had probably laughed out loud when she had left his office.

'Take the third exit at this roundabout.'

'That will take us back on to the motorway going south.'

'That's right.'

'Where are we going?'

'You'll find out soon enough.'

They were back on the noisy motorway, travelling back the way they had come. The light was fading and a drizzle was starting to fall. After a couple of attempts to find the right switch, she turned on her headlights. Green and white signboards loomed ahead.

'Take the next left.'

More signs, white arrows. She indicated left and pulled into the slip road. Her brain registered the letters on the signs, but refused to interpret them. Red and white cones on her right and left, notices apologizing for any inconvenience caused by the contractors. Did they never finish the roadworks?

'Take the track to the left.' This was Viv speaking, she was sure now. And it was Viv who had murdered Jenna.

As she swung the car over and slowed down on the uneven surface, something caught her eye in the rear-view mirror as it rolled across the back shelf. She turned her head to see what it was. A bunch of red peonies. And as the insistent signs had been telling her, this was the Oxford Exit. The drizzle was thickening to a downpour and the deserted site glistened under the lowering sky.

'Pull up here,' said Vivian.

When she switched off the engine it was silent except for the rustle of the rain on the roof and the distant hum of traffic on the motorway. Hundreds of people, driving to and from Oxford in closed metal boxes, insulated from her fear, were passing just a few hundred yards away. Even if she screamed they would not hear her.

'Grey,' said Vivian. 'I felt it was your colour.'

'What?'

She looked at what he had taken out of the glove

compartment: a new pair of tights, the colour of wood smoke.

'Just the colour of your eyes.'

She opened the door, fast, and slid out of the car. She started to run towards the motorway. If they saw her, waving her arms, shouting, in distress, surely they would stop? If she ever made it that far.

She was wearing leather shoes with smooth soles, and they didn't grip on the wet clay the way the all-weather tread on her running shoes would have done. Her skirt was clinging to her legs and slowing her down. She could hear Vivian behind her, the rustle of his shell-suit, his breathing loud, his feet sure in their trainers.

She could still get away from him. She was fit. She ran four times a week. Even in leather pumps she could run faster than most people. She hitched her wet skirt up above her knees and made an effort. Her feet slipped on the wet clay and she found herself on her knees, her hands scrabbling at the dirt. Then Vivian was on her, twisting one arm behind her back, grabbing her hair, pulling her head back. The pain from her hair lessened suddenly as he released it, but by then he had slipped the tights around her neck.

Both her hands were freed as he pulled two-handed on the tights, and she tried to get her fingers between the nylon and her neck. There was no space. She could hear him grunting with effort as the pain increased and her vision started to go black.

She was choking, dying. This was it, then. Logoff. Exit.

* * *

From a long way away a voice was shouting, 'You get him, Gav. I'll look after the girl.'

There was wet earth under her cheek, then warm cloth – a man's jacket. Her neck was on fire, her head hurt and she couldn't speak. She thought she might throw up. She recognized that she was lying in the recovery position, so someone must have rescued her.

'Are you all right?' asked Paul Taylor's voice.

What the hell was he doing here? And if it really was him, why hadn't he rescued her sooner?

'Where did you come from?' she croaked at Paul, eventually. 'Why were you driving down a contractors' track off the motorway?'

'We were following you.'

She was shivering, and he put his jacket round her shoulders.

'It's nearly as wet as I am,' she said. Then she found herself crying. This must be hysteria, the woman's complaint.

It was no warmer when Paul put his arm round her and murmured, 'Silly cow,' in her ear, but there was something comforting about it. Was this the way a brother might behave? No, not a brother. But there was no room in her life for another unsatisfactory relationship.

'Were you following me all the time? Why?' Did curiosity never end?

'From Kennedy House. Some angry householder rang the police to complain that there was always a car alarm going off in the Kennedy House car park and they were fed up with it. We heard the message on the radio and happened to be passing near, so we said we'd deal with it. The alarm had stopped by the time we got there, but we arrived in time to see you getting into Kieler's car.'

'And what made you think there was something wrong?'

He sighed. 'Your imagination must be catching: there was a bunch of crimson peonies sitting on the shelf in the back of his car. I saw them as you drove out on to the road. And you weren't driving very well, were you?'

'And you were concerned for my safety?'

'I thought: What's the stupid woman doing now? Why is she going off with a potential rapist and murderer? And I thought about leaving you to it – that was what you had told me to do, wasn't it – but then I thought of the amount of paperwork I'd have to fill in if you succeeded this time in getting yourself killed.'

'That's not a very gallant way of putting it.'

'I'm learning not to be a male chauvinist. Hadn't you noticed?'

'And why didn't you stop us long before we got to the motorway? Why did you let me go through all that grief and terror?'

'What could we have pulled him in for? Being in possession of a bunch of flowers?'

'He had a knife. Isn't that an offensive weapon?'

'A kitchen knife, which is *per se* inoffensive. He could have said that he was only intending to frighten you, not to use it.'

'Well, I think it was pretty offensive.'

'Yes, but now we've got intention unlawfully to kill,

haven't we? We couldn't have got him for Jenna Coates with nothing but that peony rubbish of yours.'

'I do hate it when you sound like the *Police Law Primer*. And I thought it was that peony rubbish that made you follow us in the first place.'

'Yes, maybe. How are you feeling?'

'Bloody awful. I think I'm going to be sick.'

'That will be the shock. You sound pretty ropy, I must say.'

An ambulance pulled up in front of them.

'Is that for me?'

'It must be the one I radioed for fifteen minutes ago.'

'Why didn't it race up with its siren blasting?'

'Maybe you're not important enough, or sick enough.'

'Huh! So why do I need an ambulance? I'll be able to walk in a minute.'

'I doubt it. And why can't you do what you're told for once without arguing?'

'Will you come with me?' She must be feeling bad to say something like that.

'I'll have to drive back to Oxford, but I'll follow you to the hospital and see you as soon as you get there. We'll need a statement from you when you can make one, too.'

Ambulancemen were approaching with a stretcher.

'I suppose you saved my life.'

'Maybe.'

'In that case, you'll let me buy you a celebratory drink down at the pub, as soon as I'm out of hospital, won't you?'

'I would, but I bet it wouldn't be as good as the fifteen-year-old single malt whisky that you've got hidden in the third cupboard from the left in your kitchen.'

Two weeks later, Kate pulled up outside her house. There was a space large enough for an expert driver to park a Peugeot in, so she drove a little further on and drove frontways into a twenty-foot space that even an idiot couldn't miss. When she got out she saw that she was a couple of feet out from the pavement at the front, and at an angle of about thirty degrees to it. Oh well.

'You should practise a bit,' said Harley, who was watching. 'We showed you how to do it, now it's up to you.'

'Oh, and thanks for the instruction on how to get into a locked car. It came in quite handy a couple of weeks back.'

'Before that bloke tried to murder you?'

'Before that, yes.' Not a subject she wanted to talk about. 'What's that thing you've got?'

'Him? He's my new dog. Dave, he's called.'

'Nice quiet animal, I suppose?'

'I swapped a skateboard for him. Mum said it was time we had a pet. Teach us responsibility, she said.'

At this moment Dave set off up the street, with Harley hanging on grimly to the other end of his lead. 'He's named after the motorbike,' came Harley's voice from the end of the street, before he disappeared round the corner. A motorbike called Dave? Harley. Dave. Davidson. She got there at last. Maybe it would keep the kid outside longer and she would have less time to listen to his music.

'Tell you what,' said Harley, as he reappeared at the

end of Dave's leash, 'I could give you some more advanced driving instruction if you like. It wouldn't cost you much.'

'How much?'

'Two-fifty an hour. I could show you how to do a hand-brake turn, if you like.'

'You didn't learn that at your Training for Citizenship class.'

'I learnt it off Darren's brother. And—'

'And where did you get all those red and white cones from?'

'Got them for you to practise your reversing with, off Clyde's dad. He works on motorway maintenance. He's not home much, but I saw him round Clyde's on Saturday, and I swapped 'em for you.'

She thought about asking what he had swapped them for, but decided against it. In principle she didn't approve of Harley's streetwise tricks, but she could see that if she was going to do any more jobs like the last one for the Security Team, she could do with learning as many of them as she could fit into her crowded schedule.

'Well, I'd be grateful if you could swap them back again. I'm not too keen on the sight of red and white cones at the moment. They bring back some unhappy memories.'

Dave was having a good time with Harley. She could hear them pounding up and down the uncarpeted stairs of number 12. Harley was shouting and Dave was barking, and she didn't think that even Bruce Springsteen would be able to win the volume contest, especially when Mrs

Toadface joined in and shouted at both of them. She put on her running shoes and made for the end of the road. If the Toadface family kept up the noise level she would get back to her normal level of fitness. For the moment she felt a bit shaky, and the bruising on her neck was still visible. She ran doggedly on towards the canal. She would keep going at this pace for twenty minutes before turning back.

She had just finished chapter twenty of *Wuthering Heights* and turned off her light when the back door crashed open and closed again at number 12. 'Get out of there, you little bugger,' shouted Mrs Toadface. Surely she hadn't chucked out the toddler. The howling soon put her right. That wasn't a child, it was a dog. He was in the back garden, complaining loudly at being excluded from the household. Maybe he only did this baying act when there was a full moon. Maybe, on the other hand, he intended to bay every night of the month, and keep her from hitting her word processor at 5 a.m. Maybe it was time to move house.

Kate knew that she would have to face Andrew Grove and Charles Trim at some time, and she was feeling well enough to take them on. She had prepared a report on the book thefts, short and inconclusive, and she didn't think that they would be very happy about it. On the other hand, as Andrew had said, she had been cheap, and it hadn't cost them a lot of money.

'Those women at Santa Luisa are refusing to give up

our Eliza Baughns and the rest of the Veil books,' said Charles, as she sat in his room in St Giles' and breathed in the familiar smell of mouldering plasterwork.

'Perhaps they're right,' said Kate. 'It must be very difficult to prove that they really belong to you, especially since Graham Kieler is refusing to give any details of the book theft network.'

'I don't think he's capable of giving details of anything that has happened in the real world,' said Andrew. 'But I don't see that that is a good enough reason for the Santa Luisa librarian to hang on to our property.'

'I do,' said Kate. 'The books are being used, and studied, in a way that their writers would have approved. What good were they doing in the bookstacks of our Oxford libraries?'

'I think that is a most immoral point of view. Andrew, take your friend away from here. We will send on a cheque to cover her services in cataloguing.'

The metal grille gave one last squawk as they closed the street door behind them.

# xii

## *Conclusion*

*I want you to start by writing down some memory of childhood. Don't worry about getting the details absolutely right, but do try to remember how you felt at the time. It is these feelings from childhood that will help you to understand how you sometimes find yourself doing things that you can't explain.*

They encourage you to write things down here. They say it's therapeutic, whatever that might mean in the circumstances. I suppose they think that it will help me to come to terms with living in this place, without normal human contact, without everything that made my life enjoyable. Everyone I meet here looks at me with a certain gently disapproving expression and sets about manipulating me into something that they want me to be. But I don't want to change. I just want the chance to get on with my stories. If they won't let me live them, I shall content myself with writing them down. It's rather like listening to a recording of Mahler instead of going to a concert. Or worse, perhaps. But anything is better than a world without music I suppose.

I tried to explain to them about music, once. The doctor said that she liked Mozart. I listened to him for years, I told her. You can put his music down on paper and draw lines round it. You can keep it locked up in a box. But the spirit, the genius, even of Mozart, raps on the lid and tries to get out. Sometimes, like in the Queen of the Night's aria, it escapes and goes shouting off down the road, unfettered, uncorseted. But mostly it's pretty tightly buttoned into its waistcoat, is Mozart. But then I found Mahler, and Stravinsky. Now you can't draw lines round *them*. They'll push your boxes out of shape until they stand free, spiky as chicken wire, and screech at you. Oh yes, life's been different since I found Mahler and Stravinsky. Take that Pulcinella. You think she's predictable and safe, with her short blonde hair and her grey eyes, but she'll surprise you. She'll creep up behind you with cymbals in her hands, will Pulcinella, and make you jump right out of your coffin.

I don't think the doctor understood me. Maybe she just isn't a musical person. She wrote some more notes on her pad and left the room. I wanted to read what she had written. To tell the truth, I shouted at her about it. If they're going to write you down on paper, they've got to get it right. All I wanted to do was to check.

I worry sometimes that if they succeed in changing me, I might never be able to get my storytelling gift back again. I would be like an actor, able only to repeat some-one else's lines instead of providing my own.

They tell me that I have to learn to distinguish between the real world and the world of my fantasies, and I am afraid that if they keep on at me like this, in their gently insistent way, that I will no longer be able to move freely between the different people who inhabit my head. And how do they know which is real, which is fantasy? If I can't tell, how can they hope to do so? But it is getting more difficult to make the pictures come into my head and walk myself into them the way I used to. This place is full of vandals. I build up a world, but before I can move into it and live there, as soon as I turn my back, some white-coated hooligan has walked in and kicked it to bits. I shall hide my next work where they can't find it, so that I can live there whenever I want.

'Tell us more about it, Graham,' they say. 'Tell us about the little boy called Viv.' They speak as though I had made him up, and when I try to recall the scent of peppermints, or the sweet heavy smell of the cats' meat boiling in the big aluminium pot, they fade into the smells of floor polish and disinfectant that permeate this place. Aunt Nell's red hair and scarlet hat go flicking away, disappearing out of the corner of my eye, just when I think I've got hold of them again.

They tell me to talk about my mother. They ask me to pretend to talk to her.

'Release your feelings,' they say.

Release what feelings?

What is the use of talking to her? She doesn't listen.

For years I wanted to get in touch with her, talk to her. I wrote her letters. Long, rambling, childish outpourings that I failed to post. I don't know where she is, and I don't suppose they do, either.

They have a teacher of creative writing who comes in and is very encouraging. I think I am quite a treat for her after her other pupils, especially the ones who find it difficult to get the words down on paper, like Joe, who sits there with his tongue sticking out of the corner of his mouth, digging his biro into the paper and stopping to ask every minute or so how to spell a word.

'Never mind about the spelling,' she says brightly, smiling with her rose-pink lips, crinkling up the corners of her grey eyes. Eyes like wood smoke, or was that someone else? I forget now. 'Just try and get your feelings down on to the paper. That's the important thing. That's what we're all here for.'

But Joe likes to have his feelings spelled right, as though this will somehow validate the things that he writes. There are some very peculiar people here, I can tell you; criminals even, some of them.

Frances, that's what our teacher is called. She's not as much fun as Emma Dolby, though she doesn't lose our homework papers the way Emma used to do, and she's not as good looking as Kate Ivory. But she does have this beautiful hair, long and reddish-brown that she wears in a thick mass on top of her head, like some Edwardian heroine, with tendrils that escape and curl invitingly in front of her ears (little pink ears, rather like the petals of peonies, and sometimes, after I've been watching them for a while, she touches them, with a nervous gesture). But one day, when we are alone, I am going to pull out all the hairpins so that her hair falls over her shoulders and down her back, right down to the ground. And then I shall be able to grasp it in my hands and bury my face in it. I shall smell the peppermints and the violet cachous and see the herringbone path and the scarlet poppies, and I shall climb all the way up the side of the tower at last, through the tangle of that lustrous hair, and in through the window to where the princess is waiting in the lamplight. At last I shall kiss away the black petals from her throat. There will be a bowl of cut peonies, white and pink and crimson, sitting on the table next to her head. And she will call for the buttered toast and welcome me back into the family where I have always belonged.

*What was that you were saying, Frances? I'm afraid that I wasn't paying attention there for a moment.*

# Oxford Mourning

## Veronica Stallwood

When novelist Kate Ivory first meets Dr Olivia Blacket, an academic at Leicester College, Oxford, the atmosphere is far from amicable. Olivia refuses to show Kate the fascinating material she is researching, even though it concerns the same esteemed literary figure that Kate is writing about. Determined to nose out the scandals that could provide her with a best-seller, Kate discovers a darker side to Dr Blacket. What are the strange obsessions that haunt her? What is her relationship with Kate's boyfriend Liam? And most of all, who would want to murder her . . . ?

Liam's name heads the list of suspects, but Kate knows that several others were in the vicinity of Olivia's rooms at the time of her death, including a bizarre 'family' of civilised squatters – four men guarding a blank-faced girl. As Kate is drawn into their circle, she struggles to understand a complex web of overlapping lives, and realises that, before she can unravel the truth, her own beliefs and values will come into question . . .

'Stallwood is in the top rank of crime writers' Mike Ripley, *Daily Telegraph*

0 7472 5343 9

**HEADLINE**

# Die in my Dreams

## Christine Green

'First rate whodunnit . . . with a convincing detective duo' *Daily Telegraph*

Ten years ago Carole Ann Forbes was found guilty of stabbing her lover to death. Released early from prison, she begins a new life in the small town of Fowchester. Then a man is found stabbed to death on a nearby river bank and suspicion naturally falls on Carole Ann.

Chief Inspector Connor O'Neill and Detective Sergeant Fran Wilson work on the case in delicate harmony – not helped by Connor's drinking problem and Fran's conflicting emotions for her irascible boss. Connor refuses to believe that the beautiful Carole Ann is involved in the riverside murder and when he reads the trial notes even doubts that she was guilty of her first crime. Then another man is found dead, also stabbed. There is no doubt that Carole Ann will be rearrested – unless Connor and Fran can work fast enough to find out the truth in time . . .

'Green has considerable talent to observe and amuse' *Guardian*

0 7472 5207 6

**HEADLINE**

## *A selection of bestsellers from Headline*

| | | |
|---|---|---|
| ASKING FOR TROUBLE | Ann Granger | £5.99 ☐ |
| FAITHFUL UNTO DEATH | Caroline Graham | £5.99 ☐ |
| THE WICKED WINTER | Kate Sedley | £5.99 ☐ |
| RAINBOW'S END | Martha Grimes | £5.99 ☐ |
| WEIGHED IN THE BALANCE | Anne Perry | £5.99 ☐ |
| THE DEVIL'S HUNT | P C Doherty | £5.99 ☐ |
| EVERY DEADLY SIN | D M Greenwood | £4.99 ☐ |
| SKINNER'S MISSION | Quintin Jardine | £5.99 ☐ |
| HONKY TONK KAT | Karen Kijewski | £5.99 ☐ |
| THE QUICK AND THE DEAD | Alison Joseph | £5.99 ☐ |

Headline books are available at your local bookshop or newsagent. Alternatively, books can be ordered direct from the publisher. Just tick the titles you want and fill in the form below. Prices and availability subject to change without notice.

Buy four books from the selection above and get free postage and packaging and delivery within 48 hours. Just send a cheque or postal order made payable to Bookpoint Ltd to the value of the total cover price of the four books. Alternatively, if you wish to buy fewer than four books the following postage and packaging applies:

UK and BFPO £4.30 for one book; £6.30 for two books; £8.30 for three books.

Overseas and Eire: £4.80 for one book; £7.10 for 2 or 3 books (surface mail)

Please enclose a cheque or postal order made payable to *Bookpoint Limited*, and send to: Headline Publishing Ltd, 39 Milton Park, Abingdon, OXON OX14 4TD, UK.
Email Address: orders@bookpoint.co.uk

If you would prefer to pay by credit card, our call team would be delighted to take your order by telephone. Our direct line 01235 400 414 (lines open 9.00 am–6.00 pm Monday to Saturday 24 hour message answering service). Alternatively you can send a fax on 01235 400 454.

Name .......................................................................................

Address .......................................................................................

.......................................................................................

.......................................................................................

If you would prefer to pay by credit card, please complete:
Please debit my Visa/Access/Diner's Card/American Express (delete as applicable) card number:

| | | | | | | | | | | | | | | | | | | |
|--|--|--|--|--|--|--|--|--|--|--|--|--|--|--|--|--|--|--|

Signature ..................................................... Expiry Date ..............